Praise for

# *Pall in the Family*

"A tightly plotted, character-driven triumph of a mystery, *Pall in the Family* had me laughing out loud while feverishly turning pages to try and figure out whodunit. This novel sparkles with charmingly peculiar characters and a fascinating heroine, Clyde Fortune, who effortlessly shuffles the reader into her world like a card in a tarot deck. Eastman is fabulous!"
—Jenn McKinlay, *New York Times* bestselling author of the Library Lover's Mysteries, the Cupcake Bakery Mysteries, and the Hat Shop Mysteries

"A kooky small town filled with eccentric characters, psychics, and murder make Eastman's Family Fortune Mystery series a stellar launch. Add a dog-walking ex-cop paired with her old flame investigator, and it's not hard to predict a brilliant future for this quirky new series!"
—Kari Lee Townsend, national bestselling author of the Fortune Teller Mysteries

"What emerges as most entertaining in this mystery by debut author Dawn Eastman is how well she slowly develops her characters and prevents them from being two-dimensional caricatures . . . The paranormal aspect is surprisingly realistic and matter-of-fact amongst the townspeople . . . Clyde proves to be a talented investigator herself with or without her 'extra' skills, and she is a very likable heroine with the humor to cope with her eccentric relatives." —*Kings River Life Magazine*

"[An] entertaining read . . . The cast of characters is a lovable bunch of kooky psychics." —*RT Book Reviews*

# Be Careful What You Witch For

DAWN EASTMAN

BERKLEY PRIME CRIME, NEW YORK

**THE BERKLEY PUBLISHING GROUP**
Published by the Penguin Group
Penguin Group (USA) LLC
375 Hudson Street, New York, New York 10014

USA • Canada • UK • Ireland • Australia • New Zealand • India • South Africa • China

penguin.com

A Penguin Random House Company

BE CAREFUL WHAT YOU WITCH FOR

A Berkley Prime Crime Book / published by arrangement with the author

Berkley Prime Crime Books are published by The Berkley Publishing Group.
BERKLEY® PRIME CRIME and the PRIME CRIME logo are trademarks of Penguin
Group (USA) LLC.

For information, address: The Berkley Publishing Group,
a division of Penguin Group (USA) LLC,
375 Hudson Street, New York, New York 10014.

ISBN: 978-0-425-26447-8

PUBLISHING HISTORY
Berkley Prime Crime mass-market edition / July 2014

PRINTED IN THE UNITED STATES OF AMERICA

10  9  8  7  6  5  4  3  2  1

Cover illustration by Daniel Craig; design element © iStockphoto/Thinkstock.
Cover design by Judith Lagerman.

*To my son, Jake, who inspired all the best parts of Seth.*

# Acknowledgments

Writing is a solitary pursuit, but the production of a novel is a group effort.

Thank you to the team at Berkley Prime Crime. I am fortunate to work with such a fantastic group. Special thanks to my editor, Andie Avila, whose attention to detail and love for the characters make each book better.

My agent, Sharon Bowers, will always have my deep gratitude for making a dream reality.

I would like to thank DP Lyle, MD, for sharing his medical expertise. And thanks to Ramona Valencia for (gleefully) helping to plot a murder and donating old EpiPens to the cause of research.

I'm grateful to my amazing writer's group, Wendy Delsol, Kali VanBaale, Murl Pace, and Kim Stuart. Their support and encouragement are priceless.

Thank you to family members Ann and Bob Eastman, Jim and Alyce Mooradian, Barb Laughlin, Kristin Morton, and Barbara Morton who have tirelessly spread the word about the Family Fortune Mysteries.

To my webmaster brother, Brent Eastman, for help with all the technology.

And finally, to Steve, Jake, and Ellie, who make my life a hilarious adventure.

# 1

**Black-robed figures circled the bonfire. Their** chanting sent a shiver down my spine that had nothing to do with the cold. Hooded and lit only by the flickering flames and silver moonlight filtering through the naked branches overhead, they were nameless except for their leader, my best friend Diana.

I felt a sharp jab in my ribs.

"When's the good stuff start?" Aunt Vi said, too loudly. Though a skeptic about Wicca she'd insisted on coming to the ceremony when she heard there would be fire *and* a cauldron. Her silver braid peeked out from under her borrowed robes and she gawked around the circle.

"Shhh!" I hissed. I felt uneasy anyway, but now several of the hooded figures had turned in our direction.

Deep in Greer's Woods on Halloween, we were a good fifteen-minute hike from the road. Diana had trekked her supplies to this spot during the afternoon. Wiccans called this day "Samhain" and she planned to summon the spirits of the dead and the Goddess of Shadows to join us for the Wiccan New Year celebration. Putting a Wiccan in charge of the Fall Fun Fest meant the usual lineup of kids' costume parade and applesauce-eating contest was joined by a midnight ceremony in the woods.

Vi tugged on my robe.

"Clytemnestra, you said we were going to see our future in the fire. I don't see anything."

"She just started—give her a minute," I said through clenched teeth. Vi was purposely using my full name to irk me.

Nearing seventy, Vi had retained what might be politely called a "childlike enthusiasm" for all things paranormal.

Diana lit the black candles on the makeshift altar and called on the four elements to join the circle. I felt the heavy brown bread we'd shared earlier settle uncomfortably in my stomach. When she reached the part about the God of Darkness and Goddess of Shadows, I moved a little closer to Aunt Vi. Diana doesn't scare me, but sometimes her ceremonies and spells do.

Until six months ago, I had been a police officer. I felt guns, criminals, and drunken idiots were business as usual. Magick, ghosts, and séances were another matter. We lived in Crystal Haven, a town known for its psychics and fortune-tellers, so I should have been used to it. But, hosting the Fall Fun Fest that included a Wiccan ceremony was new. In the midst of this spooky group with only a crescent moon and a bonfire for illumination, standing closer to Vi was only slightly reassuring. The flames cast dancing shadows on the trees, accentuating their gnarled branches. Sparks lifted up and disappeared in the darkness.

Another jab to the ribs. "Nothing's happening. What about the cauldron?" Vi said, more quietly.

Just then Diana dropped a match into her cauldron and blue flames leaped out and glowed in the center of the circle.

"Oooh," Vi breathed.

A burning stick of sage was passed around the circle. "Burn and blaze! Into the future we now gaze!" The group chanted, asking to see their future in the fire. Vi joined in with gusto. I thought longingly about séances and tarot cards. Those seemed tame and soothing compared to this.

Mesmerized by the flames, my mind wandered. Without meaning to, I stared deeply into the fire. I saw a vision of a house. The cottage was covered in vines and set back in a dense forest. I felt myself drawn to it, as if I'd been there before. The atmosphere of the ceremony and the chanting of the circle had breached my wall of protection. I habitually guarded against any messages from other realms. I shook my head to clear it of the smoky fog that had settled over me.

Vi squeezed my arm through my robe. "You saw something, didn't you? What was it?" Vi was always on the look-out for any sign that my "gift" was active.

I shook my head again, although she wasn't likely to get the signal in the dark, while I wore a hood. "Nothing, I—"

A scream cut through the chanting. One of the robed figures had fallen into the center of the circle, the face covered by the hood. The voices stopped and the inky figures blended together as they rushed to the crumpled form. Diana arrived first and pulled the hood back. It was Rafe Godwin. He clutched his throat, his face dark in the dim light of the clearing. His huge, terrified eyes made it look as if he were choking himself. Then, grabbing Diana's wrist, he pointed to his throat with his other hand.

"Is he having a heart attack?" a hooded figure asked.

"His lips are swelling, it looks like an allergic reaction," another voice volunteered.

"Call 911!" Diana said.

Gasps and concerned *tsk*ings made their way through the circle.

"Oh my," said Vi, at my side again.

"Rafe, where is it?" Diana asked.

He wrestled with his robe and Diana began pawing through the folds.

"Diana, what are you doing?" I said. I knelt down to help her.

"He's got an EpiPen in here somewhere. I think he's going into shock." She continued wrestling with his clothing and a few others knelt to do the same.

The group began muttering about bees and wasps. But at midnight in October the likelihood that an insect sting was involved seemed remote.

"Here it is!" Diana held a short tube the length of a pen over her head. She popped the injector out of its plastic holder and jabbed it into his thigh right through the robe.

Now that I stood closer, I saw the mottled dark color of his face, the swollen lips and eyelids. He fought to take weak raspy breaths.

The crowd got very quiet. I expected Rafe to take a deep breath, and for his eyes to return to normal size. Nothing happened. He stopped struggling, but otherwise I saw no change. Certainly not the miraculous recovery I had come to expect from watching television.

Diana shook his shoulders but he didn't respond.

One of the people who had pushed through to the front of the crowd began CPR. Someone else announced that an ambulance had been dispatched. As we stood helplessly watching, I realized Rafe Godwin would not be seeing the future.

# 2

**Muffled sniffles and sobs punctuated the other-**wise quiet clearing. We'd known he was dead a few minutes after CPR had started. Fortunately, one of the group members, a nurse, took over the evaluation and finally made the decision to stop CPR. Visibly shaken, he sat with his back against a nearby tree, head in hands, while the rest of us held vigil and waited for the paramedics to arrive.

Diana sat next to Rafe on the ground and seemed to be in a trance. Her hood lay flat on her back, her orange curls reflecting the glow of the bonfire. I knelt next to her, murmuring reassuring platitudes and feeling helpless. I knew how close Rafe and Diana had been.

Vi stood nearby. Her eyes glittered in the flickering light and the shadows accentuated the furrows and creases on her face.

The wail of a siren intruded on our stunned group and then we heard the EMTs crashing through the trees.

Two men burst into the clearing. One looked about fifty, red faced and breathing heavily from the sprint through the woods. The other could have kept running all the way into Crystal Haven. Surely just out of his teens, he'd need to show ID every time he bought a beer. They quickly assessed the mood of the crowd and let their equipment slump to the ground. After verifying that Rafe was dead they moved the stretcher toward Rafe's body to carry him out of the woods. Diana looked confused at their approach and leaned over as if to protect him from attack.

"Diana, he's gone," I said. I touched her shoulder.

She looked at me with wet eyes.

"But I gave him the epinephrine. Why didn't it work?"

I shook my head and helped her stand so the EMTs could do their work.

"Let them get him to the hospital," I said.

"Is there any next of kin?" the older man asked as he scanned the crowd. I saw his eyes grow wide as he took in the cloaks and hoods, the cauldron and altar.

Several people shook their heads, and turned to Diana.

"No, I'm the closest thing he's got to family." Her voice broke, and she rubbed her eyes with her sleeve. Rafe Godwin was Diana's father's oldest friend. He'd been like an uncle to her and her brother growing up, and a source of support after their parents died.

The younger EMT had shuffled closer to his partner and scanned the crowd as if he were a rabbit who had stumbled into a fox den.

"What's going on here?" the older one asked.

"It's part of the Fall Fun Fest," I said. I stuck out my hand. "I'm Clyde Fortune, and this is one of the scheduled activities."

He took my hand in a warm grip. They both relaxed at this—festivalgoers were apparently less threatening than free-range witches.

After they lifted Rafe onto the stretcher, a couple of the men in the group stepped forward to help carry it. We filed out of the clearing after them, making a procession of dark-robed figures through the woods.

# 3

⚜

**The next day, the crisp, clear November air held** just a threat of the winter to come. It brought back my best memories of growing up in Western Michigan, spending time in the woods, and it was a welcomed feeling after experiencing last night's tragedy there. I closed my eyes to let the sweet, sharp smell of the fallen leaves block out all other sensations. The midnight ceremony was meant to kick off the weekend Fall Fun Fest. So far, the great weather and promise of good food had overshadowed the pall of a death in the woods. I was helping Diana at her vendor's stall, which was doing a brisk business selling everything from herbs to jewelry. When I'd driven her home the night before, I'd offered to cover for her that morning, but she'd insisted she would feel better if she stayed busy. As the organizer of the Fall Fun Fest, she said she would go crazy sitting at home wondering if there was anything she should be doing.

I'd learned over the years that arguing with Diana when her mind was set led nowhere.

Diana owned Moonward Magick, the busiest Wiccan supply store in the area. She had also worked from mid-August to set up the Fall Fun Fest. In past years it had been held in Grand Rapids but the organizer was getting older and had health issues. Diana had been talked into running it this year and decided to move it to Greer's Woods outside of Crystal Haven. I wondered if this would be her first and last time organizing it. Based on the muttering and swearing that had occurred since early September, I was glad she didn't believe in curses.

Everyone was talking about the sudden death at the ceremony. The stories I overheard in the crowd varied widely, from seizure, to heart attack, to spirit possession. The one thing they all agreed on was that Rafe and Diana had always been close, and that she had tried to save him. I saw that she was wearing her mother's rose quartz pendant. She only wore it when she was stressed or upset, but her warm and caring manner with her customers gave no indication of her feelings.

She refused all questions about the death, and would not engage in any conversation that wasn't directly related to her business or the festival. She was a master at putting off an emotional outburst until the appropriate time, unlike me. *I* was a master at putting off emotional outbursts forever. I could tell it was depleting her energy.

"What's good around this place?" I stiffened as a familiar voice floated through the crowd.

Before I could duck behind the display board, Aunt Vi and my mom approached the table.

"Clyde, there you are!" my mom said in a tone that suggested she'd trekked the Himalayas for a week to find me.

The sisters were almost the same height, both with silver hair. Vi had hers in its familiar braid, and she wore a multi-colored skirt with two cardigans and a shawl. Mom had her hair in a bun, as usual, and wore a light blue tracksuit and sneakers. This was her venturing-into-the-woods outfit.

"I knew it! I knew all that Halloween chanting and fire gazing would lead to trouble." Vi fixed me with her fierce black eyes. I refrained from reminding her that she'd insisted on being there.

Vi, a pet psychic, and Mom, a tarot reader, had been unpleasantly surprised to learn a Wiccan ceremony would be part of this year's Fall Fun Fest offerings. Mom held a long-standing wariness of spells and potions. Vi approached the Wiccans as an entertaining subculture, but one not to be entirely trusted.

I sliced across my neck with my hand and jerked my head in Diana's direction.

Violet had taken a breath to begin her inquisition when she noticed my not-so-subtle maneuvers. The sisters glanced in Diana's direction and fell silent. Violet did something gymnastic with her eyebrows but I gave up trying to figure it out. My aunt and mother truly did communicate with glances and nods, a skill I had not developed, at least not with them.

I walked away from the booth and they followed. Once out of earshot, we began rapid-fire whispering, sounding like angry geese.

"What are you two doing here?"

"We came to support Diana in her . . . endeavors." My mother clutched her amethyst amulet for protection. "Vi told me about what happened last night."

"It's all anyone in town will talk about," Vi said. "Witches in the woods, rituals, *death*. Hey, I heard there was good food here. Where's the giant turkey legs?" Vi stood on her tiptoes.

"I think you have this confused with a Renaissance fair. There aren't any turkey legs here."

"Oh. No swords or jousting?"

I shook my head.

Violet dropped her heels and the corners of her mouth at the same time.

"Do you know any more about what happened?" Mom glanced in Diana's direction and lowered her voice. "To Rafe?"

I assured them I had no information. My status as a former police officer led them to believe I had an inside track on such things. Last spring, after shooting a suspect while working as a police officer in Ann Arbor, I had come home to recoup and think about what to do next. I had had very little time for either when Crystal Haven had its first homicide in decades. One murder led to another and by the time the crime was solved, I found myself with a small inherited house and a large inherited bullmastiff. Now that I had my own place, the ladies in the family had taken to semistalking me, a side effect I hadn't considered when I decided to stay in Crystal Haven and leave police work behind.

I described the death of Rafe Godwin to Mom with minimal detail. She walked back to the booth and embraced Diana, both of them welling up and sniffling. In spite of her feelings toward Wiccans in general, mom loved Diana.

Violet and I stood with our arms crossed, shaking our heads.

"Diana, I'm so sorry. That must have been so horrible for you after losing your parents. Now you've lost Rafe as well," Mom said.

"I never liked that Rafe Godwin," Vi mumbled out of the side of her mouth.

"What are you talking about?" I said. "Everyone liked him. He led a very popular coven in Grand Rapids, did charity work, and was a huge support to Diana and Dylan."

"No, not everyone." She shook her head. "The cats don't trust him. They say he's not as nice as he seems and *they* would know. They're very good judges of character." Vi nodded once to punctuate.

*Slow deep breath.* It was my own fault for thinking Vi would have real information about anyone. Her pet psychic abilities were highly exaggerated in my opinion, but she and my mother took it very seriously.

"Okay, well, he's dead now so the cats don't have to worry," I said and turned back to the booth.

"What's *he* doing here?" Vi said. I turned to follow her gaze.

Tom Andrews made his way through the crowd. He'd worked at his mother's booth over the weekend helping to sell her healing herbs and potions. Tom was wearing his police uniform so I assumed he must be working at his day job.

He spotted Diana and Mom and turned in the direction of the booth. At the same time, he tripped over someone's dragging robe, grabbed a passing woman for support who shrieked and stepped away, which caused the group to scatter around him like an exploding firework. He righted himself and took the last two stumbling steps to Diana's table and clutched it to keep from falling down. Diana had already rushed to help if he fell and I could still hear the crashes and grunts of the masses as the waves of Tom's klutziness spread.

As usual, Tom was unaware of the chaos in his wake and struck a pose of calm authority.

"Diana Moonward?" he said.

She cocked her head at him as if maybe he'd sustained a brain injury on his way through the fair.

"You know I am. What's up, Tom?"

He dropped his officer stance and lowered his voice. "I have to take you in to the station for questioning—I'm really sorry."

"What! I knew it!" Vi rushed to his side. "I knew Rafe Godwin was murdered!"

Tom turned to Aunt Vi. "How did you . . ."

Diana gasped and the blood drained from her face. Mom squeezed her amulet in her fist and stepped closer to Diana.

"So Vi's right? He was murdered?" Mom asked.

Tom looked from my aunt to my mother and then shot a pleading glance in my direction.

"I can't say anything. I just need to ask Diana some questions."

"Well, we're going with her!" Vi crossed her arms and stepped between Tom and Diana's table.

"No, *I'll* go with her," I said. "Diana, text Bethany to come early for her shift and Vi and my mom can cover your table until she gets here."

Diana fumbled in her pocket for her phone and handed it to me with a shaky hand.

"We can't do that, Clyde. We don't know anything about this . . . merchandise." Mom swept her arm over the table, and shook her head.

"We can do it, Rose. Selling is selling, right? We can always tell the customers to come back in an hour if we can't answer their questions." Vi was already rolling up her sleeves and rearranging the table.

"Well, okay. Thanks." Diana stepped from behind the table and grabbed my hand.

"I'll drive her and we'll meet you there, Tom," I said.

"You aren't arresting her are you?" Diana squeezed my hand, hard.

"No. I'll explain when we get there." He glanced at the

small gang that had gathered at Diana's table. "Nothing to see here, folks. Go about your business." He pushed his way through the throng, which gave him a wide berth, and we followed.

# 4

We walked to my car, an ancient Jeep Wrangler that had been brought back to life after I rolled it into a ditch last summer. We climbed in, buckled up, and bounced our way down the dirt path out of the woods.

The vehicle was eerily silent. Diana tended to shut down when she was nervous, a trait I appreciated at this moment. There was no need for speculation without substance. I'd had enough of that growing up to last the rest of my life. But I knew she had to be wondering whether Vi was right, crazy as it sounded. Once we hit pavement, I broke the silence.

"Diana, this is probably routine. They just need some more information about Rafe," I said.

She nodded and stared at the passing wooded terrain.

"Just answer the questions as honestly as you can," I said. "I'll stay with you." I reached over and squeezed her hand.

"What if your mom and Vi are right?" Diana blurted as she turned in her seat to look at me. "Who would kill Rafe?

And why do the police think I would know anything about that?"

I was wondering the same thing.

"Let's just wait and see what's going on," I said. "You know Tom loves the dramatic moment. He's probably just trying to make it look like a bigger deal than it is."

Diana gave me a small smile. I knew she didn't believe the reassurances, but she appreciated the attempt.

We parked near the station and sat for a moment before getting out. Diana took a deep breath, straightened her shoulders, and nodded at me. I took my own calming breath and opened the door.

Tom met us in the lobby and walked us past Lisa Harkness. She was the receptionist and self-appointed news distributor. Her mouth hung open as she reached for her cell phone. Tom showed us to a small interview room and left. Diana and I exchanged glances. We didn't wait long.

When the door opened again, Mac stood there. With his six feet and a couple of inches he filled the doorway. He kept his blond hair cropped short, and whether he was in his uniform or jeans, he radiated authority. His size and gruff manner fooled most people, but I knew the lines near his mouth were from an easy smile. And that the sparkle in his eyes was more often from laughter than anger.

I felt a warm flush at the sight of him. Last summer, we'd rekindled a relationship that had ended too soon, but we were keeping it to ourselves for now. In public we were all business. Especially since my family was not known for minding their own, and would likely begin planning the wedding if they knew we were back together. Mac was determined to give us every possible chance of doing things right this time. Between my family duties, his job, and Diana's festival, we'd had a rocky start to our reignited romance. It seemed the Fates were conspiring against us. I'd been looking forward to an evening alone with him. The look on his face wiped away any thoughts of a romantic interlude in the near future.

After I gained control of my smile and donned a more suitable expression of outrage that Diana had been brought to the police station, my heart sank at the realization that Vi must be right. Rafe had been murdered.

Mac worked in the county sheriff's office as a homicide detective. He wouldn't be here in Crystal Haven unless there was suspicion of murder.

"Why am I not surprised?" Mac said. "Of course you two were there when Rafe Godwin died." Mac dropped a file onto the table and crossed his arms. He had perfected the intimidation stance. And his blue eyes could become a steely gray when he was angry.

Intimidation didn't work on me. But Diana squeezed my hand again.

"Mac, what's this about?" I said. "Why did Tom drag Diana in here?"

He sat in one of the chairs and gestured that we should do the same. He dropped the tough-cop ploy and rested his elbows on the table.

"Diana, did you know that Rafe was allergic to peanuts?"

"Of course." Diana nodded. "Lots of people knew that."

"Someone has come forward claiming that they tasted peanuts in the"—Mac looked at the file in front of him—" 'bambrack' bread."

Diana and I looked at each other.

She shook her head. "No. I made it myself. I knew Rafe was allergic and the recipe doesn't call for nuts, anyway."

"What is bambrack bread?" Mac asked.

"It's a traditional Celtic bread made with fruit soaked in

tea," Diana told him. "I thought it would be a fun thing to do this year for the ceremony. My mother used to make it every Halloween."

"So, there weren't any nuts in any of the food you served?" Mac said.

"That's right. I made everything myself. I don't know how he would have been exposed to peanuts. Plus, if it was an allergic reaction, the EpiPen should have bought us some time."

"Yeah, we're looking into that as well," Mac said. He rubbed his forehead.

"Mac, it was an accident," I said. "He must have eaten something elsewhere and then reacted to it. Unfortunately, we were so far out in the woods that we couldn't get him to a hospital in time."

"He was severely allergic," Diana said. "He carried EpiPens everywhere he went, and stashed them all over the place. And he was really careful about what he ate. I don't know how this could have happened." She put her head down on her arms.

I put my hand on her back.

"Diana, you knew him pretty well, right?" Mac asked.

Diana sat up and nodded. "He was my father's best friend. Dylan and I called him Uncle Rafe. After my parents died, he was the one who helped us put the pieces back together." Her voice broke and she put her hand to her mouth.

Mac slid a box of tissues in her direction. "I'm sorry, Diana," he said, and waited.

After a loud use of the tissues, she said, "Sorry, I'm just overwhelmed with the festival and I've been avoiding thinking about him being dead."

"You've been working too hard." I put a hand on her arm. "Let Bethany take over the booth today."

She shook her head. "It's better if I stay busy." Diana looked at Mac. "Do you need anything else?"

"Whatever you can think of that would help us find out who might have wanted to hurt him." Mac held his hands out. "It's clear he ingested something in the hour or so before he died. Was he with you all that time?"

Diana sat back in her chair and took a deep breath. She nodded and looked at the ceiling, trying to recall the evening.

"He helped me set up the food," she said. "We had a small meal before the ceremony. That's where he would have eaten the bambrack. Who said they tasted nuts?"

Mac looked at the table and then at Diana. "I can't tell you."

I felt my jaw clench. If we'd been alone, I would have called him on his top secret attitude. There was nothing to indicate foul play as far as I could tell, so unless he was keeping major information from us, he had nothing to go on.

"Mac, Diana is exhausted. I'm sure she'll call you if she thinks of anything. Can we be done here?"

He nodded. "Before you leave, I'll need a list of everyone who was in the woods that night, his closest contacts, and any family."

Diana took the pad of paper he offered and began writing. Mac pulled me out in the hall while she worked.

"Did *you* see anything that might help?"

"Like, did I see someone hand him a jar of Planters?"

"This isn't funny, Clyde. I have to investigate the claim that his food may have been contaminated. Knowing Diana made it without any nuts means someone must have doctored it later."

"It's all hearsay. Some random person claims they tasted nuts and now you're launching an investigation?"

"We have samples of all the food from the ceremony.

The nurse who helped out at the scene took it all to the hospital—he thought it was a food allergy reaction and figured it might be useful to the doctors. He watches too much TV, but in this case it was actually helpful to be able to send it all off to a lab."

"You know that will never hold up in court. There's no proof he got that food from the ceremony."

"Who said anything about court?" Mac's voice got a little higher and he held his hands up like I was mugging him. "I'm just trying to figure out if this guy died by accident or not."

"Diana did everything she could to help him." I crossed my arms and held his gaze.

"No one is accusing Diana of anything." He put his hand on my arm and slipped it around my back to pull me into a hug then retracted it quickly when he remembered where we were.

I raised an eyebrow, then smiled at him. "Good." I wasn't sure why I was worrying. Mac was right, there was no reason to suspect she had anything to do with peanuts in the food, but I was getting a bad feeling anyway.

In general, bad feelings are the only kind I have. Or maybe they're just the strongest ones. I've never quite figured it out, but I was excellent at predicting trouble and doom. It was *my* special talent. Vi talks to animals, Mom reads the tarot, and I have vague inklings of badness, punctuated by dreams predicting death and mayhem. I'd trade it in an instant for a talent like singing or painting.

Diana came out of the room and handed Mac her list.

"Thanks, Diana. I'll look into this."

He walked with us back toward the front of the building and said good-bye. Mac could get very wrapped up in a case. It was unlikely I'd see him anytime soon. But, I smiled and nodded—I don't do clingy.

# 5

I insisted on taking Diana to lunch instead of returning right away to the festival. I felt we needed a dose of Alex, the third member of our little group and the designated cheerer-upper. I knew he could help me out in the support-a-friend department.

Everyday Grill felt more crowded than usual this time of year. The festival had definitely helped the tourist trade this fall. Shocked once again at the changes Alex had made to the interior of the restaurant, I surveyed the new atmosphere with appreciation. Last summer, he was just an employee and the décor ran toward 1970s dark steak house. After the events of the early summer had resolved, he'd purchased the restaurant at a bargain and was able to put some money into renovations. Now the whole place felt lighter, brighter, and more like Alex.

The menu had been fancied up as well but he left a few old standbys for the regulars.

Diana and I were well-known by the waitstaff so her iced tea and my diet soda arrived almost as soon as we sat down.

Diana sipped her tea and then pushed it away. "I'm not really that hungry."

"You say that now." I shoved a menu at her even though we both had it memorized.

I ordered the Cobb salad. Diana, who wasn't hungry, got the bacon burger with fries. It's always good to drown stress with grease and fat. I was distracting her with tales of Baxter, my bullmastiff, and his never-ending war with our neighborhood squirrels, when Alex came out of the kitchen. A few inches taller than me, he had the shoulders of a kayaker and the barely contained energy of a toddler. His dark hair was hidden under a white bandanna, but he'd removed his apron. He pulled up a chair and gave Diana a long hug.

"I heard about Rafe. I'm so sorry."

Diana nodded and attempted a watery smile.

"What have you heard?" I asked, wondering if the whole peanut thing was common knowledge.

"Only that he collapsed and by the time the ambulance guys had hiked through the woods, he was . . ." Alex glanced at Diana and stopped.

She stared at her drink as if she didn't know what it was. I put my hand over hers, and thought quickly of a way to shift the subject.

"How's Dylan doing?" I asked her. Dylan Ward was Diana's brother—Diana had changed her name to Moonward after she opened her store—and until that week, I'd only seen him once in the five years since their parents had died. He'd arrived just in time for the festival and I'd seen him briefly at a couple of the events.

"He seems fine. He and Rafe never got along very well, and he hadn't seen him in years." Diana shrugged.

I nodded, but wondered just how well Dylan was doing in other ways. From what Diana had told me over the years, he'd been drifting from place to place, picking up odd jobs along the way. He was an artist and followed the art shows around the country, trekking his wares in a beat-up old Suburban that had been his dad's. He made leather boxes, clocks, and switch plates. Diana said he did a lot of couch surfing, but it often sounded as though it was more likely he did a lot of squatting in abandoned houses until the neighbors complained. Dylan was seven years younger than Diana and was only eighteen when Elliot and Fiona had died. He had taken it hard and left Crystal Haven the day after the funeral. I'd never fully understood the relationship between Diana and her brother. She was very protective of him. She sent him money whenever he had an address and always had a ready excuse for him when he disappeared for months at a time. I would have thought they'd stick together after the death of their parents, but Diana didn't seem to mind that he went his own way.

"Dylan was in here earlier talking to Lucan Reed," Alex said. "It didn't seem friendly."

"Lucan? I didn't know they knew each other," Diana said. "He's only been in Rafe's coven for the past year or so."

"It didn't look like a happy reunion. More like a Mexican standoff."

Diana's brows drew together. "I wonder what that was about."

Just as Alex shrugged, the food arrived and he was called back into the kitchen. He headed back to work after promising to stop by the festival for its last day.

**That night, after** a trip to the park with Baxter and a reheated casserole from the last time I was at my mom's, I checked my phone for messages from Mac. He'd texted to say he'd stop by later. I sat on the four inches of couch that Baxter allowed me and picked up the remote. He groaned and fixed me with his droopy stare. After almost losing him over the summer following his superdog heroics, I had spoiled him. Now he demanded the prime space on the couch and persistently tried to take over the bed.

I'd just clicked onto an FBI missing persons show when I heard a knock on the door. It wasn't Mac's usual four-beat rhythm, but I hopped up and swung open the door.

"Finally, you escaped!" I said before I saw who was on my porch.

"I guess you could say that." My nephew, Seth, slouched in my doorway. Tall and gangly, with blond bangs hanging in his eyes, it was clear he was Grace's son. He'd always had her coloring, and now his cute-kid looks were morphing into handsome charm. Tuffy, his ill-tempered shih tzu, glowered from where he was tucked under Seth's arm. Baxter became aware of his buddy and leaped off the couch. He almost knocked Seth over in his enthusiastic greeting. After coating as much of the teen as he could in dog slime, he turned his attention to the dog. Tuffy was wagging his tail so hard that Seth had to put him down. Both dogs bounded into the living room to complete their greeting ritual.

"What are you—how did you—"

Seth cocked his eyebrow and gestured toward the living room.

"Come in." I swung my arm wide and watched him push past the dogs and drop his backpack and duffel bag on the floor.

"What are you doing here?"

My older sister and I didn't communicate often, but whenever she sent her fourteen-year-old son to visit Michigan, she definitely called to make arrangements.

"It's nice to see you, too."

"Don't get snippy with me. Does your mother know you're here?" Grace was going to freak when she found out he'd traveled half the country.

He dropped his eyes.

"She thinks I'm at a friend's cottage for the weekend."

"Where does she think this cottage is?"

"Upstate New York."

I crossed my arms and took a few deep breaths. I felt a twitch begin in my right eyelid.

"Since you're now in Western Michigan, I can only assume you took a wrong turn."

"Actually, I took a car to Ann Arbor, then a bus to Kalamazoo until they found Tuffy in my duffel bag, then I caught a ride here."

"You took a car? You can't even drive yet."

"I got a ride with a friend's older brother who goes to U of M, and then I took the bus with one of *his* friends. *That* guy had a girlfriend who was picking him up at the bus station and they drove me here."

"We have to call your mother."

Seth held his hand up. "I just texted her to tell her I'm having a great time—can't we wait until tomorrow?"

"But, why?"

"I can't go back there, Clyde." He pulled his mouth into a sad expression that he probably practiced in the mirror. "I want to stay here with you."

More deep breaths. Some counting. It was late, and I knew Grace worked long hours. She didn't need to know tonight that Seth was halfway across the country and not simply a few hours away. Plus, now that he was in my house, he was safe.

"You can stay tonight. I'll wait to call your mom in the morning and then we have to figure out what to do with you."

"Great!" Seth flashed his grin. "Do you have any food around here?"

He walked toward the kitchen with both dogs trailing behind.

I spent a few moments alone in my living room pacing and trying to calm down.

By the time I joined them, Seth had emptied almost the entire contents of the refrigerator onto the counter.

"Don't you have any pickles? How about soda?"

"No pickles. I threw them away after you left. You know—to go home and go back to school?"

"Pickles last a long time; you didn't have to dump them." He chose to focus on the food, not the lecture.

I snagged a bag of chips out of the pantry and tossed them at Seth. He and the dogs had settled into their usual places at the kitchen table: Tuffy jumped onto the seat to Seth's right, Baxter rested his head on the table to his left. The dogs patiently waited for Seth to share.

I sat down in *my* usual spot—as far across the table as I could get.

We had fallen into this pattern over the summer. After I'd inherited the house, Seth and I moved our few belongings from the ancient Victorian shared by my aunt and parents to this much smaller home. It worked out in everyone's best interests. I needed my own place and the dogs were only welcome by my mom as temporary visitors, not permanent residents. Seth came with the deal—the dogs insisted. Early August had been filled with relaxation and recovery from the events of July and by the time we were all back on our feet, Diana had recruited us to help with the festival. I suppose it wasn't that surprising that Seth had shown up just in time to attend the last day of the festival—he'd been part of the planning from the beginning. I latched on to that thought as the reason for his sudden arrival. The other possibilities were less pleasant.

I worried about Seth ever since he admitted to having some sort of burgeoning pet psychic talent earlier in the summer. I never managed to get him to talk about it after he confided in me, and that concerned me. Having that sort of a secret could wear on a kid. I knew, having been that kid myself. He was a gentle person who seemed more interested in time alone with animals than with teens his own age. I wondered how much he had shared with his parents. My sister, incapable of seeing anything awry in her life, clung to the fantasy that leaving Crystal Haven would solve all of her problems and she had never backed away from that stance.

I sighed without realizing it and three sets of eyes turned to me.

"Want some?" Seth pushed the bag of chips in my direction, and continued to devour his triple-decker sandwich. I would have thought that he had been starved on his cross-country trip but he ate like that all the time. By the time he left at the end of August he had reached his life goal of surpassing me in height. I was sure I'd be craning my neck soon to look him in the eye.

After everyone was done with his snack, I told Seth to dump his things in his old room. He and the dogs padded up the stairs and returned a few minutes later, wanting to go for a walk. We clipped their leashes on and headed out the front door.

Tuffy and Baxter were delighted to be back together again. Tuffy ran next to Baxter to match his gait, his short legs blurring with the speed. Baxter slowed his pace for Tuffy, something he never did for me.

"The last day of the festival is tomorrow, so you didn't miss it all."

Seth looked surprised and said, "Right, the festival. Cool." My shoulders slumped. He hadn't come for the festival.

"You can go with me to Diana's booth after you check in with your mom tomorrow."

"'Kay."

Seth kept up a running monologue about a new electropop fusion band inspired by video game theme songs. Ever since he had discovered my stash of boy band CDs in a box during the move, he had been on a mission to improve my taste in music. I had no idea what he was talking about and suspected this was his attempt to control the conversation.

When we returned to the house, Seth's heavy tread on the front steps conveyed his fatigue from the day of travel. We unlocked the door and released the dogs from their leashes.

"I think I better go to bed," he said.

Tuffy was at his side in an instant. Baxter threw an apologetic glance in my direction and slumped off after his friends.

I sat on the couch alone, wondering what to do with a runaway nephew.

# 6

A few minutes later, Mac's signature knock sounded on the door. "Great, *now* he's here," I muttered to myself. I had hoped for a romantic evening at home before I acquired a teenager. Mac and I hadn't had much time together since we decided to try again with our relationship. Our plan for secrecy made it all the more difficult. Seth was the only person who knew we were dating—he'd seen Mac giving me a good-bye kiss one evening and straight-out asked me about him. Then in the fall, Mac got involved in a murder case in Grand Rapids. An extended stay in Saginaw followed while he wrapped up old business before resigning from that force for good and joining the Ottawa County Sheriff's Department full-time. We'd been on a couple of dates in the past few weeks before the festival duties had sucked me back in. We were elevating the "taking it slow" idea to a whole new level.

Mac didn't wait to be invited in but drew me into a long

kiss on the front porch. My knees started to feel like liquid as he steered me inside toward the staircase.

"Oh man, this again?" Seth said from the landing.

Mac jerked away from me and I almost fell backward onto the bottom step.

"Seth?" Mac peered up the stairs.

"Hey." Seth raised one hand and let it drop. It had taken a long time for Seth to not snap to attention in Mac's presence. A few moments like this one had led him to believe Mac was just a guy after all and not someone to be feared.

Mac looked at me.

I shrugged. "Surprise?"

"I didn't know you were expecting Seth," Mac said, a formal note creeping in.

"It was a last-minute thing—"

"I wanted to surprise—"

Seth and I began at the same time. I held my hand up like a traffic cop.

"Seth wanted to come to the last day of the festival. It was a spur-of-the-moment decision." I looked at Seth as I said this so he would know it was my rapidly cobbled cover story. As usual Seth caught on right away.

"Huh. Well, it's good to see you again, Seth. Is that Tuffy up there with you?"

"Yeah, he's here." Seth gestured behind him where the dog was cowering.

"He did okay on the plane? I thought he freaked out when you flew home with him in August."

Leave it to Mac to remember every detail I wished he would forget.

"They came by car," I said, and tried to steer Mac back into the living room. I hadn't prepped Seth about not telling anyone, especially Mac, that he had basically run away. Law enforcement officers take that sort of thing seriously.

"Well, I'm going to bed. Night." Seth and his companion retreated down the hallway.

Mac craned his neck to be sure they were gone.

He put his arm around my shoulder and leaned in to whisper, "This kind of puts a dent in my plans for the evening."

His proximity and scent of pine trees had me cursing Seth's timing.

"Mine, too." I turned toward him and was just settling my arms around his neck when the doorbell rang. My porch hadn't seen this much traffic in one night since Mom, Vi, and Diana had marshaled the neighbors to do a smudging to remove any traces of the old owner's spirit after I moved in.

I opened the door to Tom Andrews. Tall and lanky, with dark hair and brown eyes, he flashed a sheepish grin.

"Clyde, sorry to bother you so late but I . . ." He trailed off as Mac stepped into the doorframe.

Tom *did* snap to attention when he spotted his boss.

"Detective McKenzie! I didn't know you were here."

"What is it, Andrews?"

"Oh, well . . ." He looked from me to Mac and back again. "I wanted to ask Clyde about something."

"You know I don't want you including civilians in another murder case. This better not be about the death in the woods." Mac took a step forward, not that any further intimidation was necessary. I cleared my throat to remind him not to threaten.

"No, sir." Tom stepped back. "I just got a report about a young teen traveling with a small dog. I came to see if Clyde thought it could be Seth."

My shoulders slumped, and I could feel the heat of Mac's stare on the back of my head.

"Why would you get a report about Seth?" Mac asked.

"I'm not sure it was Seth." Tom warmed to his tale and stepped inside. "The report just said a bus driver in Kalamazoo reported a teenager had smuggled a dog onto a bus. He thought they looked a bit lost. He went to find the kid at the bus station but couldn't. Then he got to thinking about it and reported a possible runaway." Tom took a breath to continue, looked from me to Mac, and stopped.

"Clyde, did Seth run away from home?" Mac asked.

"Not exactly." I gave Mac my most winning smile. "He came to visit me . . . without his parents' knowledge."

Mac smiled back, but in a threatening way. "Call your sister—I don't want the NYPD dealing with a false missing persons claim."

"She doesn't know he's missing yet," I said.

Mac closed his eyes for a few seconds.

"Seth told her he was staying with a friend," I said.

"When are you planning on telling his mother where he is?" Mac's jaw was clamped so tight, I was worried about his molars.

"I'll call her tomorrow." I glanced at Tom, who looked devastated that he'd caused trouble. "It'll be fine. Seth is safe, he's with family. Grace won't mind."

Mac stared at me for a moment to let me know he didn't buy that for a second.

"Um, I'll just be going now." Tom backed onto the porch and tripped over the large pumpkin left over from Halloween. He caught himself on the porch railing before squashing it.

After watching to be sure he'd made it safely off the porch, I shut the door and turned to Mac. "Do you think he suspected?" I asked.

Mac shook his head. "I doubt it. His detective skills are still in the . . . development stage."

"Wanna beer?" I asked.

Mac shook his head. "No, I should be going." He looked up the stairs. "And I have a lot of interviews lined up tomorrow on this Godwin case."

He pulled me in for another kiss and I was just forgetting everything else when I heard feet pounding on the stairs.

"Clyde—oh . . . still? I thought I heard the door close." Seth stood halfway down the stairs examining the walls, the ceiling, the banister, anything to keep from looking at Mac and me.

Mac released me. He sighed, saluted Seth, and went out the front door.

# 7

◈

**Even with the extra hour that the end of daylight** saving time had given us, the next morning was more hectic than usual with another dog to walk and a teenager to wake up. It took more than one try. Calling pleasantly from the hallway didn't work. Calling less pleasantly from the doorway didn't work. Then I tossed some dog treats onto the bed and watched the melee ensue. It brought back memories of when Seth and I had been thrust together as partners in a dog-walking business engineered by Vi. Though I gave up the dog-walking when Seth went back to New York, I regularly missed hanging out with Seth and the dogs.

After breakfast and a quick walk with the dogs, we piled in the Jeep to go pick up Diana. She'd called to ask for a ride to the festival. Dylan's junker had broken down again and he needed to borrow her VW.

Both cars were in the driveway when we pulled up, so I parked in the street.

Diana lived in a small chalet-looking house that was partly obscured by vines and trees. It was the same house she'd lived in since moving to Crystal Haven as a kindergartner. Her mother had planted herbs, flowers, and shrubs over the years. Diana loved plants and couldn't bring herself to prune or cut down anything. It showed in the spring when the vegetation launched its campaign to take over the yard. Alex had been known to sneak over to her house when she was at work and "clean up." Now, in the fall, the foliage was subdued, the beautiful colors fading. Still, the deep shadows made me feel that they were all just biding their time until their world domination.

Seth and I climbed the stone steps to the porch and I raised my hand to knock when I heard Dylan's voice on the other side of the door.

"Why can't you just trust me on this?" His voice was hard, angry.

I couldn't hear a reply.

"He wasn't as great as you thought. Seeing the good in people is one thing, being blind to true evil is another."

Seth's eyes had become round, he looked back longingly at the Jeep. Before I could offer any reassurance, the door flew open and Dylan stood there, his head turned away to shout, "Whatever!" He spun back around and I watched as his face reassembled itself from anger to confusion to an uncomfortable smile. He was my height with straight black hair that he wore spiked all over his head. He had a gold hoop in one eyebrow, which drew attention to his gold-brown eyes. Diana stood just behind him in the hallway, her orange curls and bright green eyes denying the sibling relationship. The only thing they shared was their mother's upturned nose and creative sensitivity. Diana's mouth formed a circle of surprise.

"Hi, Clyde." Dylan hooked his thumb over his shoulder and shrugged. "Just some sibling bickering."

It sounded a bit more heated than their usual squabbles but I smiled in return.

Dylan was looking at Seth, obviously trying to place him.

"This is my nephew, Seth," I said. "You haven't seen him for a while."

"Seth?" Dylan held his hand out at waist height. The last time they'd met, Seth had been wearing Harry Potter robes and clutching a wand.

Seth raised his hand in greeting.

"Sorry, dude. Don't you hate it when people remember you as only a little kid?" Dylan put his fist out and Seth bumped it with his own. The male greeting ritual complete, I gestured at the door.

"Oh, yeah. Come in." He held the door wide, glanced at Diana, and said, "Later."

Dylan bounded down the steps and hopped into the VW. It sprayed gravel as he pulled out.

Diana gave a wobbly smile. "Seth, I didn't expect you. . . ."

"Seth really wanted to be here for the last day of the festival," I said.

Seth nodded. "Wouldn't miss it. I better go check on the guys." He gestured toward the car and hastily retreated. He was remarkably good at sensing the mood in a room and avoiding uncomfortable situations.

After he shut the door, I turned to Diana, who already had her hand up.

"I know what you're going to say."

I doubted that. "Okay, what?"

"You're going to say Dylan doesn't appreciate me and he doesn't respect me and I shouldn't let him take advantage."

I shook my head. We had argued enough about her brother over the years and I had thought all that more than once. "No, I've already said all those things." I let out a breath and met her gaze. "I was going to ask who Dylan thinks is evil."

Diana twirled one of her fingers through a ginger curl and bit her lower lip.

"It's Rafe." She paused and took a deep breath. "He's had it in for Rafe since my parents died. It's the reason he left town in such a hurry after their funeral."

That explained *some* things, like why Dylan hadn't stuck by his sister, and why she had tolerated it. I gestured toward the living room. A brother hating a murder victim felt like a sit-down conversation.

"You never told me that. I knew they didn't always get along but I thought that was because Rafe tried to step in as a substitute father. I figured Dylan resented it and just wanted to get away." I sat next to her on the couch.

"I think he did feel that way. And initially, that's what I thought as well. A few years ago, Dylan came here for a long weekend. You were already in Ann Arbor by then." She stopped and looked down at her lap before continuing. "He found Rafe here having dinner and they fought. I don't even know what it was about, to be honest, but *they* sure did. Dylan said something about knowing what Rafe had done. Rafe just laughed. That made Dylan even angrier." She stared into space, her brow wrinkled. "Anyway, Rafe left in a hurry and Dylan wouldn't tell me what he was talking about—until last night."

"What?" I put my hand on hers.

She took a deep breath. "He thinks Rafe killed my parents."

I pulled my hand away and stood up. "Is he serious?"

"He claims he has proof. He came back this week to confront Rafe, not for the festival."

I didn't like where my thoughts were leading me. If the bread had been doctored with peanuts, Dylan had been given multiple opportunities to do that. He'd been with Diana for the whole week.

"Do you know if he ever did confront Rafe?"

She shook her head. "He says they never had the chance to talk alone. He says Rafe was avoiding him. It's certainly true that I didn't see much of Rafe this week while Dylan was here."

"Has he told you what this proof is?"

"It has something to do with a grimoire that my father found just before he died."

"A grimoire?"

Diana rolled her eyes at me and huffed. "A Book of Shadows? A spell book?"

"Oh, like the one you write all your spells and potions in? Isn't it just a notebook?"

Diana got up from the couch and went into the kitchen. She returned holding a spiral notebook, its pages stained, the cover filled with doodles.

"This is my working notebook, or grimoire. I write down the mixtures of herbs and the words to say for different spells. If I come up with something I like, I add it to the family grimoire. It's kind of like a family recipe book. Ours has been passed down for five generations through my mother's side. In my family it always passed to the oldest daughter."

"Why haven't you ever shared this with me before?" I sat on the couch again.

Diana shrugged. "I sort of figured you knew we had one, and I've shown you some of the books I've used in the past. But, mostly, because it's supposed to be a secret."

"Still, old secret books are the kind of thing you tell your best friend . . ." I was mostly kidding but should have known better and realized Diana would take me seriously in her current mood.

"It's not like you ever expressed an interest in anything Wicca." She sat down, hard. "Your mother acts like I'm either crazy or deeply misguided most of the time, and Vi has been secretly asking for the lottery numbers for years. She seems to think I can do a 'winning spell.'" Diana's face got pink and her hair seemed to get bigger, and curlier.

"I was just kidding. Calm down." I reached for the notebook and then stopped myself. "May I?"

She nodded and handed it over.

"First of all, my mother looks at *everyone* as if they're crazy or misguided. She looks at me like I'm crazy, misguided, *and* ungrateful. Try living with that." I thought for a moment. "There's really nothing to say about Vi."

I flipped through the book, which was filled with Diana's perfect printing. She'd even sketched some of the plants she used. When I got to a spell about how to see your future, I flipped it shut.

I took a deep breath. "I've been keeping something from you as well."

She took the book back and waited.

"I've noticed a few times in the past, when you've done spells with me, that they seem to cause the dreams."

"You mean *those* dreams?"

I nodded. Diana knew how I felt about my psychic abilities. The dreams and occasional visions came unbidden and were, frankly, unwelcome. I had been trying for years to get them to stop. It was the main argument I had with my family—they thought I was throwing away a gift. Like a singer who wouldn't sing, or a star pitcher who preferred knitting to baseball. Mom and Vi, who wished they had inherited my grandmother's talent, constantly nagged me to "focus on my gift." What they didn't understand was that rather than feeling empowered by the knowledge, I felt helpless. The dreams were always bad news and I had never been able to change the outcome.

"Oh, Clyde. I'm sorry. I only did spells with you for protection. I never did anything meant to bring on your dreams."

"I should have told you, but it didn't come up that often." I grabbed her hand. "You can't tell anyone about this. If my mom and Vi get wind of it, they'll become Wiccans. Can you imagine the spells Vi would come up with?"

Diana laughed. "They would certainly put their own spin on it."

"But what does this grimoire have to do with Dylan and Rafe?"

"Dylan claims that Rafe and my dad had a fight about a grimoire my dad found. You remember my dad had the used bookstore and he was always haunting garage sales and estate sales for old books?"

"Sort of." What I mostly remembered about Elliot Ward was his sense of humor. He loved to tell jokes followed by a deep, rolling laugh that forced you to join in no matter how terrible the joke.

"Rafe was at our house for dinner about a week before my parents died. I wasn't there, but apparently the three of them were drinking and reminiscing. Dylan was outside shooting baskets and came in for a Coke. They must not have heard him come in, because he overheard them arguing about a book."

"Why would they argue about a grimoire?"

"Dylan wondered the same thing. He walked down the hallway so he could see what they were doing in the living room. The volume was ancient and falling apart, like an old family Bible. My dad was showing Rafe something toward the back and then he slammed it shut and said, 'You're done.'"

I sat back on the couch. It sounded like a threat, but Elliot was one of the gentlest people I had ever known.

"What do you think it meant?"

"Dylan thought there was a spell in the book and my dad was threatening Rafe with it. But now he has a new theory—" Diana's phone buzzed in her pocket.

Her eyes grew wide when she answered. "We'll be right there."

# 8

**Diana and I flew out her front door and got in the** Jeep.

"I thought we had to be there by ten. I got up early. . . ." Seth let his complaints trail off when he saw our faces.

"We lost track of time," I said.

"We're really late," Diana said.

Seth slumped in the backseat and plugged in his earbuds.

"Bethany is freaking out," Diana said. "She says it feels like the whole festival is at the booth. Most of them are asking about Rafe and whether it's true that he was murdered. The few real customers are getting irritated at the long line." Diana chewed on her thumbnail. She was a consummate professional, but the weeks leading up to the festival had taxed her organizational skills. I knew she was mentally beating herself up for leaving Bethany to fend for herself. I also knew better than to point out that the festival had been fantastic, with the highest attendance in ten years.

"What about your other assistant?"

"Skye hasn't shown up and Bethany can't reach her by phone."

I focused on the road and drove as fast as I could.

When we arrived, I had barely stopped the Jeep before Diana jumped out and made her way to her booth. Seth and I followed with the dogs.

Bethany had not been exaggerating. The line leading up to Diana's booth snaked past several other tables selling everything from pumpkin pies to wands to corn husk dolls. She pushed her way through the crowd to where Bethany, a blonde, plump, twenty-something, stood, trying to placate a customer and get the line to move along.

Diana stepped in and took over. I told Seth we should spread out along the table and gestured at the next in line to move forward.

"Dude, I just got here last night. I don't know anything about Rafe Godwin," Seth said to the fourth person who had quizzed him. He handed the man his bag and said, "That'll be twelve dollars."

After about half an hour of all four of us taking orders and sending the merely curious on their way, the line had died down to just a couple of people who were still deciding on their purchases.

"Bethany, I'm so sorry you were dealing with that all alone." Diana pushed a handful of curls off her forehead.

"No prob. They were here when I came to open up—it would have been crazy no matter what. I just got worried when you didn't show up on time. You're never late." Bethany made change for a lady who bought a lapis bracelet.

Seth sidled down to our end of the table. "I think you should take this one," he said, his face reddening.

Diana nodded and slid down to the middle-aged woman.

"What's up?" I said to Seth, and nodded at the customer.

"Nothing," he said. He leaned toward me and whispered, "She wants something to stabilize her hormones." He scrunched his nose. "I don't want to know about her hormones."

I looked away so he wouldn't see my smile.

After the menopausal customer left, Diana and I straightened up the booth, which looked like a windstorm had blown through. We went to the back of the stall to get more stock.

"Hi. Can I help you?" Seth's voice sounded deeper and I turned to see who had caused the modulation.

"I work here. I'm late." The girl brushed past him to put her bag under the table.

Seth's mouth hung open. I tried to think of a subtle signal to tell him to shut it before he started drooling, when the girl stood up and turned toward him. He clamped his jaw shut.

"I'm Skye," she said.

Seth nodded and pretended to be interested in the crystal balls on the table.

"I'm Seth."

Skye spotted Diana and me and came to the back of the booth. When she approached, I realized what had Seth so tongue-tied. She had bright blue eyes in a delicately perfect face framed by dark wavy hair. She was mesmerizing—I couldn't stop staring.

"Diana, I'm so sorry I'm late. My mom insisted I go to church with her." Her words came out in a rush. "She's been acting like a lunatic since Rafe died. She hopes I'll leave the coven now." I was surprised when, rather than scolding her for leaving everyone in the lurch, Diana pulled her into a hug.

"These past couple of days must have been awful for you. I'm sorry I didn't call." Diana patted her back and released her.

"Clyde, this is Skye. You might have met her the night Rafe . . ."

I put out my hand to shake hers. I remembered her now, but meeting her in the woods in the dark had not prepared me to see her during the day. A quick glance at Seth showed a person not ready to meet her under any circumstances.

Seth turned reluctantly away when a customer tapped him on the shoulder.

"Diana, since Seth and Skye are here to help Bethany, maybe we can wander the festival for a few minutes?"

She cocked her head at me and seemed to understand immediately what I wanted to do.

"Good idea. Let's go." Diana turned to Bethany and said, "Call me if it gets crazy again. We won't go far."

I glanced at Seth, who seemed to be standing very tall.

Once we got a few booths away, I said, "What's up with Skye?"

Diana nodded and sighed. "I hired her for the festival because Rafe recommended her. She's been working on some sort of project with him and she's a computer expert. Do you remember meeting her mother at the ceremony? Bea? She's short, thin, and always wears her hair in a bun?"

I slowly nodded as I ran the ceremony through my mind. "She didn't seem very happy to be there that night. Sort of the way my mother would act if I had forced her to come."

"That's not too far off. Bea doesn't approve of Skye's choice but came to the ceremony as a show of support or interest. Anyway, the fact that someone died right in the middle of the ceremony hasn't made matters any better."

"Is Skye old enough to join a coven? I thought you had to be eighteen?"

"She turned eighteen a few months ago. Her parents weren't happy when her first act as a legal adult was to leave their church and join the coven. They blamed Rafe and things got pretty ugly for a while there. When Bea asked if she could come to the ceremony I thought it was a good sign, that maybe she had developed an open mind."

"Sounds like maybe you were wrong."

Diana nodded and chewed on her thumb. I knew she worried about Rafe's coven and some of the accusations that had been swirling over the years. Rafe liked to run things his own way and some in the Wiccan community felt he was too heavy-handed. Even within his coven there were detractors. Now that he was dead, the group would have to figure out if it would stay together or split up. Diana had avoided covens because she didn't like the politics and she didn't want to do anything that would jeopardize her business. She would never admit it but she was just too independent to join a group that would dictate how she should practice her religion.

"We need to pick up some gossip," I said. "This is the last day of the festival and then our chance disappears to find out what people are saying about Rafe."

Diana nodded. "I doubt I'll pick up any useful tidbits. Everyone here knows how close we were."

"I think we should split up," I said. "You ask around and see what people saw at the ceremony. You know everyone who was there. I'll try to find out what stories are circulating. I never thought I would say this, but we sort of need Aunt Vi."

"I'll start with Ember and Bronwyn. They're from Traverse City area. They don't have any connections to the drama in Grand Rapids."

I took a deep breath. "I'll go find Lucan Reed. If he was arguing with Dylan, he might be more likely to talk to me than you."

"See you back here in an hour?"

I nodded and watched her melt into the crowd.

# 9

I found Lucan at his booth. He made masks and costumes for rituals and ceremonies, as well as cauldrons and wands. There was a large red head with black horns growing out of it that would have terrified me if I didn't know that it was used during Beltane to symbolize the god of fertility. I had seen pictures in Diana's books. There were more scary-looking masks and some robes as well as metal cauldrons and wands.

He stood when I approached, rising in front of me like a Highland warrior. He was well over six feet tall and very broad. His hair was wild, long, and dark red. He had it tied back in a piece of rawhide string. His full beard obscured most of his face. I felt myself flinch when his hand shot out. Realizing what he wanted, I took it and shook.

"You're Diana's friend," he said in a deep rumble.

"Yes, we met the other night at the ceremony in the woods."

His face pulled down and he looked away. "What a night-mare that was."

"I'm sorry for your loss. You and Rafe were close?"

He shook his head. "Not as close as you might think. We worked together, but that was it. Still, it's hard to watch someone die like that and not be able to help."

"Did you know he was allergic to peanuts?"

"I'd have to be living under a rock not to know he was allergic. Every time he put something in his mouth he announced he couldn't eat peanuts."

"Have you heard anything more about what might have happened?"

He picked up a small knife and a long piece of wood and began to work on what would probably become a wand. "Aren't you dating that cop?"

I felt my face get hot. How did he know? If he knew, then lots of people knew. I hesitated.

"Excuse me?"

"That lanky cop. The young one." He examined my face, and I found myself wanting to defend my right to date any-one I wanted.

I was too relieved, however, to argue with him. "That's Tom Andrews. We're friends. Not dating."

His eyebrows quirked upward. "Well, Tom Andrews has already been sniffing around, asking if I saw anything."

"Well, did you? Hear or see anything?"

Lucan set the wand and the small knife on the table. "I don't want any trouble with cops or their girlfriends. Why should I talk to you?"

I chose to ignore the girlfriend comment. "Because I'm Diana's friend and if you knew Rafe at all, you'll know how close they were. She's devastated and needs some answers so she can deal with this."

He let out a breath of air, and wouldn't meet my eyes. "I like Diana. She's a great person. Maybe not the best judge of character, but she's great."

"Whose character?" I didn't know why this guy was getting under my skin but I found myself annoyed by his assumptions, and I sensed he was hiding something.

"You just said she was close to Rafe. She's either a terrible judge of character or he was a much better actor than I gave him credit for." Lucan had picked up the wand again. If he kept on with his whittling, he'd end up with a toothpick.

I took a deep breath and waited. Lucan cleared his throat. He set his knife down again. "Rafe had alienated quite a few people in the coven. He ran it like he was our fearless leader and we should all just do whatever he said. Wiccans tend to like to do things their own way." Lucan grinned. "We aren't exactly conformists."

"You aren't saying that anyone in the coven would want him dead, are you?"

"All I'm saying is Rafe had an inflated idea of his own place in this world. He said he was descended from five generations of Wiccans and since no one else had that kind of heritage, we should all listen to him. That alone was debatable since many people say Wicca only began in the 1950s. He acted like some kind of chosen one, and that can get on a person's nerves after a while. I would imagine he acted like that with other people as well. Has Diana talked to her brother?"

"I think she's pretty aware of how her brother feels," I said.

Lucan shook his head and laughed. "I doubt it."

"I could really use your help if you know something."

His mouth drew into a thin line behind his mustache. "Talk to Skye Paxton and Morgan Lavelle. They both knew Rafe pretty well. And tell Diana to listen to her brother."

Lucan turned away as a customer approached the booth. He made a big show of telling them about all of his merchandise. I took the hint and nodded at him as I walked away.

Lucan's comment about Diana listening to her brother reminded me I needed to talk to my own sibling. I walked to the parking lot for some privacy. The rustling and chattering of squirrels and chipmunks gathering food for winter, and the exuberant color beginning to fade as I crunched through the leaves made me smile and I wondered how I'd stayed away from Crystal Haven for so many years. I steeled myself for the task at hand. I couldn't go any longer without talking to Grace. She was expecting Seth to return on the train that evening. I took a few deep breaths, turned on my phone, and scrolled to her name.

"Grace Proffit." Her voice was crisp, businesslike.

"Grace, it's Clyde."

"Clyde? Hi. Your number came through as private. How are you?"

"I'm fine. I'm calling about Seth. . . ."

"Don't you have his number? He's out of town right now. He'll be home tonight if you want me to give him a message." I heard honking in the background, and Grace's voice faded in and out.

"Are you at home?" I raised my voice and put my hand to my other ear as if that would improve the connection.

"No, I'm walking to an appointment uptown, I don't have much time."

"Listen, Grace, Seth is here. With me."

"What? I thought you said Seth was with you. Wait. I'm ducking into a coffee shop, it'll be quieter."

For once not jealous of Grace, I leaned against my Jeep

fender and listened to the few remaining leaves whispering in the trees.

"What did you say?" The connection was clear now with no background noise.

"Seth is here with me. He and Tuffy showed up on my doorstep last night."

The line was silent.

"Grace?"

She cleared her throat. "Is he okay?" Her voice cracked.

"Yes, he's fine."

"He's supposed to be upstate with friends. What's he doing there?"

I shrugged even though she couldn't see me. "He showed up after hitching a ride with friends and taking a bus. I haven't pieced it all together yet. He's working at Diana's booth at the fall festival right now and flirting with the prettiest girl in town."

"I knew something was bothering him but I've been so busy with these disasters at work. It's not a good time to be working for an investment company. . . ." I imagined her with her hand to the bridge of her nose, her classic stressed-out posture.

"Grace, I don't think anything is *wrong,* but something is up and I think I can get it out of him. He's welcome to stay for a while, if you and Paul are okay with that. Maybe he can stay for a week or so until we get it figured out."

"I would normally hop on a plane and drag him back home, but something's been bothering him lately. Ever since he came home from the summer, actually."

Since she'd *never* hopped on a plane to come to Crystal Haven, I saw this for the empty threat it was.

"Why don't you let me figure out what's going on? If you can deal with his school, we'll take it from there."

"Yeah, okay. I know he trusts you, Clyde. Maybe he'll open up to you. But let me know if he needs anything."

"I'll call you in a couple of days."

"Okay. I'll talk to him tonight when I get home from work. And, Clyde, thank you."

I clicked END CALL and took another deep breath. That had gone way better than I expected. I was surprised she was letting him stay. Either she was really distracted by whatever was happening at work or she was very worried about him.

# 10

❧

I walked back toward the festival, studying the map of vendors' booths. Besides the usual baked goods and crafts, Diana had added some Wiccan vendors this year. When I had begun this project with Diana, I had no idea about all the merchandise involved in the pagan/Wiccan world. I headed toward the Wiccan section and wandered past tables full of colorful candles and incense. Diana stood a few booths away talking to a woman with long dark hair trailing down her back. I assumed it was Bronwyn or Ember. She wore dream catcher earrings that caught the light when she moved. The booth was filled with soaps, lotions, and bath salts. Not wanting to interrupt, I turned in the other direction.

I stopped at a booth selling hand-drawn tarot cards. One of them was a beautiful pen-and-ink Victorian Gothic deck I bought for Mom. Past jewelry, crystal balls, and pendulums I finally found Morgan's booth at the very end of the row.

As I approached, I could see why Diana had given her this

remote location. Morgan Lavelle was known for her hand-made athames, which were forbidding daggers used in Wiccan rituals. I had asked Diana about them the first day I walked past a booth with a display of the ritual blades. I felt like I was at a gun and knife show rather than a fall festival. She'd explained that they were used to direct energy and many Wiccans believed they should never be used to cut anything. That was a relief, but didn't make them any less scary-looking. Morgan's entire booth was draped in black cloth and a huge number of dangerous-looking daggers were arranged in half circles, or star shapes with the blades pointing outward. Dragons curled up the handles, or pagan symbols were carved into the blade. The dark, ominous feel of the booth gave me pause more than the knives themselves. Morgan wore a black cape and more eyeliner than an Egyptian princess. She was encased in a tight black turtleneck and black jeans tucked into four-inch-heeled boots. She'd pulled her jet-black hair into a tight chignon and she favored the kind of deep red lipstick that I usually saw on the covers of vampire books. Multiple necklaces and amulets glinted around her neck. Small silver skulls hung from her ears, their red jewel eyes flashing. All she needed was a riding crop to look like a dominatrix. Maybe she had one hidden beneath the table.

Diana kept to the light side of her magickal life but I knew that some people were drawn to the darker edges. The main tenet of the Wiccan philosophy was that whatever you put into the world came back to you threefold. I would think that would be enough to keep people away from what I would consider black magick. Things like sending bad luck and illness toward an enemy, or even a love potion if its intention was to enslave the subject.

Morgan clearly had no qualms about this aspect of Wicca. Along with her knives she had a selection of "spell kits" with candles and herbs packaged together with pieces of parchment. She had a kit for protection from enemies, misfortune to foes, and agony to adversaries. Behind these unpleasant titles sat a large black candle packaged with incense and what looked like human hair. It was labeled simply REVENGE.

Morgan was busy with a customer but turned to me abruptly and said, "Be careful about touching. The ingredients might rub off on you."

I snatched my hand away from the revenge candle and moved to the relative safety of the knife display. Morgan packaged up a small knife that looked tame in comparison to the rest of her wares and handed it to a young woman who quickly melted into the crowd.

"Have we met?" Morgan tilted her head in my direction.

I had to look up to meet her gaze. Her heels gave her at least a three-inch advantage on my five-foot-seven frame.

"I don't think so. I'm Clyde Fortune." I hesitantly put out my hand, but Morgan just glanced at it and I let it fall. When she crossed her arms, I noticed a charm bracelet on her wrist that seemed out of place with the rest of her scary jewelry.

"Oh yes, Diana's friend. I've heard about you." She frowned and focused on my eyes. "Your eyes really are striking. You must have some powerful visions."

Morgan referred to the different colors of my eyes. One is brown, the other pale blue. Wiccans believe that it's a sign of psychic talent. It's the only thing my mother can really get behind when it comes to Wiccans.

"I wouldn't say that. In a town of psychics, what's one more premonition, right?"

"You can't deny it forever. But, that's your journey, not mine." Her voice was flat, bored. "What can I do for you?

Looking for a more powerful spell than Diana is willing to share?" She gestured to her table of horrors.

"No!" I brought my voice back under control and continued, "No, I just wanted to talk to you." I had to carefully weigh how much to tell this woman.

"Okay, talk." She crossed her arms and narrowed her eyes.

"Diana is really upset about Rafe's death. I've been asking people who knew him if they had any theories on how he could have ingested peanuts." I didn't mention Lucan's referral, sensing it wouldn't help me.

"So, it *was* an allergic reaction? I wondered." She put one long black fingernail to her lip.

"Yes, that seems to be the theory."

She nodded. "Rafe was very allergic. He claimed he'd have a reaction just from smelling peanut butter." She smiled. "He did tend to exaggerate."

I waited for her to continue.

"I don't think I can be of much help to you. I'm sure you've heard that Rafe and I had a bit of a . . . falling-out a few months ago. I left his coven and I haven't seen much of him recently. We generally didn't like to be around each other. In fact, I avoided last night's ceremony knowing he would be there." She shrugged, and focused on polishing her knives.

"Do you mind my asking what the falling-out was about?"

She looked up and held my gaze for a long moment, stiff, unyielding, as if debating whether to answer at all. "Actually, I do mind. It was personal, but I'm sure you'll find someone willing to describe the last fight we had." A bitter smile crossed her features, and then disappeared. "Rafe liked to be in control—most of the time."

Her smirk was so suggestive I took a step back. I wondered again where she kept her whip.

I cleared my throat. "Were you involved, romantically?"

She let out a gust of air. "Romantically? There was nothing romantic about it." She looked me up and down. "We both had needs. Don't attach some fairy-tale fantasy to it."

"What about—"

"That's all I have to say about Rafe," she said, her voice icy, clear. She pivoted toward a new customer examining the knives made of bone.

Dismissed, I turned and walked away. But I felt her cold, hard stare follow me down the path.


**By the time** I made it back to Diana's booth I had discovered that everyone had a theory about Rafe's death. I'd skulked around the various stalls listening in on the gossip, a skill passed on to me by Aunt Vi. There were outraged discussions about quality control and the faulty EpiPen, there were theories about rival covens and more than a few people mentioned the Wiccan rede of a threefold return. The general sense was that Rafe deserved what he got, which was a whole different take on Rafe than the one I had always heard from Diana.

Her booth was crazy-busy again as the shoppers settled in to the last-day-of-the-festival frenzy. Baxter and Tuffy may have had something to do with the bottleneck since they sat right in front of Diana's sign wagging at anyone who walked by. They were such an odd couple that no one could pass by without stopping to pet one of them. Diana set Seth loose to explore the fair while the rest of us served the continuous stream of customers. Seth returned with a small metal dragon statue—an unusual choice, but apparently his Harry Potter roots ran deep. He shoved it in his pocket when Diana and Skye approached. Diana sent us home for dinner as long as we promised to return for the closing ceremony. She knew we had yet to tell my family that Seth was in town.

Seth, the dogs, and I headed back to Crystal Haven in silence. I was running all the rumors through my head. He was plugged in to his iPod. I thought maybe he would volunteer his reasons for being back in Crystal Haven—I had read somewhere that teenagers liked to talk in cars. Apparently, not all of them.

We pulled into my parents' driveway and I shut off the Jeep. "Are you ready?"

Seth nodded. "It's not going to get any better. Maybe Tuffy will distract them."

"Yeah, let's go with that." I got out and opened the back door for the dogs.

Baxter planted himself at the front door and gave two deep woofs. Like Mac, he had a signature knock. Aunt Vi swung the door open in greeting and stopped midsmile. "Tuffy? Where did you . . ." She looked up and saw Seth standing on the bottom step. She stepped back in the house and said, "Rose, I knew it! Seth is here!"

"Who's here?" Mom appeared, wiping her hands on a dish towel. She saw Seth and came forward with her arms out for a hug. "What are you doing here? We missed you so much!" She turned to me, hands on hips. "Clyde, how long have you been planning this?"

Seth allowed the fawning to continue. I think he secretly liked it. His blond bangs fell into his eyes as he bent to hug the ladies in turn. The truth was, things hadn't been the same since he left to go back home at the end of the summer. I'd gotten used to having him around. I guess the rest of the family felt the same.

"And Tuffy's here, too!" Vi crouched down and gave the dog the same hero's welcome as Seth. I was starting to get jealous.

Dad came to the door. Just slightly taller than me and with a shock of white hair that stood straight off his forehead, he looked perpetually surprised. "What's going on out here? Oh, hi, Clyde. Wait till you see my new police scanner. I can even pick up the Grand Rapids channels." Dad was slowly easing out of his dental practice and pursuing other interests, like spying on the police.

"Frank, Seth is here with Tuffy," Mom said.

"Oh, Seth. You should come see it, too." Dad stopped and looked at the melee of dogs and people on his porch. "Did I know you were coming to visit?" He looked at Seth.

"No, it's a surprise." Seth grinned.

"Thank goodness. I thought I was slipping." Dad scratched his head, and swung his other arm toward the door. "Well, are you coming in or what? Dinner's on the table."

We trooped inside and settled around the table in our usual spots. Mom bustled, making a production of setting an extra place for Seth. Vi sat with Tuffy on her lap, a distant look on her face.

"Tuffy doesn't like planes, and he also doesn't like your duffel bag," Vi said to Seth.

Seth just nodded.

"He wants to know how long he gets to stay before you have to travel again."

I cocked an eyebrow at Vi. "Tuffy wants to know, or you do?"

"It *is* a good question," Vi said.

"Seth just got here, Vi. Let's not rush him out the door."
Mom came in from the kitchen with lasagna in her hands.
Mom always had enough food to feed any swarm of locusts
that showed up—even Seth. "I hope you're all hungry."

The dining room fell silent after the food was dished up.
Mom had made her own sauce and the cheesy meaty combination was one of my favorites. Seth was on his second
helping before the inquiry began.

We had decided to give the same explanation to the family as we had been giving everyone else. Seth wanted to
catch the end of the festival since he'd been working on it
for most of the summer. I still didn't know why he'd arrived
on my doorstep, and something told me I didn't want to
know. But I would need to confront him soon.

The story seemed to satisfy everyone and we moved
on to other topics, namely Rafe's death. Seth had been filled
in on the particulars and listened avidly to the conversation.

"I just knew something would happen that night. I felt it.
The woods were so dark and there was this . . . *foreboding*,"
Vi said.

I looked at the ceiling. *I* remembered her asking five
hundred questions and chattering through the whole thing.
She didn't seem to be worried at the time.

"I, for one, am glad I wasn't there. I've never been happy
about the whole dark-woods-and-cauldrons combination."
Mom began collecting the dishes.

"I heard the 10-52 go out on the scanner. I have to say I
was relieved when I heard the victim was male." Dad glanced
at me. His police scanner habit meant he talked in code much
of the time and I was the designated translator.

Seth, Mom, and Vi looked at me and waited.

"10-52 is 'ambulance needed,'" I said. They all nodded
understanding and went back to their food, except Vi.

"What does Diana say about the whole thing? What did the police want? Are there any suspects?" Vi's rapid-fire questions had my head spinning.

"They don't know anything," I said. "Someone claimed they tasted peanuts in the food that Diana served and since word has gotten out that Rafe died from an allergic reaction, Mac is looking into it."

"I knew it," Vi muttered. "There was something off about that weird bread." She grabbed another roll from the basket and ripped it in two before slathering on the butter.

"Tuffy didn't like him." Seth pulled the dog onto his lap.

Heads swiveled in Seth's direction.

"How do you know that?" said Dad.

I felt my heart pound. Seth didn't want anyone to know about his . . . connection to the animals.

"Tuffy doesn't like anyone," I said, and glanced sharply at Seth.

He realized his error. "We were at Diana's once when he stopped by and Tuffy started shaking and went and cowered by Baxter," Seth said. It wasn't his best cover story.

Vi looked at Tuffy with narrowed eyes.

I felt I had to argue the point even though I wanted to get off this topic.

"C'mon, you can't be taking this seriously. He hates everyone and he's always cowering." I appealed to my dad, usually the sensible one in the family.

He shook his head. "I don't know. I think animals can sense things that people can't."

I sat back in my chair, defeated.

"*Any*way, until they find any real evidence of intentional harm, I think this is just an unfortunate accident," I said.

Everyone looked at me with varying degrees of pity at my lack of imagination.

# 11

**Seth and I stood in the backyard with the dogs. It** was much colder than the last time we'd done this and I was glad I'd thrown on a jacket. Seth shivered next to me in a T-shirt and a light hoodie.

"I talked to your mom today."

"Yeah, she texted." He kept his face turned away from me.

"What's going on in New York? Is something wrong in school?"

He shook his head and buried his hands under his arms. He looked pathetic. I was about to tell him to go inside when Vi appeared in the doorway. She spotted us and picked her way across the yard.

"Seth, you're freezing. Go inside and make a big deal out of your grandfather's new contraption," Vi said. For all of Vi's communication with other realms, she was still suspicious of anything electronic.

Seth looked at Vi with relief and raced into the house.

"I should get Seth to the ceremony. He doesn't want to miss it." I stepped past Vi.

Her arm shot out and she gripped my arm. "Stay a minute."

"What's up, Vi? I don't know anything more than I told you."

"I'm here to tell *you* something." She peered around the yard, and lowered her voice. "I don't want your mother to hear this."

I was speechless. Vi never kept secrets from my mother.

"Why can't my mom know about this?"

"Just trust me. She doesn't want to know."

"Okay. . . ."

"There's someone you need to talk to." She looked over her shoulder as if there were spies hiding in the trees. I wondered if she suspected the squirrels, or maybe it was the owls.

"I'm not investigating Rafe's death," I said, and crossed my arms. "I don't think there is anything to investigate."

"Not about Rafe. This is something else. Your grandmother would have wanted you to meet this woman."

That stopped me. My grandmother Agnes had died when I was fifteen. She'd been a gifted psychic. Some people thought she was the reason Crystal Haven had lasted so long as a spiritualist community and had become famous. She'd known I had visions and dreams and had promised to teach me how to use them instead of being haunted by them. Before she got the chance, she died of cancer. Vi knew that mentioning my grandmother was the best way to get me to listen.

"Why have you never mentioned this mystery woman before?" I had my hands on my hips now, just like my mother. "If she lives here, how come I haven't met her?"

"You know *of* her." She lowered her voice even more.

*"Neila Whittle."* Vi made the name sound like the title of a horror movie.

"The old witch? I thought she was dead."

Neila Whittle was the topic of many playground ghost stories in Crystal Haven. A recluse, she lived on the edge of town, up a private road. Her property was surrounded by a black ironwork fence. It was as if central casting had plopped a classic witch into Crystal Haven for the children to fear. The house itself was small, stone, and completely covered in vines. It sat in the middle of a grove of trees as if it had sprouted there of its own volition. Every kid in Crystal Haven had been dared to climb her fence and creep toward the house on one dark night or another. It was part of growing up here.

"She's alive and well and still . . . You need to talk to her." Vi nodded and wouldn't say any more. Holding her finger to her lips, she shooed me inside.

I found Seth in my father's office, huddled over a small black box with backlit buttons and a glowing screen. It was definitely a step up from his old scanner. Dad was giving Seth the rundown of 10-codes.

"Hey, we better get going if we want to make the ceremony," I said.

Seth had been writing the codes on a card, which he folded and stuffed in his jeans pocket.

"Okay. Later, Papa." Seth held out his hand for a fist bump and after considering for a moment Dad tapped his fist against Seth's.

We said good-bye to Mom and Vi, who were in the living room poring over Mom's new tarot cards. The dogs followed and we all jumped in the Jeep.

"That was pretty uneventful for a dinner over there," Seth said as he leaned back in the seat.

I nodded, thinking that even though the dogs hadn't eaten anything they shouldn't, and no one had gotten into a heated argument, something eventful had happened. Vi had gone behind my mother's back and pointed me in a direction I didn't even know existed.

**The lot was** packed when we arrived. Because the fair had been dismantled that afternoon, the final ceremony was to take place at Message Circle. It was closer to the road than the fair had been and would allow all the festival attendees to get out to the main roads quickly to drive home.

We picked our way along the path, which was lit with battery-powered lanterns every fifteen feet or so. Seth had launched a vocal campaign over the summer to use kerosene lamps. He had an affection for the oil lamps my mom dragged out when the power failed during storms. Diana and I had vetoed the idea for safety and transportation reasons.

"See how fake that looks? Not spooky at all," Seth groused as we walked along the path.

"It's not supposed to be spooky. And they're safer than kerosene. You can't go driving around with a backseat full of kerosene."

"Whatever," Seth grumbled. "It would look way better."

Thankfully, we caught up to some other people walking toward the circle and he fell silent.

Lit with small torches, eerie shadows jumped among the seats and darkened the trees as we approached Message Circle. Larger torches flanked a boulder draped with black cloth holding Diana's cauldron.

There was an air of celebration as people dressed in hooded robes greeted others dressed in jeans and leather

jackets. A few wore down jackets and hats. I wished I had
worn gloves. Morgan Lavelle was hard to miss. She towered
over her two companions. One was the woman I had seen
Diana speaking with at the festival. Her earrings glinted in
the firelight. The other was an older version of the first, with
long gray hair. I assumed it must be Ember and Bronwyn.

Diana was already in the center of the circle directing
people to find a seat. She wore her black velvet robes and I
was jealous of the warmth they must provide. Seth and I
shivered in our light jackets. A long-standing superstition,
I didn't pull out my winter coat until the first snow. The
longer I held out without wearing the coat, the less snow we
would get. I didn't think it actually worked, since every year
we got dumped on. But the habit persisted. Lake-effect snow
was worthy of superstition.

Seth entertained himself by watching his breath turn to
mist. He at least had Tuffy sitting on his lap for warmth.
Baxter would crush me if he sat on my lap. I tried to bury
my hands in Baxter's fur and his drool soaked through my
jeans when he rested his head on my leg. It was time to get
this ceremony going. Skye Paxton spotted us and sat next
to Seth. She introduced her younger sister, Faith, who looked
about fifteen. They fawned over Tuffy and I wasn't sure
which one was enjoying it more, Seth or Tuffy.

A hush fell as Diana stood and raised her arms. After a
brief welcome, she asked us to join hands. Ugh. I hated
holding hands with strangers. I grabbed Seth's hand and he
took Skye's hand as if his life depended on it. I turned to
my right with my hand out and was surprised to see Lucan
sitting there. He was very quiet for such a large man. At
least he wasn't a complete stranger.

Diana thanked everyone for participating, and said she
would send positive energy through the circle. It reminded

me of my Girl Scout days when we would hold hands and pass the squeeze around the circle. Then a lit sage stick made its way through the crowd just like on Halloween—Wiccans were big on clearing energy with smoke. She asked us to sit, and allowed the crowd of about forty to share some favorite experiences from the festival. This, of course, began to devolve into a discussion of Rafe's death. After a few queries about Rafe, his coven, and his allergies, Diana firmly steered everyone to more pleasant subjects, such as the workshops, food, and camaraderie. I still heard muttered comments about Rafe, but the group respected Diana enough to move on. When the comments had died down, Diana raised her arms in the center of the circle. The group fell silent.

Diana turned in a circle and said:

> Lady of Darkness, Lord of Shadows,
> Fire, wind, air, and water
> We offer love and thanks
> For this Sabbat rite.
> O ancient ones, we bid thee farewell.
> Blessed be, and so mote it be!

She threw a lit match into her cauldron and blue flames shot out. Fire was a big crowd-pleaser.

"Wicked," Seth whispered next to me.

"So mote it be," said Lucan.

Scattered murmurs of "blessed be" made their way through the crowd and people began to collect their belongings and gather in small clumps to say good-bye.

The ceremony over, Seth, Skye, and Faith approached Diana. I could tell Seth really wanted to get a look into the cauldron. It was just rubbing alcohol and would eventually burn itself out but Seth looked like he thought it was real magic. I nodded to Lucan, and Baxter and I headed toward Diana. She was guarding the cauldron from curious visitors.

"Have you ever set anything on fire with that thing?" a small, elderly woman asked with a bit too much excitement in her voice.

"No, it's really quite contained. But you need to be careful if you use it inside." Diana smiled at the crowd that was gathering. Maybe she'd sell a couple of cauldrons before the night was over.

After a few more questions about the cauldron and some passing-out of business cards, Diana was ready to go. The teens took photos of one another and exchanged phone numbers.

Diana let Seth put out the fire by dropping the lid on top. We left him to guard the cauldron while we trucked the rest of her supplies out to her car. Lucan had been standing off to the side and now stepped forward to help carry our bags. Diana smiled and nodded her thanks. By the time we returned, the cauldron had cooled and we carried it to the lot as well. I gave Diana a long hug and promised to stop by her house the next day. She said she wasn't going to the store but was letting Bethany open up. This alone told me how hard the last couple of days had been on her.

# 12

The next day, Monday, Seth slept in. I took the two dogs for a business walk and promised them a longer one when Seth woke up. Baxter groaned and slumped onto the couch when I got my keys out. Tuffy's eyebrows went up into his hairline and he did his nervous dance. He followed me, looking forlorn as I shut the door behind me.

I called Tom Andrews on the way to The Daily Grind and he agreed to meet me. Mac was never forthcoming with information on an open case. Tom was more generous. I hoped he was in the loop on the whole Rafe Godwin situation. After what Diana had told me about Dylan's suspicions, I was getting a sick feeling in my stomach. Sometimes it was hard to distinguish between regular nerves and actual "feelings" and so I ignored my gut and decided to approach the problem in a logical and controlled manner. I would gather information, examine the facts, and not get caught by Mac.

This time of year the only people in the coffee shop were regulars. We had reclaimed our town from the summer tourist crowd and now that the festival had decamped, the place was back to its quiet normal. This was good and bad. I liked not waiting in line, but growing up in a tourist town trains you to view the invaders as a necessary annoyance. Without vacationers, the economy would shut down, but it was nice to feel like we had Crystal Haven to ourselves for a little while.

Josh started making my usual latte when I walked in the door.

"Should I start Diana's tea?" he asked. His black watch cap barely contained the shaggy mop of dark hair.

I shook my head. "No, but you can make whatever Tom Andrews usually drinks."

Josh cocked his head, raised his eyebrows, and crossed his arms. He and Alex had been partners for years. They were overly invested in Mac and me getting back together and I felt guilty about keeping it a secret from them. Plus it meant they saw deeper meaning in all my actions.

I put both hands up. "We're just friends. Everyone knows that."

Josh shook his head. "Not everyone."

Fortunately, Tom swung through the door at that moment, nearly wiping out a coffee-mug pyramid, and I was able to extricate myself from the conversation.

Tom waved to Josh. "I'll have a—"

"Already started, dude," Josh said.

Tom and I had our choice of tables so I steered him to one by the window as far from the counter and Josh's ears as we could get.

"So, what's up with Seth? Did he run away?" Tom wasted no time introducing the topic I wanted to avoid.

"Not exactly. Grace knows he's here." I didn't fill him in on when she found out about his travel plans. Josh brought our drinks and I waited until he left to ask my next question.

"What's going on with the Rafe Godwin case?" I focused on my latte and tried to appear casual.

"You know I can't talk about an active case." He leaned forward and waited for me to look at him. He lowered his voice. "Mac almost fired me last time."

I nodded through my twinge of guilt. "I know. I'm sorry. I was just asking because Diana's so broken up about it. I thought if I could tell her more about how Rafe came in contact with peanuts, it might ease her mind."

Tom sat back in his seat. I could see the struggle on his face. He wanted to help Diana and loved to talk about his work. He pressed his lips together. Leaning forward, he kept his voice low. "We did hear back from the lab on that. I don't know if it will ease her mind." He hesitated.

"And?"

"Maybe you should talk to Mac about this." He sat back. "I don't want anything to get out of hand again."

Tom was referring to the standoff in the woods this past summer. He had apologized about a thousand times for getting me involved in what became a dangerous situation and was apparently still feeling guilty.

"Mac won't tell me anything. You know how he is." I heard the desperate note creep into my voice and silently chided myself for manipulating him. "Can you tell me where the peanuts came from?"

Tom sighed and looked out the window. He twisted his lip between his thumb and finger while checking up and down the street.

He leaned forward again. "They found peanut oil in the bread that Diana made."

"Peanut oil? How did they test for that?"

Tom shrugged. "I don't know. I didn't know our lab could do that sort of test, but apparently there was peanut oil on the bread."

"*On* the bread? Or in it?"

He gave me a flat stare, obviously sorry he'd given in. "It seems that the bread had peanut oil rubbed on the outside." He sat back and crossed his arms.

"What does Mac say?"

Tom shook his head. "You're going to have to talk to him about that. I don't want to get involved. Last time—"

I held up my hand. I knew where this was going. "Okay, okay. I get it. You don't want to get in trouble with Mac."

We stared at each other for a moment. If the oil was on the bread, then anyone could have put it there. There's no way Diana did it, but it didn't let Dylan off the hook.

"This means anyone at the ceremony or near the food could have done it. But, why?"

Tom nodded, his excitement winning out. "Exactly. The bread was sitting out on the table, according to the people we've interviewed so far. It was a serve-yourself kind of setup. Anyone could have—" He stopped abruptly.

"Tom?"

"You aren't going to get any more out of me." He turned in his chair to look out the window.

"Do you want some help on this?"

Tom shook his head violently. "No. I was wrong to ask for your help last summer. You have no idea what I went through after the case wrapped up." He flipped his notebook shut and shoved it into his pocket. "Mac said that if anyone had gotten hurt that night in the woods, it would have been my fault. I have a sworn duty to protect the citizens of Crystal Haven and I didn't do that this summer. I won't make the same mistake again, and not just because Mac said he'd kill me if I put you in danger again." His face flushed pink as he finished.

"Mac said that?"

Tom put up his hand. "Please, Clyde. Just let it go."

I nodded and glanced out the window at the brown leaves dancing down the street. Tom was right and so was Mac, but I needed to know what was going on. Diana was going to be devastated when she found out that her bread had killed Rafe.

**As I walked** to my car, my phone buzzed in my jacket pocket. I pulled it out to check the text. Diana had sent: *911—my house!*

Fortunately, she only lived a few minutes from the coffee shop. I ran two stop signs and screeched around the corner to her street. I pulled up behind a police car that had its lights flashing.

Rushing up to the porch, I met Dylan and Charla on their way out. Dylan appeared angry and scared in equal measure. His head was down, but he looked up and caught my eye. I read him loud and clear—*help*. Diana followed, shouting questions at both Charla and Dylan.

"Charla, what's going on?" I stepped in front of them.

"Clyde, help your friend." She gestured back toward Diana. "I'm taking Dylan in to the station. He's under arrest."

Charla had been on the Crystal Haven police force for as long as I could remember. She was the one who had convinced me to enter the police academy. And while I knew she harbored a soft spot under all the bravado, she rarely showed it. Diana's face was pale and her eyes welled with tears.

"Diana, we'll figure this out." I put my arm around her, wishing that I was better at emotions. I steered her back into the house so she wouldn't see Dylan getting into the police car.

"Clyde, I can't believe they're doing this." She turned toward me and gripped my arms. "Can you talk to Mac? Convince him he has the wrong person. Dylan could never have done what they're saying."

Mac and I thought we were being very discreet, but I wondered yet again whether Diana knew we were together. She seemed to always know what was going on in my life, whether I told her or not.

I led her to the living room and sat next to her on the couch. "What are they saying?"

"Charla said she's arresting him for Rafe's murder." Her voice broke and tears overflowed. She took a shaky breath. "I don't believe it."

I patted her back and reached for a box of tissues sitting on the coffee table. "Okay, let's go down to the station and be sure he gets a lawyer. Do you feel up to this?"

She nodded and clutched the tissue box to her chest.

# 13

Diana and I tailed the cruiser down the hill and
into town. It pulled up in front of the police station, which
was tucked between a bookstore and a palm reader. We
found a parking spot not far away—impossible during the
tourist season but there were only a few die-hard visitors
between the fall festival and Thanksgiving. Even without
the siren, a small crowd of locals had formed to watch Dylan
walk into the station, his hands cuffed behind his back. It
would be about ten minutes before all of Crystal Haven
knew Dylan had been arrested.

We followed Charla down the hall toward the one cell,
which was more like a low-priced hotel room than any
prison I had ever seen. The walls were clean and graffiti-
free, and I knew the food came from Alex's place. Ann
Arbor had been a much bigger city with a more active and
noisy prison facility.

She turned and held her hand up. "You two can wait in the

lobby or come back later. We have to get him in the system and finish the paperwork. It could be a couple of hours."

Diana released a sob when Charla said "in the system." I took her hand and led her back out to the front. Dylan had not said a word the entire time. Maybe he would be okay if he just kept his mouth shut.

"We need to find a lawyer, Diana. Do you want to go over to Rupert Worthington's office and see if he can take the case or recommend someone?"

Her eyes were glazed but she nodded. I knew she'd been keeping herself in check until the festival was over. She had said she was going home from the ceremony the evening before to have a bath and a good cry. She'd need more than that to get through this ordeal.

**We sat on** a bench outside the police station to let Diana adjust to the circumstances. When she was no longer crying in earnest, we walked down the street in the direction of Rupert Worthington's office. He'd been the one to tell me about my inheritance last summer. It was this bequest that had allowed me to give up my job as a dog walker and prompted me to abandon my plans to return to Ann Arbor and my old job as a police officer. He'd informed me I had inherited a house and cash but I had to live in Crystal Haven for a year in order to accept the inheritance—an unusual requirement of the will, and after some thought and prodding from my family, I had accepted. Of course, the money wouldn't last forever and my future career was a nagging concern.

I doubted Mr. Worthington took criminal cases but hoped he could put us in touch with someone who did. His office was near the marina, empty now and quiet. I loved the clanging of the boat riggings and the squeals of seagulls in the summer. A few leaves skittered across our path on the nearly deserted street.

The air had turned significantly cooler in the last couple of days and I was glad to step inside the law office. Diana shivered, from cold or shock I couldn't tell. We entered the office to the tinkling of a bell over the door.

"May I help you young ladies?" Rupert's rumpled look was particularly bad that day. His shirt was partly untucked, his hair stood up in small spikes around his head, and he had loosened his tie to the point that he should have just removed it.

Diana glanced quickly at me, concern in her eyes.

"Mr. Worthington, perhaps you remember me from the summer?"

He took off his reading glasses and examined me. "Oh yes. Clytemnestra Fortune. How are you enjoying your new house?" He stepped forward to shake my hand.

I took his hand. "Please call me Clyde. Everyone does." Only a few people from my childhood still called me Clytemnestra and now that I had moved back, I was systematically working to stamp out all use of that name. It had been my mother's misguided attempt at giving her daughters unique and meaningful names. Her name was Rose; her favorite roses were orange. Both Clytemnestra and Grace are orange roses. Dad must have lobbied on my sister's behalf. She got the normal name. Nine years later, he gave in and *I* have to live with it.

"What can I do for you?" Rupert asked. "The requirements in the will were quite clear and even though we *are* headed into winter, you have to stay in the house for a full year, you know. Only the tourists get to avoid the snow." He chuckled at his own wit.

I assured him I had no intention of moving out of the house. He politely waited for me to explain our presence.

"This is Diana Moonward. She needs a lawyer for her brother."

"You look very familiar, young lady. Have we met?"

Diana nodded. "You handled my parents' estate. Elliot and Fiona Ward?"

"Oh yes. I remember. What a tragedy. I'm so sorry. I'd be happy to help you. Where is your brother?" He peered behind us. "What does he need—a will, a contract review?"

"No, sir. He's in jail," Diana said. "He's been accused of murder." Her voice broke and she began crying in earnest again.

Rupert Worthington sucked in air and shook his head. He pawed through the papers on his desk until he found a box of tissues.

"Oh my. I haven't handled a criminal case in years, just years." He chewed on his lip and regarded Diana's pale, blotchy face. "But, yes. I can take care of him." Rupert patted her shoulder and bounced on his toes. "I may need to consult with a firm in Grand Rapids, but you just leave everything to me."

Diana cast a worried glance my way.

"Can you tell us what to expect next?" I asked. I had already told Diana what I knew from the arresting officer's point of view, but wanted to hear what Rupert had to say. Procedures were different in various judicial districts.

"There will be a preliminary hearing as soon as they can get it scheduled. I hope to have him released on bail but I wouldn't plan on it. Better to be pleasantly surprised than bitterly disappointed." Rupert began a smile and then retracted it when he saw Diana's stricken face.

Diana and I shook his hand again and headed back out into the brisk day.

"What am I going to do? I don't have money for bail. What if it's a huge amount?" Diana waved her arms, and her eyes were wild. "Where will he stay until trial? How can they even think he did it? They've all known him since he was a little kid. Tom Andrews was his best friend in high school."

I shook my head. I had never been on this side of the arrest before. I knew he would be booked and a charge would be entered. Then they would set a court date to decide whether there was enough evidence to go to trial.

"Let's go to my place and figure out what the next steps should be," I said.

We put our heads into the wind and, with linked arms, walked up the street.

# 14

**Diana arranged with Rupert to meet her at the** police station later that day. We convinced Alex to leave his manager in charge of Everyday Grill and go to my place with us to make a plan. I'd called Mom and Vi. I didn't think I could keep Diana calm *and* organize what to do next all on my own. My mom was great at the soothing-and-calming thing. Maybe I could convince her to do a tarot reading that was slanted toward a good outcome.

I'd also phoned Seth, who was finally out of bed at eleven, and warned him the gang would be arriving shortly.

The doorbell rang just as we were taking off our coats. Mom, Dad, and Vi stood on the porch. I questioned the wisdom of calling them when I saw they were laden with baskets and tote bags.

"I knew it!" Vi said when I opened the door. She pushed past me and dropped her bags, gesturing wildly. "I knew that whole thing in the woods would lead to trouble. I just felt it in my bones and now look at us. Dylan's in jail, Rafe is dead . . ." She got a good look at Diana and trailed off.

"Diana, come sit down. I have cookies and chamomile tea." Mom held out a basket and gestured toward the dining room.

Seth, Alex, and I followed along with the dogs, who seemed to sense the mood of the room and went quietly into a corner to lie down.

"We have to find out what really happened so we can get Dylan out of prison." Vi pounded the table and the dogs looked up.

"What can we do, Vi? We don't know anything." Mom shuffled her cards and laid them out in front of her.

"We can start by talking to whoever was there that night," Vi said.

"Vi, did you see anything unusual?" I asked.

"What *wasn't* unusual? People in robes, chanting, fire in the cauldron. I was amazed!"

"But did you see anything that might relate to what happened to Rafe?"

Vi sat back and took up her knitting. She claimed she couldn't really think unless she was knitting, but her talents only stretched to scarves and hats. Occasionally she branched out into dog sweaters, which she foisted onto her clients. This time, something very long and purple dangled from her needles.

"I saw Rafe talk to that big guy."

"Lucan Reed?" Diana asked.

"Yeah, that might be it. They didn't look friendly, almost like they were arguing. They only spoke for a minute and then Rafe stalked off to the other side of the circle. It was really dark, so I couldn't see much."

"What about you, Clyde?" Alex asked.

"I was so busy keeping track of the food and making sure things didn't blow away or get lost in the dark that I didn't pay attention to who was talking to whom. I didn't notice Rafe at all until he fell in the center of the circle. I thought he was having a heart attack," I said, and glanced at Diana. It couldn't be easy for her to be reliving that night.

Diana nodded. "I didn't pay much attention to what other people were doing, either. I was focused on the ceremony and what I needed to do."

Mom, sitting next to Diana, patted her hand.

"Look, honey." Mom sat back in her chair and scrutinized her layout. "The cards say Dylan didn't do it. If I'm reading this right it was a woman who was responsible." We all leaned forward. It did seem as though there was a female presence in the situation, but just like every other divination technique, it was open to interpretation.

"Let's get out that pendulum thingy," Seth said.

Alex put his head in his hands. A simple divination technique, the pendulum swings in a "yes" or "no" direction in response to questions. He had never been able to work the device and he was too competitive to just let it go. The pendulum had become his nemesis.

Vi picked up her tote bag, allowing her knitting to fall to the floor.

"Alex, I need to check on Clyde's alarm system. Want to help?" Dad asked. He was no fan of the pendulum, either, and the two of them disappeared.

We spent about forty-five minutes with the pendulum with no results. Vi had just taken possession of the crystal to ask another question when the doorbell rang and triggered a clamor of barking and scraping of chairs.

Vi got to the door first. After peeking through a small

crack, she swung the door only far enough so she could fill the opening.

"Hello, *Officer* Andrews." Her voice was icy. "What can we do for you?" She crossed her arms, and I could tell she was blaming Tom along with all the other police officers for Dylan's arrest.

"Can I come in, please, Miss Greer?" Tom's voice floated in from outside.

"We're really very busy right now trying to figure out how to get Dylan out of *jail*."

"I know. That's why I want to come in."

Vi glanced back at Diana, who nodded her consent. Vi swung the door wide to a somber Tom Andrews dressed in his street clothes. He raised a hand in greeting.

"Well, let the man in, Vi," said Dad. He and Alex had come to see what was happening in the front hall.

"I'm so sorry, Diana," Tom said. His foot got caught in the welcome mat and he stumbled through the door. He stood up straight and smoothed his jacket. "I had no idea they were planning to arrest Dylan. I would have warned you, which is probably why they didn't tell me. They seem to think he's a flight risk."

"Who's 'they'? And why is he a flight risk?" Alex stepped forward. He, Diana, and I had been inseparable in high school and his protective instincts were strong. Anything that upset Diana was sure to upset Alex.

"Mac and Charla. They have *some* evidence and are looking for more," Tom said. "Dylan hasn't exactly been easy to find over the past few years. He follows the art shows and even Diana doesn't always know where he is. They were afraid he'd take off again if he knew they were coming to arrest him. Basically, I'm off the case." Tom stood with his hands out, palms up. "Mac says I'm too close to Dylan and can't be objective." He let his hands fall to his side.

I gestured toward the dining room and the group moved in that direction. Dad and Alex abandoned their project and joined us. The pendulum forgotten, we gathered around the table.

Per Tom, several witnesses had come forward with stories of Dylan and Rafe arguing and someone claimed that Dylan had threatened to kill Rafe. Dylan had the opportunity to doctor the bread since he had easy access to Diana's kitchen, and another witness had seen Dylan leaving Rafe's house the day he died. Rafe had followed him into the yard and grabbed Dylan's arm. Dylan shook him off, and Rafe fell. Apparently, Dylan just kept walking. Tom ticked these items off on his fingers.

"Isn't this just circumstantial evidence?" Alex said.

Tom nodded. "But they found some fingerprints on the EpiPen. One of them was Dylan's. One was Rafe's, one was the paramedic who picked it up at the scene, and they're assuming the last set would be Diana's." His head was bowed toward the table.

"We have to do something!" Vi glared around the table, daring anyone to contradict her.

"But what?" Seth said.

"We need more suspects, for one thing," I said.

Diana took a shuddery breath. "I don't like the idea of looking to put the blame on someone else just to get Dylan out of jail. What if the other person didn't do it, either?"

"All we need is another option to stop them from assuming they have the guilty party and ending the investigation," I said. "Mac and Charla are solid cops, and I don't believe they would arrest Dylan without good reason, but I also think it wouldn't hurt to give them a few more avenues to look into."

Diana took a deep breath. "I did have a weird conversation with Ember and Bronwyn."

"What kind of crazy names are those?" Vi said.

I cast a threatening look at Vi and she picked up her knitting.

"Bronwyn is the mother and she and Ember make organic soaps and lotions. They also dabble in oils used for spells," Diana said.

"What happened?" Tom asked.

"I was asking them about what they might have seen that night and Bronwyn told me about seeing someone rummaging through the robes. Then she started to say something about Morgan Lavelle, and Ember stepped in and cut her off."

"Morgan says she wasn't there," I said.

Diana nodded. "She wasn't on the list and she and Rafe tended to avoid each other. I didn't see her there. I don't know what Bronwyn was going to say. But it was strange."

"So, any other gossip?" Vi asked. She leaned forward and glowered around the table as if we were keeping things from her.

"Lucan and Rafe have been fighting for the past several months," I said. "I heard that Lucan didn't agree with Rafe's overly controlling leadership style."

"I saw Lucan and Dylan arguing at the restaurant the day that Rafe died," Alex said. He peered around the circle and looked down. None of us were sure if that would help or hurt Dylan.

"I heard that Morgan and Rafe had a major falling-out a few months ago," Diana said. "There were rumors that they were a couple and then they fought about something and he kicked her out of the coven. She was livid and started calling all the coven members and bad-mouthing him."

"That sounds like routine drama," said Alex.

Diana nodded. "It was, mostly. Rafe wouldn't admit it, but I think he was afraid of her. He caught her going through his garbage. He thought she was looking for supplies for her dark spells."

"What?" I said. "Do the police know?"

Tom shook his head and watched Diana.

She hugged herself and shivered. "I told Mac that Rafe was anxious about kicking her out of the coven. That woman is scary. Did any of you happen to go by her booth? She sells all kinds of spell kits for revenge and power. It's not what Wicca is meant to be."

"Did you see how she dresses? She looks like a dominatrix," Vi said.

Dad's head snapped up from the newspaper he was perusing.

"A what?" Seth asked.

We all sent a glare in Vi's direction.

"You know, black leather, scary hair, long nails . . ." Alex decided to skate over the definition and describe her clothing.

"Oh, like Lady Gaga?"

"Yeah, a lot like her," Vi said.

"Skye told me her mother didn't like Rafe," Seth said. "Well, her mother hates everything to do with Wiccans."

"I knew that, but thought maybe she was coming around since she came to the ceremony," Diana said.

Seth shrugged. "Dunno. It's just what she said. I got the impression her mother hating it was part of the appeal."

"We have Lucan and Morgan in his coven," Alex said, ticking off the suspects on his fingers. "They'd been fighting with him over the leadership of the group. And Dylan—who had what reason?"

Tom sighed. "He thinks Rafe killed his parents."

A collective intake of breath circled the table. I was surprised Tom knew about this, and Diana's perplexed expression indicated she was as taken aback as I was.

"How did you know?" she asked Tom.

"He told me a long time ago, the day after your parents' funeral, right before he left. He thought Rafe had something against your dad and was sure that Rafe had arranged their accident."

"How horrible, to carry around that sort of anger." Mom had her amulet in a death grip. "Poor Dylan."

Diana brought them all up to date on the grimoire and how there was something in that book that Dylan thought Rafe had killed their parents for.

"What could be in some moldy old book that would be worth killing for?" Seth asked.

Diana shrugged. "Dylan thought there was a powerful spell in there, but he's shown it to a bunch of Wiccans who all say the same thing. The recipes are typical everyday spells that would be found in any grimoire, especially one that was passed down through a few generations."

"Then what's the big deal?" Vi asked. She dropped her knitting and leaned forward.

"There's a family tree in the back." Diana met my gaze. This is what she had been about to tell me the other day. "Dylan said he never paid any attention to it because he was convinced the secret was in the spells. The genealogy is that of Rafe's family," Diana said. "You may not know this, but one of the main reasons he's in charge of the Grand Rapids coven is because he has the longest family history of witchcraft. He's always played up the fact that Wicca is in his blood, and his followers believed him."

We nodded to encourage her to continue.

"Dylan showed the book to a friend who knew nothing

about spells, but a lot about genealogy. Apparently the symbols indicate that Rafe was adopted. His whole argument that he is most equipped to run the coven goes out the window if he's adopted."

"Oh my," Mom said.

"Do you think your dad threatened to expose him?" Alex asked.

Diana held her hands out, palms up. "I don't know. They were friends, but my dad always said that Rafe was power hungry and it would ruin him someday. Dad may have just wanted Rafe to be aware that he knew his secret. Maybe Rafe didn't even know he was adopted. . . ." Diana trailed off, the day's events finally taking their toll on her.

"We need a plan to figure out who else would want Rafe dead," Dad said.

"I can't believe that Rafe would have killed your parents over something like this—it's just ridiculous," Mom said.

"I don't know, Rose," Vi said. "He really liked being the big fish in a small pond. If he had to give that up, what would he have done?"

Glances shot around the table. We had all seen how contentious things could get here in Crystal Haven over issues like who was the best psychic, who did the best séances, etc. What seemed small to one person could be the whole world to another.

"I wouldn't put it past Rafe," Vi said. "I never . . ." she stopped when she noticed Diana's quivering lip. "I never saw eye to eye with Rafe Godwin." She took up her knitting again with intense interest.

"Let's start by looking into Diana's parents' accident," I said. "Tom, do you think you could go to Bailey Harbor and get the police report? Would they release it to you?"

Tom nodded. "I have a friend working there. I should be able to get a copy."

"We'll start with that," I said. "And we should try to find out more about Lucan and Morgan and what kind of disagreements they had with Rafe. I'm not sure why this coven is so valuable to everyone."

Tuffy jumped up on Seth's lap and pushed his face into Seth's neck. "Tuffy needs his walk," Seth said. Baxter stood up, alert at the word "walk."

"We should get home," Mom said to Vi and Dad.

"Clyde, I've got all the smoke alarms connected to your alarm company now," Dad said.

"Thanks, Dad."

Mom patted him on the back. "Parents never stop trying to protect their kids."

"Diana, stay here tonight. You don't want to be alone at home, do you?" I said.

"She can stay with me," Alex said. "You've got Seth here, and Josh and I have room." He slung an arm over Diana's shoulder. "Come on, we'll go to your house and get your stuff and then I'll go with you to meet the lawyer."

Alex steered Diana outside after the rest of the group.

As soon as the door closed, Tuffy jumped up with bright eyes and a wagging tail.

"What does he want?" I said to Seth.

"He thinks it's time for a walk and his afternoon treat."

"He gets an afternoon treat?"

"Of course. Baxter probably wants in on that as well."

We snagged their leashes off the hook and headed out into the cold, gray dusk. I wasn't used to the time change and resented the darkness encroaching so early in the day. I pulled my jacket closer and worried about what tomorrow would bring. As we walked along I thought about all the people who had apparently been at odds with Rafe. It surprised me since I had only heard Diana's view of him. It was just another example of how people put on different faces for their various roles.

Seth's phone buzzed and he checked the text. His phone was much more active than it had been over the summer. His face looked pink and I wasn't sure if it was from the cold or whatever he read on the tiny screen.

"Faith wants me to go to a movie with her," he said.

I smiled. "Oh? Okay. Do you . . . go to movies when you're home?" I wasn't sure what Grace's rules were. This had never come up over the summer.

"Yup, we have movies in New York City and I sometimes go see them."

I narrowed my eyes and probably looked like Vi. "You know what I mean."

"Yes, I'm allowed to go out." He sighed dramatically. "I have to be home by nine thirty on weeknights and eleven on the weekends."

"Okay. Do you need a ride?"

He looked at his phone. "She says her mom will drop us off at the mall."

"That's fine. I can pick you up if you want."

He shook his head. "No, Skye will pick us up."

He punched in a message and his phone buzzed again. "Oh. They're on their way; we'd better head back to the house."


**A black Tahoe** sat in the driveway. We hurried down the street to meet it. Faith must have been pretty sure that Seth would say yes.

A thin, pretty woman climbed out of the driver's seat. Her hair was pulled up into a loose bun, and bangs covered her forehead. She wore a black skirt with tall boots and a cream-colored leather blazer. In her forties, she had the whole forty-is-the-new-thirty thing perfected. She held her hand out to me as we approached.

"Hello, I'm Bea Paxton. You must be Seth's aunt." When she smiled I could see where Skye got her beauty. "I think we might have met briefly the other night. That poor man, what a tragedy . . ."

I nodded and shook her hand.

"Sorry for the short notice. Faith just came up with this idea as we were heading back to Grand Rapids. You don't mind if I drop them off? I have a meeting tonight. . . ."

Since Seth routinely took a subway alone and had managed to get all the way to Michigan from New York, I wasn't worried about his ability to navigate the mall.

"No, that's fine. Thanks for taking him," I said.

"It's no problem. Skye will drop him back home by nine thirty. It's a school night so I don't like Faith to be out past then. I looked up the movie and I think it will be appropriate." She looked to see if the teens were listening, which they weren't. They were busy listening to each other's music on their phones. She lowered her voice. "No violence or . . . sex."

"Well, thank you."

She raised her voice and said, "Okay, kids, let's go."

Seth waved good-bye to me and the dogs and climbed into the backseat.

"I guess it's just you and me, guys," I said to the dogs.

Tuffy whined, and Baxter let out a quiet groan as we watched the SUV pull into the street.

# 15

❧❧❧

**The next day, Tuesday, I took Seth to my mom's** with the dogs. Vi had decided that she and I should start interviewing anyone who had been at the ceremony on Halloween night. I had mostly agreed in order to keep an eye on her. Since the nurse who had performed CPR was closest to Rafe at his death, we decided to start with him. I wondered if he had any opinions about the failure of the EpiPen.

Daron Pagan was a Wiccan, but not part of Rafe's coven. He lived in the area and was a solitary practitioner, like Diana. They knew each other because Daron frequented her store, and they occasionally exchanged e-mail about news occurring in the Wiccan community. Diana had called to ask him to meet with us, and he'd agreed, saying he had a lunch break at eleven thirty. Diana was going to spend the morning meeting with Rupert again. I had offered to join her, but she insisted I talk to Daron.

"Let's hit the road," Vi said as soon as Seth and I walked in the door.

"Maybe Clyde wants some coffee before you go." Mom had followed Vi into the front hall.

"She's fine, aren't you, Clyde? We're not driving to Canada. We'll be back in a couple of hours." Vi pushed me out the door and pulled it closed behind us.

She took my hand and hurried me toward the Jeep.

"What's the rush, Vi?" I asked. I pried my hand from her grip.

"I had to get out of there before your father started on his home-repair list." She cast a glance at the house. "Now that Seth is here to help, he wants to fix everything in *our* house and he's working on the list for *your* house. You might want to put a stop to that." She said this with the tone of someone anticipating a train wreck.

I smiled. My dad was not the greatest Mr. Fixit but he was harmless. He'd certainly never caused any problems that I could remember.

"If Seth and Dad want to clean out some gutters and fix the leaky toilet, I'm all for it."

"I have a bad feeling about it. You just remember that I told you so." Vi wagged a finger under my nose and bustled past me to climb into the passenger seat of my Jeep. She buckled herself in and sat, waiting.

Feeling my own sense of foreboding for completely different reasons, I climbed into the Jeep and steered it north out of town.

Daron worked at an urgent care clinic between Crystal Haven and Grand Rapids. I had visited the place myself after my car accident over the summer. I didn't recall meeting him at the time, but he claimed to remember me.

As we got closer to the health center, Vi began discussing strategy.

"Mac has probably already interrogated this guy, so we won't be able to spring any surprises on him," she said.

I nodded, and kept my eyes glued to the road.

"Are you the good cop or the bad cop? We need to get our story straight," she said.

"I don't think we need a story, Vi. He already knows us, and we're not cops."

She *tsk*ed. "How did you ever catch criminals in Ann Arbor with this kind of unimaginative thinking?"

I suppressed a smile and shrugged.

"He has no reason to tell us anything. For all we know he's the murderer and he'll lie to us to get us off the track," Vi said.

I hadn't considered this, but didn't think he was a suspect. "He didn't look like he was trying to kill Rafe. He worked really hard doing the CPR. Did you see him afterward? He was devastated."

Violet tapped her fingers on her lips. "Yeah, he did seem to be trying to help. Still you can't be too careful. Treat every witness like a suspect, isn't that what they say?"

I shook my head. "No one says that."

She huffed. "So your plan is to just go in there and ask him if he knows anything and shake his hand when he says he has nothing to offer?"

"What would you like to do?" I turned and looked her in the eye. Sometimes it's easier to go along for the ride than to fight it out with Vi.

"I say we tell him there's a suspect in custody—that will relax him if he's hiding anything. Then we get him to describe everything he saw that night." She nodded to herself.

"Okay."

She swiveled her head in my direction. "Really?"

"Yup, we'll do it your way. But I don't think either one of us needs to be the bad guy."

"Okay, but if it seems like things are getting out of hand, don't be surprised if I start pushing him pretty hard."

"Got it."

I parked the Jeep and exited with some trepidation about Vi. At least she didn't carry a weapon or handcuffs. The urgent care center was in a new building set back from the road. Everything about it was shiny. Inside, the waiting room chairs gleamed in bright colors, TVs flickered from the ceiling in two corners of the waiting room, and a young boy played with a bead-and-wire game that fascinated anyone who came within a few feet. He coughed, making a deep wet sound. Vi grabbed my elbow to pull me as far as we could get from the boy.

"Stay away from the little ones. They have the strongest germs," she said.

We approached the front desk and a pretty young woman smiled at us over her computer monitor.

"Can I help you?"

"We're here to see Daron Pagan," I said. "Is he available?"

She nodded. "He told me to expect you. Let me call back there and see if he's free."

She mumbled into the phone and smiled brightly as she hung up. "He'll be right out." The monitor stole her attention and Vi and I took seats near the door to the exam rooms.

A few moments later, Daron poked his head through the door and scanned the room. He spotted us and waved.

"Ms. Fortune?" He put his hand out to shake.

I nodded and introduced Vi.

"Sorry, I know we met the other night, but it's all become something of a blur." He showed us through the door.

Daron was young. I hadn't realized that in the darkness of the woods. He must have recently graduated from nursing school. No wonder the failed CPR had hit him so hard. His blond hair was cut short and his warm brown eyes were filled with concern. He gestured toward some plastic molded chairs in the small staff break room. We took a seat at a round table with sticky spots.

"Diana said you wanted to ask about Rafe Godwin?" he began, robbing Vi of the chance to accuse him of anything.

I sat back in my chair to avoid touching the table. "You may have heard the rumors that it wasn't an accident. Diana and Rafe were close family friends, and she wants to find out whatever she can about his death."

"She probably saw everything I did." He spread his hands out in a helpless gesture. "I don't know what I can do to help. I already told the police everything I know."

Vi sighed loudly, and jabbed me in the ribs. I shot a glance in her direction.

"Did you see anyone near the food, or talking to Rafe?" I asked. "Was there anything about the allergic reaction that seemed strange to you?"

He lifted a shoulder and reminded me of Seth. "I already mentioned this to the police, but I did think it was strange that there was no click when Diana administered the EpiPen. Those things are spring-loaded to give the dose into the muscle. I saw her pull out the pen and swing it toward his leg, but there was no click."

"Do you think there was something wrong with it?" I asked.

Vi had found a wet wipe and scrubbed at the table.

"I don't know." He watched Vi, and pointed to a trash can when she finished her cleaning. "It's something I only thought about after the fact. At the time I was more concerned about why the epinephrine didn't seem to be working and running the resuscitation procedure through my mind. I had never performed CPR out in the field like that. In fact, I had never done a code all on my own before." He stared into space for a moment and then met my gaze. "I feel terrible about what happened. I wish I had been able to do more."

"I didn't hear a click, either," Vi said. She rested her elbows on the now spotless table. "I *knew* something was wrong."

"You weren't anywhere near Rafe. How would you have heard a click?" I turned to her, realizing I was now interrogating my own partner.

"He said there should have been a click." She waved her hand toward Daron. "It sounds like it should have been pretty loud. Spring-loading makes a loud click. I didn't hear a click." She crossed her arms and nodded at Daron.

He smiled at her but it disappeared when he looked back at me. "I think the paramedics took the EpiPen with them when they left. Maybe they kept it with his things when they brought him to the hospital."

I nodded, thinking that Mac and Charla had probably already covered that base. Plus, I had no authority to inspect the EpiPen. I'd be lucky if Mac never heard of my interview with Daron.

"Anything else strike you about that night?"

Vi coughed.

He shook his head. "No, it was a pretty classic allergic reaction. It was a really rapid response but it's not unheard of. It's why they often tell you to bring two EpiPens just in case one malfunctions."

Vi shuffled her feet.

I turned to her. "Do you have something you'd like to ask?"

She nodded and took a deep breath. "Do you have any pets?"

Daron's eyes grew wide and he glanced at me.

"No, ma'am. No pets."

"You don't like animals?"

Daron shifted in his seat. "I like animals. I had a dog growing up. I live in an apartment now, so it's not allowed."

The pretty receptionist poked her head in the door. "Daron, they need you in exam room three."

He nodded to her and stood. "I hope that helps. I can't think of anything else right now." He stole a quizzical glance at Vi and skirted around her to the door. "Tell Diana I'll come by and see her soon."

We watched him leave and then I turned to my germophobe aunt.

Before I could speak, she said, "That went great! We make a good team. We should do more of this. We could go into business." She started ticking things off on her fingers. "We could help find things, locate lost animals, or solve burglaries. I've been studying up on how to tail someone without getting caught."

Hoping to distract her from this conversational direction, I said, "Why did you ask about pets?"

"I thought I could get corroboration from a dog or a cat. But we'll just have to take his word for it that he tried his best to help Rafe."

# 16

Violet was quiet on the ride home. It worried me. She was only quiet if she was sick or plotting something.

"You should go see Neila right now." She turned in her seat to give me the benefit of her full stare.

"Now? I'm right in the middle of trying to help Dylan and Diana. I don't have time to wander memory lane with one of grandma's old friends."

"I'm getting a feeling you don't have time not to. Drop me at home, and I'll cover for you. You know how to get to her house?"

I nodded. I hadn't agreed to her plan, but she plowed on ahead as if I had.

"I'll tell them you had to run an errand for Diana."

"Vi, I *do* have to run some errands for Diana. I don't have time for Neila." I also didn't want to go to her spooky house all by myself. I thought if I had to go I would drag Alex or Seth with me.

Vi shook her head. "You have to go alone. She won't talk to you if you bring anyone else." It never ceased to annoy me when Vi seemed to read my mind. She always knew when I was planning to ignore her instructions. I suspected she was picking up on some sort of cues I was sending out but I'd never identified exactly what it was that tipped her off. Of course, *she* would claim it was all part of her talent.

I breathed out slowly. Maybe it would be easier to make a quick trip up there, say hello, and be done with it than to continue to dodge Vi and her "feelings."

"Okay, I'll drop you off."

A few minutes later, Violet stood on the gravel driveway outside my Jeep. "If I don't hear from you in two hours, I'm coming up there searching for you."

I started to laugh but stopped when I saw the serious look in her eyes. I nodded instead and put the Jeep in gear.

Neila lived on the outskirts of town at the top of a hill. Her house sat alone on this particular rise and the road dead-ended at her driveway. I remembered from my teen years that the driveway rose steeply after the road and then flattened out about one hundred yards into a dense, treed lot. My Jeep bounced over the bumpy dirt driveway and then lurched around the last corner. This time of year the house was visible through the trees. Their naked branches stretched like bony fingers over the roof and the absence of leaves on most of the trees allowed a weak filtered light into the yard. The house itself was small, and completely covered in vines and other vegetation that I didn't have the knowledge to identify. The few areas of visible wall showed that the house had once been yellow. The back of my neck prickled and I realized this was the house I had seen in the bonfire on Halloween.

It had a couple of evergreen sentinels on both sides and the oaks and maples also had vines wrapping up their trunks. Her yard consisted of more vines and ground-cover plants; no real grass would grow in what was essentially a forest. I parked and got out of the Jeep, letting the door close quietly. My approach must have alerted all the birds and squirrels because it was silent in the small yard. The house had a missing shutter on one window and a second shutter was hanging by one nail, lending a haphazard look to the front. I stepped onto the porch and felt a chill as I moved out of the last shaft of weak sunlight.

The silence and air of neglect had me wondering yet again at the wisdom of showing up here unannounced. I had only my aunt's assurance that the old lady was even still alive.

I raised my hand to knock when a voice said, "Come on in, it's open." I jumped and nearly fell backward off the porch. I looked around for the source of the voice but couldn't see where it had come from.

The knob turned easily, and I pushed the door inward on creaky hinges. The front hall was dark, and I squinted into the gloom.

"Ms. Whittle?" My own voice bounced back to me. I caught a glimpse of something white to my left and spun to meet it. It was just the sheer curtain lazily shifting in the breeze from the door.

"Clytemnestra?" The voice came from behind me and was so like my grandmother's that tears stung my eyes before I'd turned to see who had spoken.

For a moment I thought Aunt Vi had set up an elaborate prank. A clump of fabric stood in front of me. It was draped in all shades of gray and brown shawls where its shoulders should be, a gray rough fabric as a skirt, and a dingy apron that had once been white. At five foot seven, I was used to being taller than many women, especially in my family. But

I was a giant compared to this creature. She barely came up to my chest, and I thought Vi had hired a third grader to trick me into bolting out the door and down the hill like so many kids had done over the years. Then it moved and I saw the hunched little woman smile. Expecting the smile of a jack-o'-lantern, I was surprised to see a full complement of teeth, and when she stepped into the light, her cool gray eyes glimmered.

"Ms. Whittle, we haven't met. I'm—"

"I know who you are, Clytemnestra Fortune. I'm surprised you don't remember me. You used to play in the yard when you were no higher than my hip. You loved my sugar cookies." She came a bit closer, tilting her head to look into my eyes. "Blue and brown. I told your grandmother you would be a great seer with eyes like that. You should have come sooner."

I skipped over the fascination with my oddly colored eyes, and the creepy pronouncements, and focused on the part where I had been here before.

"I've . . . been here?"

"Well, you came with the rest of the teenagers when you were about fourteen, but didn't linger. None of them do. But yes, you used to come here with Agnes. She was my friend. I still miss her every day." A gust of wind blew the door all the way open and it slammed into the wall. I jumped, but Neila just went to the door and clicked it shut.

She tilted her head toward the back of the house and walked down the hallway. She didn't look back. I caught myself wishing I had Baxter with me. Armed robbers I could handle, but creepy old ladies and their haunted houses were not my thing. *She's just a little old lady,* I chided myself. *What I need is a grip, not a dog.*

Her kitchen looked like a cross between a mad scientist's

laboratory and a historic village kitchen circa 1820. I had never seen a fireplace so big outside of a field trip to Greenfield Village in Detroit. She'd hung cast-iron pots and pans from hooks in the ceiling. In the middle of the fireplace sat a metal frame and hanging from it was a large cauldron. There was a low fire burning beneath and steam rose out of the large round pot. I braced for the stench that I was sure would emanate, but then smelled—beef stew. Neila gathered her fabric around herself to lean over the cauldron and the aroma almost made my knees buckle. I realized I hadn't eaten since a banana at breakfast.

She turned and pointed to a chair. "Hungry?"

I nodded.

"I made a big batch. It seems I have more visitors than one might expect for a haunted house." Her mouth moved into a grin and she was suddenly more like my grandmother and less like a witch.

"Is your house haunted?" I glanced around the kitchen to avoid looking in her eyes.

"No, I don't think so, but every town needs a legend." She moved about the fireplace, grabbing bowls from a low table, and began spooning up the savory mixture. She crossed the room, and as I followed her movements, I saw the modern stove and oven tucked into a corner near the refrigerator. She bent and pulled fresh rolls from its depths. I felt my whole body relax.

She sat across from me with her own bowl and the room was quiet except for spoons scraping on crockery.

Disregarding all of my mother's training in manners, I mopped up the last of the stew with the bread. Neila chuckled.

"Want some more?"

I felt like Oliver Twist, but nodded.

Finally, I was so full I wasn't sure I would be able to walk out the door.

"Thank you, Ms. Whittle. That's the best stew I've had since . . ."

"Your grandmother passed?" She smiled kindly. "It's her recipe. I always make it this time of year. It's one of my favorite things about heading into winter—knowing I can have your grandmother's stew."

"Why don't I remember you?" I said.

"Well, you were very little and an awful lot has happened between now and then."

"Still, I've tried to remember everything about my grandmother."

Neila nodded. "She was a great woman. Should we get started?"

I was startled by her question and must have looked it. She smiled and patted my hand.

"My aunt Vi told me to come and talk to you. Honestly, I don't even know why."

"Violet loves her mysteries, doesn't she?"

I thought about that and realized she was right.

"I suppose, but I don't know what her intentions were in regard to visiting you. Have you heard about what happened out in Greer's Woods a few nights ago?"

Neila's eyes glistened, and I thought she was about to cry. She cleared her throat. "Yes, I heard about Rafe Godwin. But I don't know anything about that."

I tried to think of the least offensive way to ask my next question. Psychics don't like to have their talents challenged.

"Ms. Whittle, did you ever talk to my grandmother about my . . . visions?"

"Oh yes." She nodded. "She was very impressed with

your talent. She said you had a true gift, and I wasn't surprised. She was worried about you, though. That's why I thought you would come. She told me to help you with the visions but to wait until you came on your own."

This was classic Greer/Fortune family behavior. I tamped down the anger that rose in my chest at my grandmother's methods. I should have expected it since they were the same as my mother's methods. My dismay must have been clear because Neila stood and started clearing the dishes in a businesslike manner.

"Don't be mad at your grandmother. These things take time, and a person can't be helped until they're ready."

"If you can help me to stop having the visions, then I was ready about fifteen years ago."

Neila hesitated. "I can't stop the visions. I can only teach you how to interpret them and how to use them."

*Now* I understood. Vi didn't tell me *why* I needed to see Neila Whittle. This was just one more attempt on the part of my family to get me to pursue the psychic way of life.

I stood quickly. "I'm sorry, Ms. Whittle. I don't need that kind of help. Thanks for the stew and the conversation."

I hated to offend this poor little old lady, but I had to get out of there. As I walked down the hallway, a deep sense of grief passed through me. It didn't feel like my own, it felt primal and vast. I had to concentrate to breathe, and I grabbed the wall to steady myself. I didn't hear her come up behind me, but when she placed her hand on my back the relief was astonishing.

"You're fine now. Go." She pushed me gently toward the front door. "But think about what I said. You won't be able to stop the dreams, the feelings, the visions, but you can learn to use them. You can learn to control *them*, so they don't control you."

Regaining my sense of manners, I shook her hand. "It was nice to meet you—again."

I ran to my Jeep, jumped in, and locked the door as if I could somehow lock out the feeling that I would never escape from the expectations of my mother.

# 17

Pushing all thoughts of Neila Whittle and my family out of my mind, I focused on the problem at hand, which was how to get Dylan out of jail and find closure for Diana.

I texted Seth and told him to meet me out in the street in front of my mom's house. I wasn't ready to talk to Vi or my mother yet. I didn't know whether Mom was in on this latest attempt to make me "accept my destiny," but I felt like avoiding both of them for now. Turning the corner, I saw Seth and the dogs loitering at the curb.

"What's with the stealth?" Seth said after he loaded the dogs and buckled his seat belt.

"Let's go get Alex and see what we can find out about Rafe," I said.

Seth shrugged and said, "You're driving." One thing I loved about Seth was that he was always up for whatever came along.

Alex was more difficult. It took a bit more explaining, coercing, and downright whining to get him to leave the restaurant and get in my Jeep. It was well after the lunch rush so he didn't have that excuse but liked to have a plan in place before gallivanting off on an adventure. Since I didn't have a plan, it made convincing him problematic.

"Let's just figure it out when we get to Rafe's house. We have to do something," I said when I finally had him moving toward the Jeep.

He stopped on the sidewalk and peered into the vehicle's windows.

"I'm not sitting in the back with the animals," Alex said.

Seth sighed and got out of the Jeep. "Be my guest," he said, sweeping his arm toward the front seat.

"Which Hardy Boy are you?" Alex asked.

"Hardy who?" Seth pushed the dogs out of the way and folded himself into the backseat. "Is that a new group?"

Alex sighed and shook his head. "Why don't you Google it?"

"Not that interested, dude."

I turned on the radio to stop the bickering, and headed north.

Rafe had lived in a small bungalow on the outskirts of Grand Rapids. One of those neighborhoods unsure of whether it was moving up or down in the world. Adorable cottages with flowers in the window boxes and fresh paint on the porches sat next to houses with boarded-up windows, peeling paint, and broken rakes and lawn mowers in the yard. I parked one block over just in case a vigilant neighborhood watch was in place.

Rafe's small house was painted a cheery yellow with white trim. He had crammed an herb garden and a flower garden onto his small lot. On this leaden, cloudy day, the brown plants and scattered leaves looked forlorn. The house had already settled into benign neglect. Flyers for pizza delivery and cleaning services cluttered his welcome mat. Leaves skittered over the porch and down the steps. The windows were dark and reflected the gray of the sky.

Diana had told me there was a key above the windowsill to the right of the door. I found it easily and slid it into the lock. I hesitated a moment before turning it, feeling guilty about intruding into this man's life. Then I remembered Dylan and twisted the small piece of metal with a satisfying *click*.

Alex glanced nervously up and down the street. "Are you sure this is legal?"

Oblivious to our conversation, Seth's head bobbed to his iPod soundtrack.

"No, I'm *not* sure," I said. "There's no police tape or note on the door saying to stay out. We have a key. I think we would be able to talk our way out of any trouble."

"Maybe in Crystal Haven where you have Mac twisted around your finger, but not here in Grand Rapids," Alex said.

I put my hands on my hips. "I don't have Mac twisted around anything."

Seth snorted. Maybe he was less oblivious than I thought.

"Let's just get this over with," Alex said, and stepped inside.

It felt like a violation to walk into the house without the owner there. All of his belongings watched us, waiting to see what we were up to. Literally. Artwork of various pagan gods and goddesses followed us with their eyes. A quick perusal of the living room revealed Rafe's altar draped in a deep rust cloth embroidered with a pentagram. Pumpkins, gourds, and candles sat on top. I recognized the arrangement from Diana's house. She always decorated with seasonal items as well. She explained it was a way to bring nature into the house.

"What are we looking for, anyway?" Alex asked. His eyes darted warily from item to item.

I shrugged. "I'm hoping we'll know it when we see it."

Seth took his earbuds out. "I don't know what to look for." He peered around the entryway. "Ooh, kerosene lamps!" He stepped toward the mantel, where the lamps stood beneath a pentagram wreath made of twigs.

I put out a hand to stop him. "You take the kitchen and the bathroom," I said. "Just look for anything that feels out of place or that might indicate Rafe had a problem with anyone."

I pointed Alex upstairs to the bedrooms. I took the office and living room. Other than the altar and the kerosene lamps, the living room contained a threadbare couch and chairs draped with throw blankets. A battered table held a beautiful Tiffany lamp with a Celtic knot pattern that looked to my untrained eye like an antique. Next to it sat a small square leather clock that had to be one of Dylan's. What Rafe had saved on furniture, he spent on electronics. A large flat-screen TV took up the wall opposite the altar.

Rafe's office looked like a band of monkeys lived there. Piles of magazines claimed the space around the perimeter of the room, obscuring the baseboards. His large desk hulked in the corner under the weight of notebooks, dried herbs, candles, and a sleek laptop. My shoulders slumped at the sight. This was the room most likely to yield results but it would take days to sort through everything. I mentally rolled up my sleeves and got to work.

An hour later, I sat back and stretched my arms over my head. I'd been hunched over Rafe's desk, sorting through piles of paperwork and stacks of sticky notes with reminders to pick up dry cleaning or to increase the proportion of rosemary in an herbal poultice and everything in between. Rafe had stuffed one of Morgan's revenge kits between a book on Wiccan rituals and a Grand Rapids guidebook.

Seth wandered in and said he'd found nothing "unusual" in the kitchen or bathroom. "I did find this on the top shelf of the pantry. I thought it was a recipe book but maybe not." He produced an old, worn, leather notebook.

I flipped through it and recognized that it must be Rafe's grimoire, based on my recent education in those specialty notebooks.

"Thanks, Seth. This might be useful."

Alex wandered in, yawning, and reported he had found nothing except fancy soaps and incense. He held out a bar of soap with a handmade label that said EMBERMYST. I recognized it from the festival but couldn't remember who had sold it.

"He had a bunch of these in the upstairs bathroom," Alex said.

I took the soap and inspected it. It smelled of mint and lavender. I shrugged and set it on the desk.

"I'm not having any luck, either," I said. "I can't find any information that might lead to knowing who would want to hurt him."

"Were you expecting a threatening letter or blackmail note?" Alex asked.

"No." *Yes.* "I just thought there would be something here to point us in the right direction. One strange thing was this." I pushed a lever under the desktop and a panel slid open in the top desk drawer.

"Wicked," Seth breathed. He stepped forward to try it for himself.

"I found his will here in the secret drawer. He left everything to Diana and Dylan."

"Really?" Alex took the stack of papers from me. "This won't help Dylan's case. Didn't Rafe have any family?"

I shook my head. "Apparently not, at least no one he'd leave his house to. I also found a family-tree diagram with the will."

I had just turned back to pull that file out of the drawer when we heard a car door slam outside. I froze. Seth ducked down along the wall and slowly raised his eyes above the windowsill for a peek.

"Oh, crap," Seth said. "You aren't going to believe this, Clyde."

I was sure I would believe, just maybe not like it. I waited, and when I didn't reply he continued.

"Mac is here with some other cops I don't recognize."

I felt my eyes grow big and my stomach dropped down around my knees. Alex's panicked look mirrored my feelings.

"We have to get out of here," I said.

"They're talking by the cars right now, but I think they're coming in," Seth whispered.

Alex grabbed my arm, gestured at Seth to follow, and dragged me through the kitchen toward the back door.

We tiptoed quickly to the back of the house and were about to open the door and bolt through the backyard when a man wearing a blue uniform came into view. We all ducked and turned around. We made it back into the front hall just as the doorknob started to turn. Seth squeezed my arm and pointed up the narrow staircase leading to the bedrooms. I shook my head no—I didn't want to be trapped in the house with Mac doing a room-by-room search.

Alex sided with Seth and we were all at the top of the

staircase when we heard Mac's voice enter the house down below.

I had noticed that the bungalow had a third-floor window and figured there must be attic space somewhere. I would just have to hope that the cops didn't need to do a very thorough search. They were probably here on the same mission as we were—to see what had been going on recently in Rafe's life. No one put their important stuff in the attic, right?

Alex found the small door in the ceiling and we popped it open quietly and lowered the ladder without it squeaking. I sent a quick thank-you to Rafe for keeping his hinges oiled.

After we were in the attic, which was dim and gloomy on this late autumn afternoon, Alex pulled the ladder up inside and replaced the door. We sat hunched by the opening, listening to footsteps in the rooms below. I mentally smacked my forehead when I realized I had left the grimoire sitting downstairs on the desk. I'd managed to put the other documents back in the secret drawer . . . maybe I'd get a chance to come back later.

Rather than waste time getting a leg cramp and worrying, I clicked on my handy penlight and crept around the area. Alex followed. The usual assortment of junk languished in the corners. Two trunks looked promising, but contained only old musty clothing from a previous owner, unless Rafe was also a cross-dressing '60s hippie. A dressmaker's form stood alone in a far corner—was that a required fixture for an attic? A further perusal of old bicycle tires, baseball mitts, and hockey pads turned up nothing useful. I wasn't even sure any of it had belonged to Rafe.

Seth, who had been stationed by the trapdoor, waved his arms like a drunken air-traffic signaler. Alex and I tiptoed back to where he stood.

"They're talking about coming up here." He said it so quietly we both had to lean toward him.

"What should we do?" Alex mouthed.

Seth pointed to the small window at the far side of the attic. I could barely make out tree branches through the grime. The window faced the backyard but it was three stories up. I have only a couple of fears. Guns, bad guys, small spaces, even snakes didn't bother me. Spiders I could tolerate at a good distance. Heights did me in.

I shook my head and backed away. My foot found the one creaky floorboard in the whole attic.

"Did you hear that?" a male voice floated up from the floor below.

"It's just the wind." That one was Mac. They moved off to the other end of the house.

"How are we going to get Dylan out of jail if we're all sharing his cell?" Alex said.

"You won't have to climb, Clyde. We'll just wait there on the roof until they go. It's better than being killed by Mac." Seth pulled on my sleeve.

At least Seth and Alex could hide out there. I'd decide when the time came whether I needed to join them or not.

We tiptoed again across the attic and no squeaky floorboards gave us away. I was sure that the window would be stuck and save me from needing to climb through it. But, no, it swung open easily as if it was used all the time. Now I was cursing Rafe and his general home-maintenance tendencies.

Seth was the first out, fearless as only a teenager can be. He poked his head back in. "It's fine, there's plenty of room. The roof is kind of steep, but it's not slippery."

Alex waited for me. He knew I'd never follow them out. He narrowed his eyes, tilted his head toward the window, and pointed. I felt my shoulders slump. Then we both spun in the direction of the trapdoor as it dropped open and weak light from the floor below leaked upward.

Alex began moving his hand in a circular, "hurry up" gesture. I took a deep breath and put my foot on the ledge. I barely had time to steady myself before I felt a huge push from behind. Good thing Seth was there to grab me or Alex would have pushed me right off the roof. We quickly found our footing and I looked straight ahead into the tree branches. Alex scrambled out right after me and pulled the window closed. He stood on the other side of the window, legs spread for a better grip on the steep roof, hands grasping the siding.

We plastered ourselves against the wall of the house and waited. I heard Mac and the other guy moving around the attic. They weren't tiptoeing. They were certainly taking their time, however.

A cold drop of rain hit me right between the eyes. Of course. I had a brief moment to hope for a light drizzle before a full-on autumn rain began in earnest. We were soaked within two minutes. I couldn't wipe the water out of my eyes because I was busy clutching the side of the house, trying not to shift my weight for fear of sliding off the roof.

How long were they going to search the attic? There was nothing up there.

"Clyde?" Seth whispered.

I turned my head in his direction.

"I really have to pee."

I looked heavenward and got a few huge raindrops in my eyes.

"You'll have to wait, obviously," I hissed at him.

"The rain is really not helping. I think I can climb off the side and drop onto the first-floor roof." He began to sidle toward the edge.

"Seth! Come back here," I whispered, loudly.

He slipped and grabbed my hand. I took a moment to convince my heart to stop racing and realized I couldn't hear Mac and the other officers inside anymore. I leaned over to peek through the window and almost lost my balance when I saw Mac's face peering back at me. He rolled his eyes and shoved the window open.

"Come on. I wondered how long you would stay out there." He put his hand out through the window. I took it and he pulled me inside. So glad to be safe and not sliding down the roof, I clung to him for a moment. I also thought that would remind him of how he really didn't want to arrest me. I hoped the guys were safe—that he hadn't seen them—but then he pushed me away and stuck his head out the window again.

"You guys coming or are you enjoying the weather?"

Seth and Alex climbed back into the attic and waited, casting nervous glances from me to Mac and back again. Their clothes dripped quietly onto the floor, and they stood as still as possible. They both knew better than to say anything.

Mac crossed his arms. Seth shuffled his feet and continued to study the floor. Alex pushed his hands in his back pockets and looked at the ceiling.

"How did you know we were out there?" I said.

"Your Jeep is easy to spot and there's this." Mac passed his phone to me—there was a picture taken from the backyard of the three of us standing on the roof before it started raining.

I handed it back. "Charla?"

Mac nodded. "*She* was smart enough to come in when the rain started." He left the rest of that statement alone.

I waited. I knew Mac wouldn't be able to hold off for very long.

"What are you doing here? How did you get in? I should be taking you all down to the station."

"I think we'll leave you two alone," Alex said and snagged Seth's sleeve. They both raced down the ladder to the floor below.

Mac turned slowly to face me.

"We had a key so, technically, we didn't break in," I began.

Mac pinched the bridge of his nose.

"We wanted to help Dylan. He *couldn't* have hurt Rafe. We were just looking for some other reason why someone would want Rafe dead."

Mac nodded and then shook his head. He took a deep breath and I sensed he was maybe counting to one thousand.

"I can't do this again," he said. "You and your gang of amateur operatives have to back off and let me do my job."

"But—"

"No. I almost lost you last summer. Seth could have been killed. Do I have to remind you of the danger?"

I shook my head.

"If I have to put all of you in a jail cell to keep you protected, I will. Fortunately, I think Dylan *is* the murderer and he's already in prison so you're safe for now." He put his hand up to stop me from interrupting. "If that changes and I sense any risk to any of you . . ." he dropped his hand. "Help me out here, Clyde."

I didn't want to see him so worried and harassed. But he didn't ever listen. Once his mind was made up, he was like Aunt Vi with a mission—unstoppable. I nodded, indicating acquiescence that I didn't feel.

# 18

**Seth, Alex, and I left Rafe's house under Mac's** watchful eye.

The rain had slowed and we walked to the car, where we were greeted by the wagging and woofing dogs. Baxter ran the length of the backseat, causing the vehicle to rock. So much for subtlety. We climbed in and I started the Jeep and put it in gear. Before I had a chance to pull away from the curb, a black Tahoe barreled past.

"Hey! That was Skye!" Seth said from the backseat. "What's she doing here?"

I turned to look at him. "Are you sure?"

He nodded.

I suppressed a grin. Seth had mentioned Skye at every opportunity since he met her, but he did have a good point. What *was* she doing in Rafe's neighborhood? I couldn't imagine that she had been involved in his death, but she might have insight into what was happening in his life just before he died. I pulled out to follow her.

I wasn't sure whether this was a good idea. Mac had just extracted a promise that I wouldn't involve myself. But how dangerous could a teenage girl be? We caught up to her at a stoplight and Seth jumped out of the Jeep before I could stop him. He knocked on the passenger window and gestured to a parking lot up ahead. He jogged back to the Jeep and climbed in.

"She's gonna pull over in that gas station."

We parked the Jeep right behind Skye's Tahoe and got out, to the loud objections of the dogs. Tuffy jumped into the front seat and put his front paws on the dash, barking the whole time. Baxter sat more calmly in the back and volunteered a low woof whenever Tuffy stopped to take a breath.

Skye climbed slowly out of the driver's side. Faith hopped out of the passenger seat and zipped around to where we stood. Skye gave us a dazzling smile.

"Hey," Seth said with the air of someone passing in the hall.

"Hi, Seth. Hi, Clyde." Skye put out her hand to Alex and introduced herself.

The preliminaries out of the way, I was searching for a way to ask her what she was doing in Rafe's neighborhood.

"We saw you drive past us just outside of Rafe's house. What were you doing there?" Seth asked.

Her smile faltered. She stole a glance at Faith, who was busy watching the dogs in the Jeep. "Promise you won't tell my mom?"

Alex and I exchanged a glance and nodded.

"Mom doesn't trust anyone these days, including me.

Ever since I told her I had joined the coven, she's been on edge. It's not really what she wanted for me."

Faith snorted. "I would say it's not something she ever imagined."

Skye glared at her little sister. "She'll get used to it."

"Yeah, when hell—"

"Anyway," Skye interrupted, "I'm supposed to be picking Faith up from school and going straight home. But I left a flash drive at Rafe's house and I wanted to get it back."

"Do you have a key?" I asked.

She shook her head. "He leaves one over his door. I thought I could just zip in there, get the drive, and get out. But there were police all over the place. What's going on?"

"The police are investigating Rafe's death. They think maybe it wasn't an accident," I said.

Both girls drew in breath at the same time.

"Oh, no," Skye said.

"Diana said you were working on a special project with him. Is that what the flash drive was for?"

Skye's face became pink, which made her even prettier. She fidgeted with a bracelet. "I don't know if I should talk about that."

"Skye, Rafe is dead. Diana's brother has been arrested for murder. If there's anything you can tell us about what Rafe was doing in the time before he died, it might help us figure out what happened to him."

Skye looked at her sister, who met her gaze and nodded once. "I was helping Rafe with a genealogy project. We'd been talking at a coven meeting a few months ago and I told him how it was kind of a hobby of mine. There's all this great stuff now on the Internet and you can trace your family back for generations."

"What was the project?" Alex asked.

"That was the weird part. It wasn't his family, the Godwins, that Rafe wanted me to research. It was Neila Whittle."

Seth's eyes snapped up from whatever he was doing on his phone. Even *he* had heard of Neila Whittle.

"Neila Whittle? Why?" I said.

"I don't know." Skye shrugged. "He told me not to tell anyone, that's why I wanted to get the flash drive back. But, I guess it doesn't matter anymore."

"Do you have the information you found?"

She nodded. "It's all on my computer. I can e-mail it to you if you want. There're quite a few files."

"That would be great," I said. "Can you tell us anything about the night Rafe died? Did you see anything unusual? Was he acting differently?"

"I don't remember anything unusual." Skye leaned against her SUV and stared at a point over my head. "He had a little fight with Lucan Reed but, believe me, that wasn't unusual. I was surprised that the EpiPen didn't work. He had told me that it was a lifesaver. But then, I'd never seen him use it."

"Is there anything else?" I asked.

Skye shook her head.

Faith said, "Why don't you tell them about Daddy and what he thought you were really doing over at Rafe's house?"

Skye shot a dirty look at her sister.

"My father followed me to Rafe's one time about a month ago," Skye said. "He didn't like that I was spending so much time with Rafe."

"He thought Rafe was a dirty old man," Faith piped in.

"Shut up, Faith." She turned back to look at me. "He wasn't."

"Your father thought there was something going on with you and Rafe?" I said.

Skye wrinkled her nose and nodded. "He was being superparanoid and ridiculous. As if I'd ever get involved with someone . . . ancient."

"We should get back, Skye." Faith held her phone out for Skye to see. "Mom is wondering where we are."

Seth, Alex, and I returned to the Jeep and climbed inside to the excited greetings of the dogs. I pulled back out into traffic, realizing we were no closer to figuring out what happened than before we began this covert operation.

# 19

❦

**I pulled into my driveway thinking about a hot** shower and some tea when I noticed someone sitting on my front porch. It was Tom.

Seth hopped out of the Jeep with the dogs trailing behind. He went inside, raising his hand in greeting as he passed Tom. So much for a relaxing shower and a few moments to myself. I heard Seth inside talking to the dogs and then the back door slammed.

Alex and I climbed the steps slowly. Tom stood as we approached.

"I have the accident report," he said. He followed us into the living room, where Alex flopped into the side chair and ran his hands through his damp hair. "What happened to you two?" Tom asked.

"Just a monsoon, an angry cop, and a low-speed car chase," Alex said. "Oh, and don't forget climbing around on a roof."

Tom looked at me. "Was Mac the angry cop?"

I nodded.

"Glad I was in Bailey Harbor all day."

"I need some tea," I said and waved them into the kitchen.

Seth was there with the dogs, passing out treats and munching on a bag of chips. I went to the stove and filled the kettle, taking a moment to get lost in the ritual of making tea. Alex and Tom were trying to get the bag of chips away from Seth. I got a box of cookies out of the pantry—they pounced on that instead. After the water boiled and I set the tea to steep I sat at the table with the hungry horde.

"What have you got?" I asked Tom.

He slid the report across the table to me. "It looks like a cut-and-dried accident. It was wet, they took the turn too fast, and the car rolled." I shivered, thinking of my own similar accident last summer.

"Did they check the car to be sure there was nothing wrong with it?"

Tom nodded. "The brakes were intact, the tires were fine. They couldn't find any reason why the car would have rolled except driver error. You know that turn. It comes up quickly and even in good weather I've seen cars go off onto the shoulder. There are enough skid marks to indicate it's a dangerous turn if you're going too fast. They put up a guard-rail after the Wards' accident, but there was nothing to stop them that night."

I got up to get my tea. Tom's description of the accident was just as I remembered it and just as I had seen it in my dream. A car going too fast, a scream of brakes, and the car rolling, rolling. I had tried to warn Diana's parents without actually telling them I had seen their deaths in a dream. A shiver went up my spine. I'd never been able to stop the premonitions from coming true and sometimes I misunderstood the visions. I had spent so much effort trying to avoid them that I had never perfected interpretation. Was it fair to have the individuals living in fear for the last months of their lives? I had yet to answer that question.

"No chance that Rafe could have had anything to do with it?" I said.

Tom shook his head. "Not according to the report. It looks like they were very thorough. If Rafe set up the crash, he did a fantastic job of making it look like an accident."

Alex put his head in his hands. "We're not getting anywhere. Even if Rafe did set up the accident that would just make the case against Dylan even stronger. We need to find out who would have wanted Rafe dead, besides Dylan."

Alex was right. Regardless of what had happened between Rafe and the Wards, we needed to find someone who was angry enough with Rafe that he or she would want him dead. I had hoped to clear up any remaining mystery about the Wards' death because I knew it was killing Diana to think that Rafe had done anything to harm them. But, right now, we needed more information on Rafe.

"It doesn't matter what the report says," Tom said. "Dylan believes Rafe was responsible for his parents' death. It's all he talked about for months afterward. Now I know why he never got anywhere. There was no evidence." Tom flipped the pages of the report over as if the answer would jump out at him.

"Did Dylan ever say *how* he thought Rafe had caused the accident?" I asked. I set the tea mug in front of me and wrapped my hands around it for warmth.

Tom shook his head. "No. He was obsessed with figuring out what was in the grimoire that would have caused the fight between Rafe and Elliot. He used to pore over that thing, writing out the spells, comparing them to other books. There were several that dealt with power and he thought

Rafe just wanted a spell. It wasn't until recently that he figured out Rafe wanted to *hide* the book, not use it.

"Where's the book now?" Alex asked.

"I think Diana has it. Dylan showed her the family tree in the back—she must still have it," I said.

"Oh, I just remembered," Seth said and headed toward the front door.

I shrugged when Alex looked at me for an explanation.

Seth returned, reached under his sweatshirt, and pulled out the book he had found at Rafe's place. "What are we going to do with this?"

I jumped up and hugged him. I'd assumed it had been left behind. Alex and I looked quickly to Tom, but he didn't even react to a stolen grimoire.

"Let me see it," I said.

Seth handed the book to me and went back to his snacking. The grimoire was made of thick black leather with a pentagram embossed on the front. When I touched it, I got that creepy feeling in my gut that told me I didn't want to know what was in the book. I flipped it open and immediately knew I would need some help. There were symbols and foreign-sounding words, lists of ingredients, and recommended moon phases. I would need Diana to interpret.

I pushed the book over to Alex and Tom; they both seemed to have the same reaction I did. They turned the pages gingerly and finally gave up with a shrug.

"I'll call Diana." Alex pulled out his phone.

Seth's phone buzzed and he pulled it out of his pocket. His eyebrows shot up when he saw who the text was from, then he quickly recovered and his thumbs got to work.

Alex walked into the living room to talk to Diana. Tom flipped through the accident report again, probably hoping he missed something the first ten times.

"I'm going up to change into some dry clothes," I said. Tom and Seth nodded without looking up from their tasks.

Alex clicked his phone off when I entered the living room. "She'll be here in about an hour," he said. "I need to go get some new clothes."

I tossed him the keys to my Jeep and he said he'd be back before Diana came over.

I grabbed some comfy yoga pants and an Ann Arbor Police Department sweatshirt and turned on the shower. The water felt great as I started to feel warm again. My brain always went into a different mode in the shower. Instead of being linear and controlled, it wandered and picked up pieces of information and sensations that I would normally ignore. This time it focused on who would want to kill Rafe. I came up with a longer list than I would have expected only a couple of days previously. Morgan Lavelle was a possibility. She and Rafe had fought and she seemed capable of just about anything. Lucan Reed had also been arguing with Rafe over the coven politics. Was that enough to kill for? Dylan hated Rafe and blamed him for his parents' death. But I didn't want to focus there. I thought of Skye and her battle with her parents over joining a coven. But she didn't have any reason to kill Rafe. Who was I missing? I realized I had been showering too long when the water started to get cool. The hot water heater in this older home was not large enough to solve the mystery.

Just as I finished drying my hair I heard the doorbell ring and the uproar of protective dog barking. I heard Seth shushing the dogs and then Diana's voice floated up from below.

**I walked down** the stairs and hesitated near the bottom when I saw what Diana had in her hand. She clutched her bulging, clanking tote bag that always contained trouble.

She raised it and said, "I know you don't like it, but I have to do something to help Dylan and this is all I know how to do."

I felt my shoulders slump at the same time I saw Seth's face light up. I'd avoided Diana's spell-casting once I realized that her spells invariably brought on the dreams that I tried so hard to block. Seth on the other hand loved anything to do with psychics, séances, or on a slow night, witchcraft. Alex walked in from the kitchen, holding a slice of pizza, and noticed the bag as well. His posture echoed mine. Both of us had been dragged into Diana's spell-casting many times over the years. Alex usually needed a couple of shots of whiskey to participate.

"Maybe we can try one of the spells in Rafe's book," Seth said.

"What book?" Diana asked.

"The one we found at his house," Seth said. "It's got cool symbols and stuff inside."

Diana glanced in my direction. "Can I see it?"

Seth bounded off to get it from the kitchen. Tom had followed Alex into the living room and we sat on the couches after evicting the dogs with some difficulty. Baxter was not pleased that his normal routine had been disrupted by all the visitors. Late afternoon was his prime napping-on-the-couch time.

While we finished the pizza Alex had brought, Alex and I told Diana the tale of Rafe's house. She laughed a bit too hard at the part about being stuck on the roof but I figured she needed it. Seth handed her the book and she placed it carefully in her lap. She ran her hand over the cover and I saw her brows come together. She flipped it open and scanned the spells. She was about halfway through the book when she slapped it shut.

"I'll have to take some time with this." Her voice shook on the last word.

"What is it?" Alex asked.

She shook her head. "Just too much to take in all at once."

But I knew what she had felt. There was evil in that book and the fact that it had belonged to Rafe Godwin had to be upsetting for her.

"I think we should get started," Diana said.

Alex shifted in his seat and stole a look toward the kitchen, where I kept the alcohol. Tom cleared a place on the coffee table, as if this was a common occurrence. Seth's eyes were bright and he asked Diana what she needed.

Diana smiled at him and said she brought everything in the bag.

Realizing this was going to happen whether I wanted it to or not, I took the chair farthest from the coffee table and waited for her to set up her supplies.

She pulled out a piece of paper with Dylan's name on it, and set up five white candles in the shape of a star.

"This is perfect. There are five of us and if we each light a candle it will make the spell more powerful than if I do this alone." Diana got up to turn out the lights. It was past six o'clock and fully dark outside, but a gray-silver light slipped in through the windows from the streetlights.

"I call on the powers to the north." Diana walked to the north side of the room. She continued calling on the powers until she had cast the circle just as she had done in the woods. When she was finished, she sat on the couch between Alex and Tom and took their hands. She nodded to Seth and me to scoot closer and complete the circle. That left Seth and Tom holding hands, which was something I never thought I would see. Seth looked only briefly pained and then he turned his attention back to the candles.

I held Alex's hand on one side and Seth's on the other. When Diana told us to close our eyes they both squeezed a little tighter. I felt a stiffness begin in the back of my neck. I rolled my shoulders to stretch it out. She again called on the powers of air, fire, earth, and water and we lowered our hands and opened our eyes. She struck a match and touched it to the candle closest to her seat. She passed the box over to Tom, who did the same, and then handed the container to Seth. Seth had to strike the match a couple of times to get a flame and then he passed them to me. Once all the candles were lit, Diana said her incantation.

*O Goddess, we ask for protection of Dylan in his time of need.*
*Protect him from word and deed*
*From harm and from all we fear.*
*For all that we hold dear,*
*I thank the Goddess for helping me.*
*I trust in Her aid*
*So mote it be!*

Diana nodded that we should each blow out our candles in the order that we lit them. I breathed out and felt myself relax.

"Is that it?" Seth asked.

"What were you expecting?" Diana said with a smile.

"Maybe some lightning, howling winds, or at least flickering candles. . . ."

Diana shook her head. "It's not quite as exciting as it is in the movies. It's more about sending good intentions into the world."

Alex was up and had moved away from the candles. Everyone stood and milled about for a few minutes waiting for an opening to change the subject. Seth took the leashes from the hook and Alex grabbed Baxter's, not trying to hide his desire to get out of the house for a few minutes.

Tom announced he had to get home and said his good-byes as the leashes were snapped on to the exuberant dogs.

When they had left, I turned to Diana.

"What do you think of the grimoire?"

She looked down at her lap, where the book had sat. "I think I'm about to learn more than I want to know about Rafe."

# 20

❦

*I am climbing up, up, up and feeling dizzy. I try not to
look down but I can't help myself, then the spinning nausea
hits and I have to lean against the wall. I don't recognize
this stairwell, which is lined with stone like an old castle
tower. I know that I have to get to the top. I can hear the
wind. I'm almost there.*

*I burst through the doorway to the roof of this tower and
the wind nearly knocks me back inside. Seth is there and I
run to him but the more I run the farther away he gets. Then
I hear a woman laughing, almost cackling, but I can't see
her and I don't recognize the voice. I lean against the short
wall on the roof and look over the edge. The whole world
tilts and I can't tell which way is up—I'm falling, falling
and screaming Seth's name.*

I woke drenched in sweat in the deepest dark. I took a
moment to calm myself. My heart was beating so hard it felt
like it was bruising my ribs. I ran my hand along the bed

for Baxter but he wasn't there. Then I remembered that he had shunned me for the more attractive sleeping arrangements with Tuffy and Seth. I stumbled out of bed, tripped over the jeans I had left on the floor, and opened my door. Weak light from outside filtered into the hallway. I had to check on Seth even if it meant disturbing the dogs. His door was closed and I crept down the hallway, still not recovered from the dream.

The doorknob turned easily, even though my hand shook, and I eased the door open. Seth had left his window shade partly open and the streetlights shone into the room. Tuffy let out a low growl when I entered. Baxter picked his head up and thumped his tail twice in greeting. Seth was sound asleep, somehow sprawled among the dogs. I backed out of the room and pulled the door closed.

I took great gulps of air as I leaned against the wall outside Seth's room. When would I learn not to let Diana do her spells around me? I hated these dreams of doom. I'd never had one about Seth before. Maybe he was in more trouble in New York than I realized. I would have to pin him down the first chance I got. I straggled back to bed, but didn't fall asleep for a long time.

**The next morning,** Wednesday, I woke up late with that sense that I had forgotten something. My eyes were scratchy. I got dressed quickly in the same yoga pants and AAPD sweatshirt and opened my door. A glance down the hall told me that Seth was already awake. It was almost a miracle that he was up before I was. Then I smelled bacon. And sugar. I heard Alex's voice from the kitchen and remembered. Seth had begged Alex for his chocolate chip pancakes and Alex had offered to teach Seth how to make them. The proposal was met with a lukewarm reception, but Seth finally agreed. Tom had angled an invitation as well. I told Alex I wasn't sure Seth knew how to cook anything and maybe they should start with boiled eggs, but Alex had that gleam of determination in his eye so I'd left them to make their plans. But after a largely sleepless night I wasn't in the mood for Cooking 101 in my kitchen. I felt a dark storm cloud gather over my head. I took a deep breath and stomped down the stairs.

There was clanging and banging, some singing, and it sounded like Seth had hooked his speakers up to his iPod for musical inspiration. My spirits lifted as I entered the kitchen and smelled coffee. They plummeted again when I saw the pot was empty. Flour coated the countertop, a carton of eggs sat on the table near a set of mixing bowls covered in batter, and Seth stood at the stove, spatula in hand. Realizing that almost every pan and utensil was in use, I hoped they'd made a pact to clean up after they were done. It looked like I'd missed the mixing part, but the flipping-the-pancake lesson was just beginning. Tom was again studying the accident report, as if multiple reads would change the contents. I grunted at them all, then mouthed a surprised thank-you to Alex when he shoved a mug of coffee into my hand and ushered me out of the kitchen. Fifteen minutes later Seth announced that breakfast was served. They had set up the plates in the dining room—apparently this was an event.

I sat in front of my plate and inhaled the buttery sweet aroma of syrup drizzled over pancakes. They were crisp on the outside, while the inside melted into sugary heaven. Seth watched me and then tried his own. His face lit up with the thrill of a job well done.

"These are awesome!" he said.

"It's the secret ingredient," Alex said, and held his fist out for Seth to bump.

After a few more minutes of exclaiming over the pancakes and congratulating Seth, I turned to Tom. "Have you heard anything more about the oil and the bread?"

Tom shook his head.

"What oil?" Alex asked.

Tom explained about the peanut oil on the bread and how anyone could have done it.

"It would have to be pretty fancy peanut oil," Alex said.

"What do you mean?" I turned to Alex.

"Most peanut oil is safe for people with allergies. The processing destroys the protein that causes the reaction. A lot of people still avoid any peanut products to be safe, but only some of the gourmet oils that still have a peanut taste and smell and are processed differently are supposed to be actually dangerous."

"How do you know all that?" Tom asked.

"I have to stay up on food-allergy issues to run a safe kitchen."

"So, this isn't regular grocery store oil?" I asked.

Alex shook his head. "No, more the kind of thing you'd get in a specialty store or online. Also, there isn't any smell or taste to regular peanut oil, but the fancy stuff does retain more peanut-y flavor."

"Thanks, Alex," Tom said. "I'm not sure Mac and Charla know about this. It might be useful."

"Glad to help," Alex said and loaded up his plate again.

More coffee, incredible pancakes, and an entertaining rehash of the cooking lesson allowed me to shrug off my concerns of the night before. We were laughing and arguing over the last pancake when I noticed the smell. Something was burning. Just then a shrill noise shrieked in our ears.

"What *is* that?" I shouted, with hands to the side of my head.

"It must be the new smoke detectors your dad put in," Alex yelled back.

We all jumped up and ran to the kitchen to see what was burning. The stove had been left on with three more pancakes in the pan; they were black and smoking, filling the room with an acrid stench. I opened a window and fanned the smoke outside. Seth grabbed a broom and poked at the smoke detector to get it to stop.

For safety, my father had hooked all the detectors together somehow, so they all started alarming. I thought I heard the phone ringing but couldn't tell over all the noise. Alex had turned the stove off and I was considering how best to deal with the pan—and the flames beginning to reach upward—when Tom shouted.

"Clear the way!" He had my fire extinguisher in his hands and before I could stop him, he squeezed the handle.

In seconds, the stove was covered in foam. The nozzle stuck and when Tom lowered his arm the thing kept spraying. Tom was so surprised that he turned away from the stove, coating the floor and the rest of us in white. As he wrestled with the nozzle, he continued to coat the kitchen until the canister ran out of chemical.

We stood for a moment staring in horror at each other and the mess that used to be my kitchen. The pancake-related disaster looked as if it had been caught in a blizzard. My favorite sweatshirt was likely ruined, the dogs whined at the doorway to the kitchen, and Seth stood with his arms out, apparently afraid to move. Tom alone had escaped the foam. His eyes were huge as he made squeaky apologetic noises. Alex was the first to laugh and soon we all had tears streaming down our cheeks. I felt almost immune to the shrieking smoke detectors when another sound came to me. Sirens.

The phone call must have been the alarm company calling to check on us. Now the volunteer firefighters were on their way. I heard them pull up outside and ran to stop them, but slipped and fell in the now-melting fire extinguisher froth. I told Seth to keep the dogs out of the kitchen before they got covered in the chemical as well. Alex helped me up and we both went through the dining room to the front door to stop the firefighters.

I got to the door just as the first rescuer hit the porch, carrying an ax and the business end of a hose. I put my hand up like a traffic cop.

"We're fine, false alarm," I said.

The firefighter looked at Alex and me, covered in white, and said, "You don't look fine."

"No, really," I said. "We had to use the extinguisher and it got a little out of hand."

"We're here now." He gestured to the other two who had joined him on the porch. "We have to check the premises. Protocol." They trooped past us into the house.

"I see you beat us here, Andrews," one of them said as they entered the kitchen.

I caught a quick glimpse of Tom turning bright red and decided to let him handle his buddies. He was also on the volunteer squad, and would likely never live this down. He didn't need me as a witness.

I turned back to Alex and was just breathing a sigh of relief when the air caught in my throat. A bright orange smart car careened down the street and screeched to the curb behind the fire truck. My mother and aunt flung open the doors and rushed up to the porch. I saw Dad's ancient Buick take the turn at the corner at a much safer speed, but still fast for Dad. He also hopped out and made his way to the stairs. Thankfully, the alarm switched off just as they made it to the front door.

"We heard about the fire alarm on your father's scanner! I knew something like this would happen. I was so glad he put in that alarm." Vi paused to take a breath and I jumped in.

"Everyone's fine. It was just a small kitchen fire." I thought about the small kitchen fire's large cleanup requirements and sighed.

"Oh, thank goodness!" Mom's left hand fluttered over her amulet while her right patted my shoulder.

"How long was the response time?" Dad asked. "I've heard they're almost as fast as a paid fire department. Were they here pretty quick?" He stood on tiptoe to look over my shoulder into the house.

"It's a good thing you aren't their driver," Aunt Vi said to him. She turned to me. "He couldn't find his keys, and you know how slow he drives. We had to leave him behind."

Dad kept his face neutral, as usual, during Aunt Vi's tirade.

The volunteers clomped back out, dragging the hose behind them. "Everything looks fine now." The man hooked a thumb over his shoulder. "We've left our best guy behind in case anything else starts smoking." The other two chortled and stomped off the porch. I sent a glare in their direction for Tom's sake, but couldn't really blame them. Tom did tend to get himself tangled up in less than stellar situations.

"Let's see what happened," Vi said.

I swung my arm wide in an "after you" gesture. I caught Alex's eye and he shrugged. We were stuck with them now until they had deemed the house safe.

**I was covered** in dusty foam when Mac burst into the kitchen.

"Clyde! Are you all right?" He was out of breath and his eyes were worried.

"I'm fine. Are *you* all right?" I was surprised by his harried appearance.

He reached for me and pulled me into a hug, completely disregarding the extinguisher foam that covered every inch of me.

"I just got back into town and heard the fire department had been dispatched to your place. What happened?" He pulled away and surveyed the destruction.

"It was a small kitchen fire and a large fire extinguisher. Didn't they tell you everything was okay?"

"I guess I didn't let Lisa tell me the whole story . . . I just . . . I wanted to hear it from you." His voice had gotten quiet and warm. A slow tingle crept along my spine.

I smiled. "I'm glad you did. I've missed you." I moved back toward him, not caring at the moment that my family was in the living room trying to get the tracked foam out of the carpet, and was enjoying our reunion when someone coughed nearby.

Seth stood in the doorway, averting his gaze with a pained look on his face.

"Sorry, I need to get the ladder from the basement. Papa is working on the alarm in the hallway." He looked over his shoulder and then turned back to whisper, "They're getting suspicious out there."

I reluctantly pulled away from Mac and gestured toward the basement door, where the ladder lived.

"I'm gonna be tied up for the next couple of days," Mac said. "Can we get together later in the week? Maybe for dinner?"

I nodded. "Yeah, I'd like that."

I walked Mac out to the front door and he left to go back to work. I pointedly ignored the stares and raised eyebrows of Mom and Vi.

"Clytemnestra, I need to speak to you." My shoulders tensed and I turned back toward my mother. My mind raced with excuses and lies to distract her from me and Mac.

"I really need to finish the kitchen, Mom."

"I'll do it," Vi said. "You two go sit on the porch."

Mom and I stepped outside and I breathed in the crisp air. Someone was burning leaves a few streets over. I wondered why the firemen weren't harassing *them*.

"Clyde, come sit." Mom patted the space next to her on the wicker couch.

I sat and waited.

"You think you can fool me, but I'm your mother and I know you better than you think I do."

I took a deep breath and prepared to tell her about Mac. But she wasn't done.

"I don't think Seth came out here for the festival. And I doubt Grace would let him ditch school for a week to come to Michigan when he just spent the whole summer here."

I felt a little dizzy as the conversation took this unexpected turn. I wasn't sure which topic was more uncomfortable.

I nodded. "You're right. Seth came here without telling Grace. But I called her the morning after he arrived and she's agreed to let him stay for a little while."

Mom blew out a gust of air. "I was worried about this. The cards have been telling me for months that there is something wrong in New York. I thought it had more to do with Grace than with Seth."

She played with her amulet and stared past me toward the street.

"Mom? I don't get the impression that Seth is in any trouble. I think he's just trying to figure out where he fits in, and he doesn't feel as comfortable in the city as he does here."

Mom turned and put her hand over mine. "Do you really think that's all it is?"

I nodded, feeling guilty at reassuring her when I was worried myself.

"I hope so," she said. "I can't tell you how much I worry about you girls, and now I find I'm worrying about Seth, too. I'd do anything to protect you kids."

"I'll talk to Seth and try to figure out what's bothering him. But, he's safe here with us. Nothing is going to happen to him."

Mom smiled and patted my hand. We walked back inside together to face the rest of the cleanup.

# 21

⁓∞⁓

**After a couple of hours with everyone pitching in,** the kitchen was clean. Seth had gone to my mom's house with the dogs because she'd promised him brownies. Alex and Tom had departed for work. Alone in the house for the first time in days, I sat on the couch clutching a cup of coffee as I replayed the dream I'd had the night before.

It had seemed so real, climbing to the top of the tower and searching for Seth. Just thinking about it I felt the familiar spinning sensation I got whenever I stood too close to the edge of a balcony, or even a window in a tall building. I tried to deny that it felt like one of those dreams that foretold the future, but I gave up and decided I needed to face it and figure out what it had been trying to tell me.

Seth was in the vision, but unharmed. I felt my shoulders relax a bit as I examined the sequence of events in the light of day. In the past, if I'd envisioned a death or injury, it had been more obvious. In the most recent dream, I felt I needed to help him but I couldn't be sure he was in real danger. This was one of those times I wished my grandmother were still alive. She would help me interpret the dreams because I so often jumped to the worst conclusion.

I sat up quickly and almost spilled my coffee. Neila Whittle. She could help. She'd practically *insisted* on helping. I downed the last of the coffee and grabbed my keys.

The drive to her place was less spooky this time. The house still appeared abandoned, but this time I knew what lay inside. My knock echoed within and I heard shufflings and scrapings on the other side of the door. It finally creaked open and Neila stood there, wearing what looked like the same pile of shawls and rags as last time.

"Clytemnestra, this is a surprise," she said. She didn't open the door farther.

"Ms. Whittle, I've been thinking about what you said last time I was here. I need your help." I looked over her head into the entryway. I thought I saw a shadow move on the opposite wall.

"Oh my. You've had a scare?" She stepped back from the doorway and motioned me inside.

I glanced around the hallway and the hair on my arms stood up. Something wasn't right. I sensed we weren't alone.

"Let's head back to the kitchen for a cup of tea," Neila said a bit loudly. She pointed toward the back of the house and I walked down the dark hallway again toward the relative light of the kitchen.

When I got there, I saw that the cauldron was steaming again and my stomach rumbled. I turned to ask what she was cooking but the hallway was empty.

"Ms. Whittle?" I took a step back toward the front door and she appeared in front of me.

"Let's get settled and we can have a nice chat," she said.

"Do you want some stew? I still have some left from last time."

I started to decline, when my stomach chimed in again. I felt my face get hot and nodded. She smiled and took a bowl out of the fridge. She bent down and placed it in a microwave I hadn't noticed before. It seemed out of place in this rustic room.

"What are you cooking today?" I pointed at the cauldron.

"Oh, nothing much. Not something you can eat, anyway. Just mixing up a bit of this and that." She waved her hand to deflect any further inquiry.

She placed the bowl of stew in front of me and when the tea was ready she sat down with her own thick brown mug and a delicate teacup for me.

"What's got you spooked?" she asked.

I didn't love her choice of words but I told her about the dream, the vertigo, and the anxious rush down the hall to check on Seth.

"Hmm. That is a tough one. You didn't recognize the stairwell?"

I shook my head, and spooned up some stew.

"Have you always been afraid of heights?" she asked.

"For as long as I can remember," I said. "I know I used to climb trees as a kid but somewhere along the line I developed this spinning sensation whenever I got too high."

"What happens when you travel in an airplane?"

"I don't like to take plane trips, but if I do, I sit on the aisle so I don't have to look out the window."

She nodded. "From what you've described, since it feels so real, like other premonitory dreams, I'd have to say this is a prediction." She wrapped her hands around the mug. "You'll likely recognize this place when you see it. I can't tell if Seth is in danger or not. It sounds like you thought he was and were trying to save him even though you had to climb up high to do it."

"What about the woman I heard laughing?"

"You're trying to figure out who killed Rafe Godwin, aren't you?"

I nodded.

"Maybe the dream is trying to tell you something about that."

"Trying to tell me what? That a woman did it and Seth is in danger?" I pushed the bowl of stew aside, no longer hungry.

"It's always difficult to tease out the warning or the message in a dream. It really depends on how you, the dreamer, interpret it."

I pressed my lips together. Neila was giving me the party line. Focus more, jump to conclusions less. But I wanted to know *now* whether Seth was in danger and how to get Dylan out of jail.

"Did you know they've arrested Dylan Ward?"

She looked down at her tea and took a long sip. "I heard. I think they're wrong and he'll be out of jail soon. But from what I've heard, someone set up the situation so that Rafe would succumb to his allergy."

"What have you heard?"

"Just that he was very careful about what he ate and that his medicine didn't work."

I wondered how a recluse could be so tapped into the town gossip, but after years of listening to Vi quote cats and horses, I wasn't sure I wanted to know her sources.

Neila interrupted my thoughts. "Can you tell the police about your dream?"

I snorted. Her face fell and I apologized.

"I'm not laughing at you. I'm laughing at the thought that

Mac would put any stock in what I tell him based on a dream."

"Phillip McKenzie? Lucille's boy?"

"That's the one. He goes by Mac and he doesn't believe in anything."

"Everyone believes in something. What would be the point otherwise?"

I looked into her gentle gray eyes and knew why she had been my grandmother's friend.

"You're right. He believes in things that can be measured and quantified. Fingerprints, ballistics, tire tracks, autopsies . . ."

"You must be wrong. Any child of Lucille McKenzie would believe in things beyond our understanding."

I didn't want to insult her by explaining that it was Mac's mother's blind faith in all things psychic that had turned him into such a skeptic. After his father's death she'd spent a huge chunk of her life savings trying to contact him. She never succeeded, as far as Mac was concerned. Lucille would say she'd seen glimpses and hints that he was trying to make contact. It was a sad story in the end. She never really moved on and Mac blamed the mediums in town for her single-minded pursuit of her dead husband.

"I don't think they see eye to eye on the subject of psychics."

"Hmm."

"Anyway, I need help figuring out what the dream might mean. I don't want to just wait until I find myself in a stone stairway running to rescue Seth. Maybe I can keep him safe beforehand if I can understand what it means."

Ms. Whittle was already shaking her head. "You don't know enough yet. Have you discovered any techniques that help the dreams to come?"

I looked down at the table. I'd spent the last fifteen years or more trying to learn techniques that *stopped* the dreams. I shook my head. "The only thing I've noticed is that when my friend Diana does a spell, it seems to trigger the dreams."

Neila nodded. "If you are truly open-minded to your friend's spell-casting that could be enough to invite information."

"I need to learn witchcraft?"

"Oh my, no. I don't get the sense that it would be a good fit for you. You need to become more open-minded to the idea of receiving information. If we're lucky, you'll get a more specific message if you are open to it."

I nodded and finished my tea. The moment I set down the cup, Neila stood.

"I don't want to rush you, dear, but this . . . potion is at a delicate stage."

She steered me back to the front door and I found myself on the front porch, with more questions than answers.

**After my abrupt** dismissal from Neila's house, I felt unsettled. Seth texted to say he was back at my house. I drove slowly back home, thinking. So much had happened in the five days since Rafe had died. I felt like my life had been upended. Diana was frantic about Dylan, I had hardly seen Mac, I was in the middle of a murder investigation again, and Seth had appeared and was apparently planning to stick around.

Seth. I had been avoiding thinking about why he might have run all the way from New York to here. He seemed to be doing just fine, but no kid just picks up and travels cross-country on a whim. Do they? I was feeling a good amount of auntly guilt for not pursuing this earlier. I told myself I would have if it hadn't been for everything else that had been going on, but I wasn't buying it. I was a coward. I didn't want to pry into Seth's life and I almost didn't want to know what the problem was because then I would feel compelled to fix it. But after that dream I knew I had to find out what was bothering him. If he was in danger, I had to know why and I had to help.

I found him in what I considered to be his room. He thought of it that way as well, if the detritus on the floor and every flat surface was any indication. The dogs were watching him in rapt attention as he ate popcorn and clicked away on his computer.

"Working on homework?" I said from the door.

"What? Oh, yeah."

I entered the room and he flipped his laptop shut. Hmmm.

"Should we take the guys for a walk?"

Both dogs jumped up at the word "walk," and they seemed to struggle with whether to focus on the popcorn or the possible adventure outside.

"Sure." Seth hopped up and the dogs got in line behind him.

One of the officers I'd worked with in the past had two teenagers. He had always said the best way to talk to a teen is to do something else to distract them from the fact that you are actually conversing. Driving in the car, doing the dishes, and for Seth and me it was the dogs—either walking them or playing with them.

Once we were a block or so from the house I began my interrogation.

"Have they sent you much homework from school?" I asked. Grace had texted me that the school would be e-mailing assignments on a regular basis.

Seth lifted a shoulder and let it drop. "Not too much."

"Heard from any of your friends from school?"

He shook his head. "Not really."

I threw all the advice out the window and went for the straightforward approach.

"What's going on, Seth?"

He gave me a startled look.

"What do you mean?"

"I mean, why did you appear out of the blue on my front porch?"

"I thought you were cool with it. Should I go to Nana Rose's house?"

"No, that's not what I meant. I like having you at the house. It's just . . . shouldn't you be in school and hanging out with your friends?"

He exhaled. "I like it better here. I wish I could just stay—"

My phone buzzed. It was Diana's ringtone.

"Sorry, just a sec," I said and answered.

"Clyde, can you come right over? Please?"

"What's wrong?"

"Just . . . come. If you can."

I put the phone back in my pocket.

"Something's up with Diana. I need to get over there."

"I'll deal with the dogs. They aren't going to want to go home yet."

I nodded and walked back toward the house, sure I hadn't imagined Seth's relief at his temporary reprieve from questioning.

# 22

❧❦❧

I hadn't spoken to Diana since her spell-casting
the night before. She'd sounded panicked on the phone so I
chose to drive the five blocks instead of walking. I pulled
onto her street and saw a police cruiser outside her house.
My mind raced and dire thoughts came unbidden. Maybe
they had more evidence. Maybe there was a break in
the case. The car wasn't Mac's; I was pretty sure it wasn't
the one Tom usually drove, either.

I parked in the street, behind the cruiser, and took the
steps two at a time onto Diana's porch. I knocked and
bounced on my toes, both because it was cold and because
I was anxious to find out what the police were doing there.

Diana's face was pale and drawn when she pulled open
the door. I started to worry that Dylan had been hurt.

"Diana, who's here? Are you okay?" I stepped inside and
gave her a brief hug.

Diana nodded. I assumed that meant she was fine.

In the living room, I saw Charla sitting stiffly on Diana's couch. We nodded to each other.

"Come in, Clyde. You should hear this as well." Diana led me into her living room. "Charla was just telling me that things are not looking good for Dylan."

"I shouldn't even be here." Charla stood up. "I just wanted to prepare Diana for the worst. With the hearing today and the evidence we have, I think they'll end up pursuing the case."

Charla didn't let things get to her. I felt my own anxiety rising as I thought about what would be bad enough for Charla to break the rules and come to Diana.

I sat in the armchair. "What is it, Charla?"

"Diana can fill you in. I really need to get going. I don't want the neighbors gossiping about my car out there in the street. You kids are going to have enough trouble in the next few days." She quickly made her way out the front door and down the steps.

Diana sat with her head in her hands. She shook her head and looked at me. "I don't know what to do."

"Tell me what's happened."

"Charla came to tell me to prepare for a court case. She said if Dylan pleads not guilty they will have to go to court and the evidence against him is mounting."

"What can they possibly have? He didn't do it. You and I both know he's not a killer."

She nodded. "I know. She said the EpiPen had been drained of medicine and the needle was snapped off."

"That's why the medicine didn't work. No epinephrine was delivered." I remembered Daron saying he hadn't heard a click when Diana administered the medicine.

Diana nodded. "I didn't notice it at the time. I'd never given him an injection. I was so upset about how bad he looked that I just took the pen out and jammed it against his leg."

I reached over and squeezed her hand.

Diana looked up to the ceiling, her eyes welling over with tears. "He never had a chance. Someone deliberately damaged his medication and then exposed him to peanuts."

"Dylan wasn't even there that night," I said. "How could he have done it?"

"They have his fingerprints on the EpiPen, at least on the outer casing. The pen itself was wiped clean—all they found were my prints on that part." Her head dropped to her hands again, orange curls obscuring her face. "I don't understand."

This made sense based on what Daron Pagan had told us. The pen comes in a case to protect it from accidentally releasing the needle. When ready to inject, the cap is removed and the pen has to be quickly and firmly pressed into the victim's thigh. I had seen Diana do that. Daron said there was no click of the needle popping out of the pen. I would expect Diana's prints to be on the pen, but anyone else who had handled it should have left prints as well.

"Is that all they have? He could have touched that casing anytime."

"Charla says the evidence points to Dylan tampering with the EpiPen prior to that night and then doctoring the bread I made so that there were peanut allergens in it."

"What does that mean, 'peanut allergens'?"

Diana shrugged. "I guess there weren't any actual peanuts in the bread after all. There was some sort of peanut oil on the bread. Rafe was very allergic. That must have been enough to trigger an allergic response."

I nodded, remembering that Alex had said the oil would

have to be special. Perhaps that could help Dylan. I hadn't known there were different kinds of oil, maybe Dylan didn't, either. Of course, how would he prove a *lack* of knowledge?

I needed to research peanut allergies and find out more about what happened that night. In the meantime I had to calm Diana and come up with a plan to get Dylan out of jail.

**I paced to** the front door and back. I sat down and then stood again. During all of my nervous energy release, Diana sat still and quiet.

Finally, after what seemed like days but was more like minutes, Diana turned to me.

"Will you go with me to the police station? I need to talk to Mac."

Relief flooded through me. I was thrilled that she was taking this so calmly and I was sure Mac could explain things. I hadn't suggested it because I wasn't sure how much Diana blamed Mac for Dylan's arrest.

"Of course," I said. "We'll go now. I'm sure Mac can give us some more information." I picked up my coat and shrugged it on, pulling my keys out of the pocket. "Sometimes he plays these things very close. Charla might not have all the facts." I looked at Diana's ashen face and decided that the quietly supportive approach might be better.

Diana put her coat on after I held it out to her. She followed me down the front steps, got in my Jeep, and buckled her seat belt. She stared straight ahead and didn't speak for the whole ride to the police station.

We went inside and I approached Lisa Harkness. Her smile faded when she saw Diana up close. She nodded to my request that Diana and I wait in one of the interview rooms until Mac could see us. I saw her pick up the phone and whisper into it as we passed through the door separating the front desk from the rest of the police station.

I chose interview room one for its larger table and better chairs. We took off our coats and sat. Diana still hadn't spoken.

I heard footsteps in the hall but they weren't Mac's. He has a very determined stride, but still limps a bit after a gunshot injury from when he worked narcotics in Saginaw. This person stopped, backed up, turned again, and finally approached the room, the steps slowing as they got closer. Tom Andrews peeked around the doorframe.

"Can I get you anything while you wait?" he asked.

I shook my head and looked to Diana. She was studying her lap and didn't respond.

"Thanks, Tom, we're fine."

"Okay. Detective McKenzie is on his way." Tom's footsteps receded and we were left in silence once more.

I didn't mind being quiet. In fact, I preferred it, but this was an unnatural quiet and I was getting concerned. I was about to try again to get Diana to talk to me when I heard Mac striding down the hall. There was no hesitation, but every other step had the slightest drag.

Mac filled the doorway as he stood, evaluating the situation.

"Diana, Clyde." He nodded to each of us. "How can I help you two?"

"Diana wants to—" I began, but Diana put her hand on mine to stop me.

"I want to make a confession," she said.

"What?" I turned to look at her and held my hand up to stop Mac from coming in the room.

It didn't work. He shut the door behind him and sat down

across from Diana. His glance slid away from me as he reached into his jacket pocket and pulled out a digital recorder.

"I'll need to record you." He placed it on the table between us.

"No. No, Mac, she doesn't know what she's saying." I stood up and tried to pull Diana up with me. "She's been under a lot of stress with Dylan and the festival and Rafe's death."

She took my hand and pulled me back down into my seat. "This is the right thing to do, Clyde." She gripped my hand even tighter and turned to Mac. She nodded.

Mac reached out and pressed a button on the device, a green light blinked on.

"Please state your full name and address," he said.

I felt dizzy and nauseated as Diana identified herself and rattled off her address.

"You're here of your own volition to make a statement?" Mac asked.

"Yes." Diana nodded. I took deep breaths and tried to figure out how to get us both out of this room.

"Okay, what information do you want to provide?"

"I killed Rafe Godwin. I put peanut oil in the bread I made, knowing he was allergic. I broke the EpiPen so it wouldn't work. I just pretended to give him the injection so no one would know." Diana hung her head. "I did it all by myself. My brother, Dylan, is innocent."

I thought I was going to be sick. The room spun and it was only when Diana turned to me with tears spilling down her cheeks that I was able to pull myself together. Mac had already turned off the recorder and was out of his seat, calling for Tom. Diana scrubbed at her cheeks and dried her eyes on her sleeve. She sat quietly while Mac read her her rights, and Charla came to lead her down the hall to be fingerprinted again.

My hands were shaking and I was still sitting in the interview room when Mac returned. I was running the last half hour through my head. I knew Diana was innocent, but couldn't figure out what she thought she would accomplish by this stunt.

"Are you okay?" he said.

I shook my head.

"I'm going to postpone Dylan's hearing until we get this sorted out," he said. "I'm really sorry, Clyde." He came around behind my chair, put his hands on my shoulders, and leaned forward to kiss the top of my head. And then he was gone.

**After Diana was** taken away for booking, I stumbled out of the police station and stood catching my breath in the frosty air.

The shock passed and was quickly replaced by anger. I was furious with Diana for what I was sure was a stunt or a misplaced sense of duty. I didn't believe for a moment that she had killed Rafe. Mac should know better. How could he arrest her when it was obvious she was lying? I didn't know what to do next, so I went to find Alex.

If I had been thinking clearly, I would have realized that Alex would need his own support when he heard the news.

I found him in the kitchen of Everyday Grill getting ready for the dinnertime rush. He glanced up as I walked in. One look and he rushed forward and helped me to a chair.

"Clyde, what happened?"

I put my head in my hands, took a deep breath, and then

felt myself coming back together. I couldn't help Diana if I fell apart. I looked up to see Alex's staff hovering nearby.

"Let's go to your office."

Alex nodded and led the way. I fell gratefully into his visitor chair.

"It's Diana," I said after he shut the door.

"Is she hurt? Where is she?" He grabbed the doorknob, ready to go.

"She confessed. She's at the police station."

"Confessed to what? She hasn't done anything." He crossed his arms and glowered as if *I* had arrested her.

I explained the visit from Charla and Diana's request to talk to Mac.

"I thought she just wanted to try to get some information from him about Dylan and what kind of a case they had against him," I said. I rubbed my arms to ward off the chill that was creeping up my body. "I had no idea she was going to confess and get herself arrested."

Alex nodded. "She didn't do it."

"I know that."

"Mac must know it as well. Why would he arrest her?"

I shook my head. "He must be following some sort of protocol. You know how he is about following the rules. I don't remember what the procedure would be for something like this. It never came up when I worked there." I had worked in the Crystal Haven department for a short time before going to Ann Arbor after police academy but no one had confessed to murder while I was there.

"Okay, we have to figure out how to get her out of jail." Alex sat in his chair and pulled his desk phone closer.

"I don't think he'll be able to keep her long without evidence, but a confession does warrant investigation."

"How bad does it look for Dylan?" His hand paused over the phone. I had no idea who he thought he was going to call.

"I don't know. We never got that far. She just said she wanted to talk to Mac and then confessed. She must think she can protect him somehow."

"Can you get anything out of Mac?"

I shook my head. "He's likely going to tell me to get her a lawyer and keep out of it."

"Maybe Tom?"

I shrugged. "Maybe."

We made a plan to call Rupert and assign him the task of getting Diana out of jail, and to meet at my house that evening after the dinner crowd.

I walked to my Jeep feeling shaky and unfocused. Knowing I'd have to tell my family the news in person, I drove to my house to pick up Seth and the dogs. I just hoped to get to my family before the gossip chain reached them.

# 23

There was no way to prepare for my family. Even after years of perfecting my technique, they always surprised me.

My announcement was met with a stunned silence, which was astounding in itself. Then, everyone started talking at once.

"I did *not* see this coming," Vi said.

"It wasn't on the scanner," Dad said.

"The cards haven't shown anything like this."

Only Seth was silent. He sat with Tuffy and Baxter on the floor, all three with long faces and sad eyes.

"What should we do?" Mom asked.

"I want to go back out to the woods where Rafe died. Maybe I'll remember something if I'm there," I said.

Seth stood. "We'll come with you." He gestured to the dogs, who looked like they sensed a walk was on offer.

Baxter knew a lot of words and "woods" was one of his favorites.

I glanced out the window at the rapidly setting sun. "It's too late now. It'll be dark soon. We'll go in the morning."

Mom insisted we stay for dinner. The dogs seemed to follow the conversation, sensing that they would be getting my mom's cooking rather than dog food for dinner.

After agreeing to stay, we trailed into the dining room. Mom managed to produce a couple of roasted chickens, mashed potatoes, gravy, carrots, and green beans. I'd have to increase the exercise or decrease the visits to my mom's this winter. She believed in a hearty meal once the temperature dipped below 50 degrees. I wondered what she did with all the food on the nights I didn't show up with a famished teen.

We settled in to the feast with a loud clatter of scraping chairs and clanking cutlery. Dad sat next to me and seemed glum in comparison to Aunt Vi's high color. I wondered if they'd had another disagreement over the relative usefulness of their respective careers.

Vi maintained that dentists were no longer needed in today's society. She'd read somewhere that the dentists had "made up" the need for six month checkups and were all in cahoots to stir up fear of periodontal disease. *Her* profession, on the other hand, had always been and always would be necessary as long as people and animals coexisted. Ever since she had first broached this topic, it didn't take more than a few words before my dad was taking deep breaths and looking longingly at the liquor cabinet.

My hopes that it was just another family squabble were dashed when Dad leaned toward me and whispered, "Red alert, 10-55."

This was our own 10-code that meant the ladies were in

full-on psychic mode and had plans to drag me into it. We'd established this protocol at the end of the summer when I realized that Dad was aware of much more than he ever let on and that he could be a useful informant in my struggle with Mom and Vi.

The plate of chicken and vegetables looked much less appetizing now. I focused on the food and tried to push my worries aside. How bad could it be? I'd gotten used to the addition of the pendulum to many family gatherings and Mom's tarot cards could be entertaining if looked at in just the right light. . . .

Seth, as usual, had checked out completely once the food was served and I expected he would be no help to me until he'd made it through his second serving. I watched the ladies carefully, trying to sense what they were up to. I hoped it wasn't another séance. The last time we'd done that, over the summer, Vi had either faked a manifestation, or had truly received a message from beyond. Either choice made my skin prickle.

We were just finishing the last round of potatoes when Vi took a deep breath and I braced myself. The doorbell rang. The cacophony of barking broke the mood and I leaped up yelling, "I'll get it!" over the noise. I was so happy to postpone Vi's announcement that I thought I might hug whoever was at the door.

It was Alex—lucky for me, less so for him. I grabbed his hand and dragged him into the dining room.

"Look who's here," I said.

"I drove by your house and it was dark so I thought I'd try here," Alex said.

I apologized for forgetting to let him know where we were.

"No prob. You aren't that hard to find," he said.

"Do you want something to eat, dear?" Mom gestured at the platters of food. "We have plenty."

"No thanks, Mrs. Fortune. I ate at work."

"I'm glad you're here, Alex," Vi said, and gestured at an empty chair across from me. "Rose and I have an idea to help Diana." Her brilliant smile should have signaled Alex to run, but he didn't.

Alex pulled out the chair and sat. "Great! We have to get her out of there."

Vi nodded. "We need to see how this is all going to play out."

Alex hesitated. "You mean, like, ask the pendulum?" He glanced at me, looking for backup.

"No, we've tried the pendulum." Vi crossed her arms and shook her head. "It can only answer yes or no questions and at this point we don't know *what* to ask. We know Diana and Dylan didn't do it but we don't have any more suspects."

Alex nodded warily. Seth leaned forward. Dad poured himself a whiskey that he produced from under the table. I hadn't even seen him get up to nab it.

"It's finally getting dark enough, Vi," Mom said. "Should I go get it?"

Vi nodded and patted her hand. She turned to the rest of us.

My stomach felt like a hard ball of ice. I knew what they were up to and why Dad had called it a red alert. They were going to use the crystal ball.

"What?" Seth asked and bounced in his seat. "What are they going to do?" He could tell by my reaction that I wasn't thrilled, which seemed to excite him even more.

"She's going to get Grandma Agnes's crystal ball," I said

to the table. I didn't want to look at either one of them. Sort of like not meeting a teacher's eyes when she's looking for volunteers in class. I decided to go ostrich on them and hope they picked on someone else.

"Oh," Alex said. He became focused on the pattern in the tablecloth as well.

"Well, we're desperate, aren't we?" Vi said, her hands out, palms up. "We really don't know what else to do."

"I love crystal balls!" Seth said. "Diana has a bunch in her store. How do you use it? I've never seen anyone use one."

Vi cast a severe glance in his direction. "You have to be very careful. Some people see all sorts of future events in a crystal ball, some see only possibilities. Others get so lost in the future that they forget about the present."

Alex and I glanced at each other. We'd heard the same speech when we were about Seth's age. Mom had caught Alex, Diana, and me consulting it about a crush Diana had and whether he would ask her to the dance. The event stuck in all our minds because it was the only time my mom had been mad that I was *trying* to use my talents. I sensed that she was afraid of the seemingly innocent orb. She'd taken it away and I still didn't know where she kept it. She left the room to go to her secret hiding place.

Alex sighed heavily. "I'd rather do the pendulum."

**Vi mobilized the** rest of us into clearing the table. Mom breezed back into the dining room, out of breath and dusty. She carried a battered wooden box about half the size of a shoe box. I wondered again where she was hiding the thing.

She set the box in the middle of the table with the reverence normally reserved for religious ceremonies. Dad slid his chair back.

"Don't go wandering off, Frank," Mom said without looking at him. "We need all the energy we can get."

Dad's shoulders slumped.

Seth wore the gleeful expression of a five-year-old on Christmas morning. Alex regarded the box as if it might contain poisonous snakes. I gripped the table and waited for Mom to open it.

She flipped open the lid to reveal a clear crystal sphere nestled in black velvet. Lifting it out, she also pulled away a square of velvet to polish the surface. After she was done, she set a round metal stand on the table, draped that with the velvet, and set the ball in the stand, all without touching the surface of the crystal. Mom and Vi were very particular about fingerprints. I was reminded of crime scene techs handling evidence.

Vi had been rifling through the cabinet that sat in the corner of the dining room and now returned to the table with several candles and a lighter. After the tapers were lit, Mom turned off the overhead light and plunged us all into the warm glow of candlelight. I didn't feel cozy.

Seth's eyes gleamed in the flickering lights and he resembled one of his manga comic book characters, all big eyes and angles. Alex had instinctively pulled back from the crystal and he regarded me warily from across the table. Mom and Vi looked at me expectantly.

I closed my eyes. I was already getting a headache right in the middle of my forehead.

"I hate scrying," I said. Scrying uses fire, smoke, or reflective surfaces to help see visions of the future.

"You were fine when it was a bonfire in the middle of the woods," Vi said.

"That didn't give me a headache the way this does."

"Just give it a try," Mom said. "You haven't looked at it in years. Maybe it will be better this time."

"I'll do it." Seth's hand shot into the air. "Tell me what to do."

For a kid who was all worked up about his ability to talk to animals, Seth was certainly enthusiastic about every other method of seeing the future or communicating with other realms. I would think talking to Tuffy would seem tame compared to a séance or viewing the future. But I've never gotten a message from an animal.

"Let Seth try," I said, rubbing the spot between my eyes.

Vi *tsk*ed. "He doesn't have any abilities."

Seth and I exchanged a panicked look. Had they figured out Seth's Dolittle tendencies?

"I thought anyone could at least try," Dad said.

Vi glowered at him and then shrugged. "Fine, give it a try, Seth." She carefully slid the ball toward Seth.

"Seth, you have to look deep into the crystal and be patient," Mom said. "Sometimes the surface will get cloudy or misty and you have to move beyond that to see what lies inside. It doesn't work every time, but give it a try."

The sphere seemed to glow from within in the dancing candlelight. Next to me, Seth leaned forward and stared at the ball. The black fabric absorbed extraneous light and minimized distractions. The candles provided just enough light to see the future in the crystal. I glanced across at Alex, who appeared a bit ill.

Seth's eyes started to bulge. I leaned over and told him he was allowed to blink. I stole a glance at the ball and it already looked foggy to me. I rubbed my forehead again and blinked. The light fog had become a swirling mist and I watched in fascination as the tendrils parted. A figure stood in the distance and I leaned forward to get a better look. It was a man, backlit, so I couldn't see his face. He was big, with broad shoulders, and his hair was pulled back into a ponytail. I was about to pull away when his face swam into view. Lucan. The room felt like it was spinning and my stomach flipped over. My head exploded in pain and I leaned back in my chair, almost forcing it to tip over.

"Clyde, are you okay?" Alex knelt next to my chair. Dad stood behind with a hand on my shoulder.

I shook my head and the pain cleared. Vi was across the table, grinning. Mom had her hands clasped under her chin; her eyes glistened with unshed tears.

"I knew you could do it," Mom whispered.

"What did you see?" Vi asked. "We know you saw something. You spaced out for ten minutes."

Seth was holding the ball with the velvet wrapped around his hand. He held it close to the candle flame and looked through it. "I still don't see anything," he said.

Vi rapped her knuckles on the table and glowered at us all.

"Give her a minute, Vi," Dad said. "She doesn't look so good."

Alex slipped a glass of whiskey into my hand. I set it on the table, sure my stomach would rebel if I tried to drink it.

"I'm okay." I shook my head to clear it. "I didn't see much."

"You saw something, though, right?" Vi said.

I nodded. "I saw Lucan."

"What was he doing?" Mom said.

"Nothing. He was just there. I saw his face and that was it."

"I knew it!" Vi said, and punctuated with a sharp clap of her hands.

"What did you know, Vi?" Dad said, with barely disguised annoyance.

"I never liked him," Vi muttered. "He looks like an invading Viking warrior."

"Invading who?" Seth asked.

"Invading anyone." Vi flapped her hand, summing up a thousand years of history. "That's all they did. Invade. He looks just like them."

I glanced at Mom, wondering how to handle this latest proclamation. She darted glances between Dad and Vi, ever on the lookout for another dustup.

"I didn't know Lucan was a Viking," Seth said. "He seemed pretty nice to me."

"I don't know him very well, but I'm sure he doesn't command an invading army," Alex said and stood up. He rested his hand on my back. "I think Clyde should get home now."

Vi nodded. "Okay, this is very helpful. Now we have a name to investigate. Rose, get your cards and we'll see what we can figure out."

I stood up and tilted my head toward the door to signal Seth that we were leaving while we still had the chance. He reluctantly replaced the ball in its box and snapped his fingers at the dogs. They jumped up and came to his side, waiting for further instructions.

"Are you sure you're okay to drive home?" Dad asked.

"It's only a few blocks, Dad, I can make it."

Alex, Seth, the dogs, and I moved toward the front door. Mom waved good-bye but Vi was already mumbling about pendulums and tarot cards and didn't seem to notice when we left.

# 24

❦

**The early morning sun slanted through the trees** as we trudged out to the site of the Halloween ceremony. Normally, I loved walking in the woods this time of year, the smell of old leaves and a distant wood fire mixing with nostalgia would leave me feeling relaxed and content. Not this time.

I wished for a moment that I had brought my guns. Target shooting always helped clear my mind, but I kept them at the local shooting range now, locked up. It wouldn't be safe with the dogs along, anyway. After last summer, neither one tolerated the sound of a gunshot.

The dogs had no pressing concerns about murder or friends in prison and bounded happily through the leaves, exploring all the scents of the forest. Seth dragged his feet to punctuate how very exhausted he was from getting up before ten. Once we were a good distance from the road, we unclipped the leashes to let the dogs explore without pulling us along.

Seth trailed after me into the forest as I tried to find the path that led to the small clearing where Diana had set up the ceremony. That night I'd followed her without really paying attention and she'd set up helpful lanterns along the way for the attendees to follow.

After about ten minutes of trying to find the clearing and keep track of the dogs, I stopped to get my bearings.

"I thought you knew where you were going," Seth grumbled.

"I *do*," I said. "Just give me a second." I held up my hand.

I mentally retraced our steps from the road and tried to remember which way we had turned that night as we followed Rafe's body out of the woods.

"It should be right up here past those two big trees," I said and led the way forward. Baxter sensed my direction and ran ahead like a canine bodyguard securing the area.

He gave a short bark and I heard him crunching among the leaves. We finally came upon the clearing. The area where the bonfire had been was still obvious. Diana had been careful to clear a space for the fire and she'd surrounded it with rocks. Charred logs remained in the center. It had been almost a week since that night. The last leaves had fallen from the twisting branches overhead and the rain from a couple days ago had soaked everything. I wasn't sure what I was looking for and didn't even know if the police had already been out to the area.

According to Tom, Lucan had cleaned up that night. He'd willingly turned over the trash bags to the police, but in view of our new suspicions, I wondered how useful any of that evidence would be.

Seth found a sodden napkin and a plastic fork underneath a tree. I found a lump of black wax with a burned wick. We put them in a plastic bag. Otherwise, Lucan had done a pretty good job of erasing all traces of everything that happened out here. I walked the perimeter of the clearing trying to remember where everyone had been standing.

Baxter rushed out of the trees with something in his mouth.

"Seth, what does he have?" I hoped it wasn't a dead bird.

"Come here, boy, let's see it," Seth said.

Baxter trotted over to Seth and dropped the thing at his feet. I was always amazed at the way Seth could get the dogs to do whatever he wanted. That was another thing to follow up on and worry about. Seth bent to pick up Baxter's find. It was bright orange and not quite round.

"It's an old rotten orange," Seth said, holding it up for me to see. He got ready to toss it back into the trees.

"Wait, don't throw it," I said. "He'll just chase it again. Put it in here." I held out the bag and he added it to the ball of wax, the fork, and the napkin.

I gave Baxter a treat for bringing us a nasty old orange and one to Tuffy for moral support. Another ten minutes in the clearing yielded only more trash. I turned to tell Seth we should finish up.

He was kneeling on the ground in the area that I remembered the robes had been piled. He stood and turned to me, cupping something in his hand. I walked to him to see what he had found.

"Look at this." He held his hand out to me.

In it was a small silver disk. It looked like flower petals around a green stone. A silver six-pointed star was embossed into the stone. A cold shiver ran up my spine. I had a charm just like this. It was on my chakra bracelet that Diana had given me and I never wore. I had seen a bracelet just like it on Morgan Lavelle's wrist.

I tried to recall the scene in my mind. She'd worn scary skull earrings and multiple necklaces. She'd crossed her arms and I saw the charm bracelet. Was a charm missing?

"What is it?" Seth asked.

"It might be Dylan's ticket out of jail," I said. "Great job, Seth. We better head back before Papa gets to the house." Seth nodded and we walked back out of the woods with the dogs, a bag of trash, and a new plan to help Dylan and Diana.


**Dad arrived just** as we pulled into the driveway. He climbed out of his ancient Buick with his tool kit and a thermos. He'd promised to come over and inspect the alarm system, to be sure it was still working after the kitchen fire and the multiple attempts to shut off the alarm with a broom handle. The thermos accompanied him on all repair jobs, even if he was in his own house. I often wondered what he kept in there.

Once inside, Dad succumbed to the exuberant greeting of the dogs, who had forgotten that they'd just seen him last night. Baxter inspected Dad's pockets for treats while Tuffy leaped straight in the air in his greeting ritual. Seth raised one hand and let it drop and shuffled toward the kitchen. The dogs trailed behind expectantly.

"How's it going at the house?" I asked.

Dad raised his shoulders and shook his head. "You know how it is. Tarot cards, pendulums, dire predictions. Vi's making a list of any animals that might know Lucan. The usual."

"You want to hang out here for a while?"

"They're talking about following Lucan around town to

see if he does anything suspicious," Dad said. "It might take me quite a while to fix your alarm." He winked.

"Have at it. Take as long as you need," I said.

Dad grinned. I smiled back but was worried. The last time Vi followed anyone we almost got arrested.

**After a thorough** inspection of the alarm system, Dad and I discussed Mom and Vi while Seth tapped away on his laptop. He claimed he was doing homework but he seemed too happy, and the typing was ripping along at a social-media pace rather than a boring-essay pace. If he stayed much longer, I figured I'd have to get involved in policing his homework situation. Grace had convinced his school to forward three weeks' worth of homework. That would get us to Thanksgiving break. I hoped it wouldn't take that long to figure out what was going on with him and to come up with a long-term plan that didn't include the boy and the dog showing up on my front porch without notice.

Dad was just getting wound up for a good Vi vent when my phone vibrated. I had set the text-from-Vi alert to the unmistakable *Twilight Zone* theme. All three of us watched the phone buzz on the table and I realized they were waiting for me to answer it. I clicked open the screen and was greeted by a blurry photo of Lucan getting into his truck. Another picture rapidly followed of the pickup pulling away from the curb, then an even fuzzier image of the vehicle on the road. I could only assume that Vi and Mom were in pursuit. I groaned and handed the phone to my dad. He stabbed at it with his index finger and handed it to Seth, who showed him the pictures.

The phone buzzed again. Seth held it up for me to see.
*we r in pursuit. stnd by*

I put my head in my hands and hoped Lucan wouldn't call the police about the erratic orange smart car that was tailing him through his day.

I took the phone from Seth and dialed Vi's number.

"What are you doing?" I said when she answered.

"Didn't you get my texts? These phones are so slow. I sent you pictures."

"I know. I got them. What are you doing?"

"We're tailing Lucan, what do you think?"

"Vi, you can't just go around following the citizens of Crystal Haven. Mac is not going to be so lenient this time."

"Mac will never know. I've been reading up on techniques. We're staying well back from him, and blending into traffic. He won't even notice."

I doubted that. There wasn't nearly enough traffic in Crystal Haven, or Detroit for that matter, to hide two little old ladies in an orange smart car.

"Vi, tell Mom to turn around and you can come here." Dad's eyebrows shot up and he started shaking his head violently. I turned away from him and said, "We'll talk about it and come up with a plan."

"What? I can't hear you—you're breaking up." *Click.* Vi had used my own tactics against me.

"Are they coming?" Dad asked.

I shook my head. "I don't think so. They had better not cause too much trouble."

I was treated over the next couple of hours to pictures of Lucan going into the grocery store, filling up his car at the gas station, and getting lunch at Everyday Grill. The only interesting shot was of Lucan going into the police station.

Dad had finished with the alarm system and began checking out the plumbing. He seemed to have a checklist of things to do in the house that he'd never gotten around to when we'd lived there while I was a kid. Vi's warning echoed in my mind, but as with many things Vi says, I ignored it. Seth moved on to some sort of explosion-y game on his computer.

I called Rupert and tried to get information on Diana. Straight to voice mail. I hoped that meant he was busy getting her out of prison.

It was midafternoon when the urgent summons arrived on my phone.

# 25

❦

**Vi had texted that I should come immediately, but** stealthily, to Message Circle. Seth and I left the dogs with Dad and jumped in the Jeep. I wanted to ensure no one got arrested. Seth seemed most interested in perfecting his surveillance skills. I spotted Mom's orange car from the road and drove into the lot to park. There was a truck there—a Ford pickup—I recognized it from the photos as Lucan's. Mom and Vi were absent. I sent a "where are you" text and waited.

*halfway to mc. come quietly*

I showed my phone to Seth and we set off down the path toward Message Circle. The circle would be quiet this time of year. Outdoor gatherings for messages ran from Memorial Day to Labor Day. We were partway there when I heard hissing coming from the woods to the right of the path. The city had planted burning bushes and other shrubbery along the walkway and I spotted Vi and Mom crouched behind one clump that hadn't lost all of its leaves yet. Message Circle was just past the turn in the path. I walked to Mom and Vi and bent over the bush.

Vi squatted like a duck and slowly lifted her head over the bush to watch the path. Mom sat on the ground, knees to her chest, shivering, and casting mutinous glances at Vi.

"We need to spread out and keep an eye on him," Vi whispered. "When I sent you the message I thought he was heading back to the scene of the crime. But then he went to Message Circle instead."

Mom sighed.

"Do you think he's Wiccan *and* a psychic?" Vi asked.

I shrugged and walked away from them farther down the path to stand behind a large evergreen. Seth followed and we both peeked around the tree. Feeling ridiculous, I pulled out my small binoculars. Lucan was sitting in the back row of the seating area, staring into space. I turned back toward Vi in time to see her crouched and moving quickly through the spindly tree trunks to another evergreen tree. Mom followed, standing straight and walking at a normal pace. Vi gestured at her to hurry up. Seth breathed heavily in my ear as he looked around the tree at Message Circle. I stepped away from him and handed him the glasses.

Squinting and huffing while trying to adjust the binocs and find Lucan at the same time, he didn't notice another figure enter the area from the opposite side. She must have come from the stone bridge which was farther into the woods and near a different parking lot. I hated to admit it, but Vi was right this time. *This* was interesting.

I pulled on Seth's sleeve and pointed him in the right direction. His eyebrows popped up over the eyepieces of the glasses. He lowered the binoculars and turned to me. I shrugged and glanced across the path to see Vi waving at us and pointing. Just then, my phone buzzed.

*see, I told you*

I nodded at Vi and gave her a thumbs-up. I didn't want to move any closer. If it had been Seth and me, or even Mom and Vi we could have explained to them that we just happened upon them. But all four of us?

We weren't close enough to hear what they were saying, but Skye's head was so close to Lucan's, I didn't think we'd be able to hear them even if we were sitting in the open. Then Skye pulled away from Lucan and said, "No! Of course not."

Lucan murmured in response and Skye started to cry.

Vi's helpful text arrived.

*looks suspicious*

Skye's head was down with her forehead pressed into his chest. Lucan had one arm around her. I didn't like the way this looked.

"Whoa, that's just not right," Seth said in my ear.

Suddenly, Skye pushed away from Lucan and ran into the woods toward the bridge. Lucan hopped up and followed her, but more slowly.

I heard him shout, "Skye, wait!"

I thought this was the perfect time to get out of the woods. Neither one of them would be pleased if they caught us here. I was just about to signal Vi to head back to the parking lot when I saw another figure step into the circle. It was Bea. She looked down the path. She held a camera in one hand, and checked her watch. Then she walked down the path, following Lucan and Skye.

"So? What do you think?" Vi asked as Seth and I approached.

I shrugged. "I don't know what to think. They could have had a very good reason to meet here."

"Why was her mother following her?" Seth asked. "The whole thing is sketchy."

We walked back toward the parking lot. I set a rapid pace, worried that Lucan would return to his truck and find us all milling about.

Seth checked his phone as we got into the car.

"Can I go with Skye and Faith to the Big Buy?"

"Skye and Faith? What are you talking about?"

"Faith says they're going to the Big Buy in Bailey Harbor. They'll come pick me up."

"Okay. Maybe you can find out what Skye was doing with Lucan."

Seth looked out the window and shrugged.

"When are they coming to get you?"

He checked his phone.

"In about ten minutes."

I pulled onto Singapore Highway and turned the Jeep toward home.

**After Seth left** with the Paxton girls, I pulled out my laptop. Skye had sent the promised genealogy information. According to her notes, Neila Whittle had just as long a pedigree as Rafe's adoptive family. I wasn't sure how Skye had unearthed all the information but her family-tree diagrams had all sorts of notes beyond just the births, marriages, deaths. Broken lines, squiggly lines, double and triple lines all connected different members of the family. Plus she had found anecdotes about different branches of the tree. It made for fascinating reading but nothing jumped out at me that would help with the problem at hand.

Dad had moved to the upstairs bathroom and was clanking away on the pipes. I decided it would be a good time to get out of the house. Feeling uncertain that the building would still be standing when I came home, I patted the front door in a reassuring fashion and hopped into my Jeep.

I drove slowly down Main Street toward the police station searching for either Mac or his car. I wanted to talk to Lisa Harkness, the receptionist, without Mac's interference. After parking down the street near Alex's restaurant, I walked against the wind toward the police station. The streets of Crystal Haven were less hospitable this time of year. The festive flags that flapped in the summer breeze had been put away, the pumpkins and scarecrows that welcomed shoppers just before Halloween were looking sad and beyond their sell-by date. The holiday lights had not yet been turned on, so it was a gray and blustery trek through town.

I poked my head in the door of the station and waved to Lisa. "Is Mac here?"

She shook her head. "You just missed him. He didn't say where he was going—I might be able to catch him if it's urgent." She reached for the telephone as I stepped in the door.

"No! I mean, that's okay. I'll catch up with him later. How's it going around here?"

Lisa crossed her arms. "I can't tell you anything about Diana or Dylan."

I regarded her carefully and switched tactics.

"Oh, I didn't mean the Rafe Godwin case. Just wondering how things are going for you. How are the kids?" I gestured toward the photo on her desk.

She narrowed her eyes at me, but her kids were still young enough that she always had something she wanted to report about them.

I patiently listened to the litany of funny things the two-year-old was trying to say and the clever things the four-year-old was able to do. I laughed in all the right places and admired the newest pictures. This seemed to melt the frostiness she had exhibited initially. I didn't blame her for her cool reception. Over the summer she'd gotten an earful from Mac about gossiping and the need for discretion in her job as receptionist at the police station.

She bit her lower lip and took a deep breath.

"You might want to talk to Tom if you're wondering about Diana. He's down the street at Millie's again."

Sighing inwardly, I realized I was glad I didn't have Tom's job. So much of it must consist of breaking up the same arguments and warning the same people to behave. Police work had turned out to be less exciting than I'd imagined. It consisted of piles of paperwork, dealing with rude and grumpy people, and the random injection of pure terror to mix it up.

I nodded to Lisa and strolled casually out of the police station. As soon as the door swung shut behind me I power walked down the street and around the corner to Millie's Book Nook. The last time I had found Tom there he was trying to avoid arresting Howard for vagrancy. Howard was Millie's husband and that time he'd fallen asleep in her comfy reading area. She'd called the station and insisted they send someone over to deal with the "good-for-nothing bum."

This time there was no crowd gathered on the sidewalk outside. Millie didn't seem to be shouting at Tom or Howard. This made me more anxious than a scene in front of the store.

"I want a restraining order!" Millie said as I pulled the door shut against the wind.

"I can't do that, Mrs. Fessler." Tom had his hands out and

barely kept the frustration out of his voice. "Only a judge can do that and then only if there is a real threat."

"Of course there's a real threat. She's crazy and she's after my husband!"

Howard sat behind the counter, shoulders slumped, looking like he'd prefer to be anywhere else.

"Hi, Mrs. Fessler," I said.

Millie wheeled around on her orthopedic shoes and took a deep breath, probably to start another tirade. Then her face broke into a smile.

"Clytemnestra! I haven't seen you since the summer. Why don't you ever come to visit?"

"I've been kind of busy with the festival, Mrs. Fessler."

"Well, you're never too busy for a good book. You just take your time, dear, and pick out a good one." She waved her arm toward the fiction section and spun around again to face Tom.

Tom shot a pleading glance in my direction. Howard had perked up and his eyes sparked with excitement. He must have been expecting me to talk her down again.

"Why do you need a restraining order?" I asked, ignoring her directions and walking over to stand near her.

Millie put her hands on her hips. "That *woman* has been bothering my husband. She trespassed in my store and I want it stopped."

I looked to Tom for an explanation.

"Mrs. Fessler thinks—"

"No, I *know*."

"Mrs. Fessler is worried that Neila Whittle is 'after' Howard here," Tom said.

I knew Neila had a reputation as a witch and that the kids in town were half afraid and half fascinated by her, but was surprised that Millie had an issue with her.

"Neila Whittle?" I said.

"The witch that lives in the woods," Millie said. "She was here yesterday and I want it stopped."

"Maybe she needed a book," I said.

Millie shook her head.

"No, she waited for me to leave to bring my bank deposit down the street and then she slipped in here to talk to my Howard." At this, she cast a look that combined adoration and menace in almost equal measure.

"She didn't—" Howard began.

"Fortunately, I had forgotten the deposit slip on the counter and when I came back in to get it, I caught them in the act."

My stomach dropped at the thought of Neila and Howard in the act of anything together.

"We were just talking. I haven't seen her in years," Howard said.

Millie made a disgusted noise. "I don't blame you, dear. I know she's a witch and probably put a spell on you or something." She turned toward Tom. "Is there a restraining order for spells? Because I want one of those, too."

"Mrs. Fessler, have you asked Howard what they were talking about?" I asked. "Maybe she really just wanted a book."

We all turned to Howard, who became pink while moisture beaded on his smooth head.

"See? That's what he does," Millie said, pointing at Howard. "If that isn't suspicious, I don't know what is."

I had to admit Howard wasn't helping himself with the blushing and sweating.

"Mr. Fessler," Tom said, "you don't *have* to answer, but maybe you could tell us what you were talking about and reassure your wife it was all innocent. Then we can move on."

Howard took a deep breath. "We didn't talk about anything. She came in, and said hello. I said it had been a long time, and asked how she was. She said she'd been better and then Millie burst in like a lunatic, accusing her of all sorts of things."

Millie sniffed.

"Neila barely escaped while I held Millie back." Howard's voice rose as he described the scene.

I felt a smile beginning and viciously suppressed it. The thought of ninety-one-year-old Millie brawling with Neila, also ancient, all over bald, pudgy Howard was actually kind of sweet.

"You can't get a restraining order against someone for entering a business if they haven't ever threatened or harmed anyone." I could tell Tom was trying to keep his voice even but the aggravation crept in.

"Why do you think she came here after all this time?" I asked Howard.

He glanced at Millie and shrugged.

"She had her chance and she blew it." Millie crossed her arms. "Now she's after him again."

I raised an eyebrow at Tom. He lifted a shoulder and grimaced, clearly no closer to understanding the issue than I was.

Howard blew out air. "We . . . courted a long, *long* time ago. It didn't work out. Then *much later*"—he paused to cast a meaningful glare at Millie—"I met Millie. I can't be held responsible for going steady with someone before I even *met* her." He hooked a thumb in Millie's direction and crossed his own arms.

Tom shuffled his feet and looked uncomfortable. I covered my grin with a cough. The thought of eighty-year-old Howard going steady was about to cause a fit of giggles.

"Maybe we should leave to let you two work this out," I said.

Tom and I backed out of the store and I flipped the sign to CLOSED before shutting the door behind us.

"Wow, those two really keep you busy don't they?"

Tom nodded and smoothed his shirt even though it looked freshly pressed. "She kind of scares me," he said.

"I couldn't tell," I lied.

"Have you heard anything more about Diana or Dylan?"

He shook his head. "I shouldn't be talking to you about this. I don't really know anything for sure, but I think Mac is going to let Diana go. He let her stay at the station last night, mostly because she refused to leave, but he doesn't believe her confession."

The tightness in my shoulders melted at this news. I knew Mac couldn't have been fooled by her confession. It unfortunately made it look like Dylan's own sister didn't believe in his innocence, though. When I mentioned this to Tom he just nodded and sighed. I realized that Dylan's arrest must have been hard on him as well. He and Dylan were always together when they were in school. He must have wanted to help him somehow. But once he was off the case, he had no more influence than the rest of us.

We'd walked almost back to the station and I stopped to let him continue on his own. If Mac was considering letting Diana go, I didn't want to interfere and get into a stubborn contest with him.

I climbed into my car as my phone buzzed. A text from Seth read: *Heading home—I'll walk the dogs.* I smiled and realized how glad I was to have him here in Crystal Haven.

I had just put the Jeep in gear when someone knocked on my window. I jumped and the phone flew out of my hand.

Mac was there and I rolled down the window.

"You probably shouldn't text even while sitting at the curb," he said with a grin.

"People don't usually sneak up on me while I'm in my parked car," I said.

His smile faded. "I need your help at the station."

# 26

**"So, what do you need?" I had to quicken my pace**
to keep up with him. "I have a lot of theories about what
happened. I'm so glad you don't suspect Dylan or Diana
anymore. That was just crazy. . . ." Mac stopped and I had
to backtrack.

"That's not the kind of help I need," he said.

"Oh. What then?" I tried to hide my disappointment with
a bright smile, but could tell by the way Mac held my gaze
that he'd seen it.

"It's Diana. She won't leave."

"What do you mean? I thought you arrested her." I pretended innocence, not wanting to get Tom in trouble.

Mac started walking again. He explained that he'd been
trying to release Diana for several hours but she refused to
go home. He admitted that it had been a mistake to arrest
her in the first place.

"I never bought her confession, but I thought I could use it to threaten Dylan," Mac said.

"You told him she had confessed?"

Mac nodded. "I thought he would admit he'd killed Rafe if he thought Diana was in trouble. It didn't work. Either he's really innocent, or he saw through the plan and figured I'd have to let her go eventually."

"You still think he did it?"

"I think he's the best suspect we have." Mac stopped walking and faced me. "He thought Rafe had killed his parents, he had access to the murder weapon, and he knew how allergic Rafe was." Mac ticked his points off on his fingers.

"Everyone knew Rafe was allergic, many people had access to the murderous bread, and he had more enemies than just Dylan," I ticked back.

Mac took a deep breath and continued walking. "You've gotten yourself involved again, haven't you? I asked you to stay out of it. As if I don't have enough to worry about . . ." Mac pushed the door to the station open and waited for me to enter.

Lisa smiled at us until she got a good look at our stormy faces. She took a very intense interest in her computer as we walked toward Mac's office in silence.

"Okay, tell me what you know," Mac said after shutting his office door.

I was unprepared for this. In the past he had just warned me off and refused to listen to anything I had to say. I took a moment to gather my thoughts. Mac's blue-gray gaze didn't help me to focus.

"First of all, I've known Dylan practically my whole life and he's not a killer."

Mac snorted and took a breath to respond, but I held up my hand.

"Also, there were several other people in Rafe's life that had an issue with him. Just because Dylan thought Rafe had killed his parents doesn't mean he was the only one with a motive."

"I'm listening."

"Well, Lucan Reed didn't like the way Rafe ran the coven. They fought about it all the time."

"You think Lucan would have killed Rafe because he didn't like the spells he cast under a full moon?" Mac didn't hide his sarcasm.

"And Morgan Lavelle was recently thrown out of the coven for similar reasons. She'd been dating—or something—Rafe and they had a big fight."

"Okay, that sounds more interesting. What else do you know about Morgan?"

I shook my head, wishing I'd known I would be giving a presentation. I would have done more prep work.

"She's creepy. And she sells knives and nasty spell kits."

Mac smiled. I did love to see his smile, but this one wasn't as friendly as most. This was one of a cat that had cornered a mouse. I didn't enjoy feeling like a cornered mouse.

I crossed my arms. "If you'd given me warning, I would have come up with some better answers." I took a deep breath. I had planned to have more proof when I told him this part, but here was my opportunity. "She's a liar. She was at the ceremony that night, and I can prove it."

"Go on." Mac sat back and watched me.

I pulled the charm out of my pocket. I'd wrapped it in plastic as soon as I got it home in case there were any fingerprints left after Seth had handled it. I dropped it onto his desk with a flourish.

"What's this?"

"Seth and I found it out where the ceremony took place in the woods. It's from a charm bracelet that Diana sells in her store."

"So? You aren't trying to pin this on your best friend, are you?"

"No. That charm came off of Morgan's bracelet. I saw her wearing it the day after Rafe was killed and it was missing this charm. I'm sure of it."

Mac rubbed his chin and leaned forward to look at the charm.

"Okay. I'll look into it." He leaned back again. "By the way, Charla and I *are* looking at other people, but we had to arrest Dylan because, right now, the evidence points to him and he has a history of disappearing. That's between you and me. Don't tell anyone else, including anyone related to you, Diana, Alex, or Tom Andrews."

I nodded.

Mac slipped the charm into an envelope and scrawled something illegible across the front.

"I'd really like to go to dinner with you and not talk about the case," Mac said. He came around his desk and put his arm around my shoulders. "I thought if we could get all of this out in the open then maybe we could talk about . . . more interesting things . . . at dinner."

I felt a little thrill down my spine at the thought of more interesting things. I really didn't want to fight with him *or* talk about murder. I nodded agreement.

"Will you help me get your friend out of here?"

I followed him to the back, where Diana sat in one of the interview rooms. I looked through the window in the door. Someone had brought her a sleeping bag and a pillow. It looked like Alex had been sending take-out meals to her as well. The door wasn't locked when I reached out to turn the knob. I looked at Mac and he cocked an eyebrow in an "I told you so" way.

"Diana?" I peeked around the doorframe.

She was sitting at the table with her head in her hands. Even her curls were droopy. She quickly looked up at the sound of my voice. She stood and rushed over to me.

"Have you found anything that can help Dylan?" she asked.

I nodded. "Maybe."

"I can't leave here until I bring Dylan home with me. He's all the family I have. I have to get him out of here." She took my hands and squeezed.

"I know." And I *did* know. She'd taken over the care of Dylan when their parents died. Even though they were both technically adults, the seven-year age difference meant that Diana felt responsible for him. She'd always been more organized, more driven, and more grown-up than Dylan. They fell into a way of relating that was less sibling-sibling, and more parent-child.

"Mac says he can't let Dylan leave yet. We have to find out what really happened," Diana said.

"Let me take you home. You can get cleaned up, take a shower, and help us figure this out. It's not doing Dylan or anyone else any good having to worry about you at the jail."

In the end, Diana barely had time for a shower.

# 27

❧❧

**We turned the corner on the way to Diana's house** and saw fire trucks on my street. With a sinking feeling I detoured to see what was happening. As we got closer, I realized they were parked in front of my house. Two firemen were outside chasing Baxter.

I left my Jeep in the street, and ran to the front yard. The alarms were sounding again from inside the house. Seth called to Baxter, who seemed to be having too much fun dodging the firemen. I looked at the porch and saw that Seth held Tuffy at arm's length and the little dog had light blue paint on his feet and belly.

"Oh my." Diana held her hand up to her mouth. I suspected she was covering a smile.

Dad came out of the house with Baxter's leash, and stopped dead when he saw me.

"This isn't as bad as it looks, Clyde," Dad said. He held his hands out to stop me from progressing toward the house.

Baxter spotted me and bounded over to say hello. The firemen gratefully followed while Dad snapped on his leash.

The two guys looked nervously from me to my father. One of them said, "Everything seems . . . safe, so we'll be going now."

Vi's warning about Dad's home repairs echoed in my head.

The firemen climbed into their truck and waved.

"Good luck, Frank!" one of them yelled. The other one laughed and beeped the horn.

"What's going on, Dad?"

"Maybe I should go . . . ," Diana said, but I shook my head and held up one finger.

Dad gestured toward the house. "I had set the burglar alarm to test it—I was waiting for Seth to come home so he could pretend to break in and I could time how long it took the alarm company to call."

I crossed my arms and narrowed my eyes.

"I decided to fix the toilet roll holder in the downstairs bathroom while I waited," Dad said. "I noticed it was a little wobbly the other day when I was here." He caught my eye and quickly looked away. "Anyway, the holder fell off and I slipped and dinged up the wall a little bit."

"That's fine, Dad. How did the fire department get involved?"

"I'm getting to that. I got out the paint to repair the wall and then Seth arrived. He didn't know I'd set the alarm, so when he came in, the alarm went off."

I nodded.

"Tuffy didn't like the noise and apparently he likes to hide behind the toilet when he's scared."

I was starting to see where this might be headed.

"I went to turn off the alarm, and Tuffy ran into the

bathroom and fell into the paint pan." Dad looked at his shoes. "Tuffy doesn't like paint, either."

Seth stepped off the porch, still trying to keep Tuffy's feet away from his clothing. "In Tuffy's defense, he'd never stepped in paint before. The poor guy was freaked."

"In the process of trying to catch Tuffy, I missed the phone call from the alarm company."

"So they sent the fire truck, again," Seth said.

Dad's face brightened. "The response time was really impressive."

Dad finally allowed me to go inside. The front hallway was covered in tiny blue footprints. The path of Tuffy's flight was well marked from the bathroom, down the hallway to the front door, where the prints began to fade and then disappeared, presumably where Seth had picked him up.

"I'll help clean up," Diana said. "Hot soapy water should be enough since it's still wet."

I took a deep breath and rolled up my sleeves, ready to clean up the mess.

Seth stopped me and reminded us that Rafe's memorial was that evening. Skye and Faith had taken him to Big Buy, where they picked up supplies for the memorial.

Diana was horrified and embarrassed that she'd forgotten.

Lucan had put himself in charge of the plans when Dylan was arrested. He'd called Diana and said he would take over while she dealt with her brother. According to Diana, there wasn't much actual planning to do since Rafe had left very specific instructions as to how his service should be arranged. We left Dad and Seth with a bucket and a mop and Diana explained the process as I drove her home to get ready in time.

The first part of the service was to be held at dusk in the

woods with Rafe's coven-mates and close friends. I wasn't going to be a part of that ceremony. Diana said they would encourage Rafe to continue his journey if any part of him still lingered. Apparently both Lucan and Diana felt there was a strong chance of this since Rafe died so suddenly and because he was a control freak. Rafe wanted to be cremated, but his body hadn't been released yet. They planned to bury his ashes near his parents' graves in a Grand Rapids cemetery.

My whole family would attend the reception afterward. That was supposed to be a time for anyone to say good-bye. Alex had been working on the catering for the event.

By the time I returned from Diana's place, Seth and Dad had made a good dent in the cleanup. We put Tuffy in the tub while Dad went home to warn the ladies that the reception was that evening. Before leaving, he extracted a promise that we keep this little mishap to ourselves. He said living with Vi was difficult enough without handing her ammunition.

Seth and I left a damp Tuffy and an exhausted Baxter at home and went to my mom's for chili while we waited for the reception. Even though I told her we'd have plenty to eat once we got there, she had been planning to serve chili and so we were going to eat the chili.

I wasn't surprised when the dinner conversation turned to pointed questions about what to expect at the reception.

"Will there be a fiery cauldron again?" Vi asked.

"I don't like what Vi told me about invoking goddesses and elements," Mom said. "It just seems dangerous to me, messing with all of that." She waved her hand in the air to encompass all of the Wiccan philosophy.

"I wish we could go to the woods with Diana," Seth said.

"*I'm* glad we don't have to," Mom said.

Dad focused on his food.

"What will they do at this reception thing?" Vi asked.

"I don't know," I said. "I think it's just like a regular reception after a funeral. Talking and eating."

"Did Alex say anything about drinks?" Dad asked.

I shrugged and focused on my food, hoping they would move on to other topics. Then I regretted that thought as they began discussing Diana's release, Mac's inability to make a reasonable arrest, and who might have had a grudge against Rafe.

After a lengthy monologue on Wiccans and their cats and whether they were reliable sources of information in the murder of Rafe, Vi finally pushed her bowl away and announced we should stop dillydallying. Seth sputtered at the implied accusation and Mom patted his hand and subtly shook her head.

The Reading Room was in an old city building that had been converted into an assembly hall space. It was used by psychics during the tourist season for readings that had been scheduled and for walk-ins. Some of the psychics had people visit them in their homes, but more and more had begun to opt for the more anonymous Reading Room. That way they kept some distance between themselves and their clients. It could fit about one hundred people. I thought that would be plenty of space but Diana was worried.

We arrived and saw that she was right to be concerned. The streets were packed with milling clumps of mourners and Dad had to park several blocks away. He muttered to himself about how it would have been easier to walk from the house and Mom patted his arm as the two walked on ahead toward the reception.

"Wow, that Rafe was more popular than I thought," Vi said.

"Ooh, look—some of them are wearing robes." Seth pointed to a couple of people in black, hooded robes walking toward the building.

"I wonder if there'll be fiery cauldrons again," Vi said.

"I hope they don't have that burning spice stick this time," Seth said. "That thing smells."

"Shhh!" I said. "You two are acting like . . . tourists."

Vi's intake of breath demonstrated her shock and outrage at such an insult. Seth ducked his head and shrugged.

The crowd was rowdier than I had expected and the noise level grew as we walked closer. I spotted Diana's bright orange hair through the crowd and pushed my way through the throng, pulling Seth and Vi with me.

Diana spun around when I tapped her shoulder and I could see she'd been crying. But she smiled and said, "Isn't it great that so many people came to say good-bye?"

I nodded, and Vi gave her a hug.

"I got worried earlier that maybe with all the talk about people arguing with Rafe that not many would show up, but look at this." She held her arms out toward the crowd and I remembered how much she had loved Rafe. I had begun to think of him as just another victim, and a not very nice one at that, but Diana had seen another side of him and I was glad for her that so many people agreed with her. However, I was picking up a tense feeling from the fringes of the crowd. They didn't all have their solemn funeral faces on. In fact some of them appeared to be heckling the crowd. One clump of boys in their early twenties had clearly been drinking and were still passing a couple of brown bags around, taking sips, and getting louder.

Then I looked the other way, down the street, and saw a small group of people with hand-painted signs: PAGANS GO

HOME! REPENT! FEAR GOD! WICCA: SATAN'S LIE! My chest tightened. *Protesters.*

I tried to usher Diana inside before she saw them, but I was too late.

"What are *they* doing here?" she said.

"Who? What?" Vi said and looked around.

"There's Skye," Seth said, and pointed.

Skye, dressed in a long black robe with a hood, approached the crowd with her hands up. The group stopped. Skye spoke to the woman standing in the front of the group.

"Is that her mother?" I said to Seth.

He nodded. "I think so." Seth's phone buzzed. I glanced over his shoulder and saw a text from Faith: *Have things gotten interesting yet?*

He switched off his phone with a disgusted snort. "She knew," he said to me.

# 28

⊷⧽⧼⊶

**The sound of breaking glass caught everyone's** attention. Someone had thrown a rock through the front window of the Reading Room. I spun around, ignoring the protestors for the moment, to focus on the gang of drinkers.

Lucan Reed pushed his way through the crowd, shoving people out of the way if they didn't move fast enough. He approached the clot of rowdy twenty-somethings. Vi, Seth, and I moved closer to them to hear what they were saying. I clutched Diana's hand in my own and dragged her with us.

"That's going to cost you, son," Lucan said to a lanky kid with sandy brown hair that fell into his eyes. He grabbed him by the scruff of the neck and the rest of his friends backed away.

"Owen! What are you doing here?" Skye left the protestors, circled the crowd, and ran up to Lucan and his prisoner.

"Why do you have to hang around with these freaks?" Owen said to Skye. Lucan gave him a little shake.

"Lucan, you can let him go. He's not dangerous," Skye said.

"Oh, is this your *new* boyfriend?" Owen slurred his words and stumbled a bit when Lucan let go of him. "The old guy kicked off so you've moved on already." He flung his arm in Lucan's direction. "I know you've been meeting him in secret."

"Owen, go home. We'll talk later." Skye had her hands up and was trying to calm him down, but Owen was on a roll.

"I'm not afraid of him, Skye. Everything was cool until you got into this . . . *group*." Owen stepped forward and took a wild swing at Lucan, who easily sidestepped him and placed him in a headlock as the kid spun around.

"Wicked," Seth whispered next to me.

"Oh, no," Diana said.

I heard muttering from the small group of activists and turned to see Charla approaching from the police station.

"All right, that's enough." Charla pushed her way through the throng and approached Owen and Lucan.

I noticed some of Owen's confederates on the outer edges of the crowd peel away and walk back down the street, the way they came.

"What's going on here?" Charla directed her question at Lucan.

"Thish guy attacked me, offisher," Owen said to Charla.

Lucan rolled his eyes and crossed his arms over his wide chest. He pulled himself to his full six-foot-plus height and glowered at Owen. Owen slid behind Charla.

The signs had disappeared, and the anti-Wiccan activists murmured amongst themselves. Charla walked toward them and said, "Move along now. Unless you're here to pay your respects, you can just keep moving."

Bea's lips pressed into a thin line but she turned away

with the rest of her group and within a minute only Owen and Lucan remained.

"Someone threw a rock through the window and it looks like there may have been a demonstration planned," Lucan said.

"No. I had nothing to do with them," Owen said. He waved his arm toward the retreating group of demonstrators. "I came here for Skye."

"Okay, no one's been hurt, that I can see," Charla said. She pulled out her pad of tickets. "I'm giving you a citation for disorderly conduct." She ripped it off and handed it to Owen. "And you can pay for the window."

"Oh, man," Owen whined.

"Is there anyone here who can get you home?" Charla asked. "I better not catch you driving yourself or you'll spend the night at the jail."

"I'll take him." Skye stepped forward.

"Are you sure?" Lucan asked her.

"Dude, she said she'd take me. Back off," Owen said over Skye's shoulder.

Lucan narrowed his eyes, but didn't respond.

Diana stepped forward, took Lucan's hand, and steered him away from Owen. "Let's go inside."

He turned toward the Reading Room with Diana and didn't spare another glance at Owen.

"Are you sure you're okay?" I said to Skye.

She nodded. "He's harmless. I'll get him home and come back in a little while." She lowered her voice. "We broke up a few months ago. He's not taking it well."

I noticed that Seth's phone had been intermittently buzzing during this whole altercation and he was currently typing furiously with his thumbs.

"What is Faith up to?"

"Hmm? Oh, nothing. She knew her mom would be here."
He slipped the phone into his pocket.

I lifted an eyebrow at him. He shrugged and turned to head into the reception.

"Charla, where's Mac?" He had a gift for showing up just when things were getting interesting.

"He took Neila Whittle home."

"What?"

"Neila Whittle. She lives on Rowan Street, at the top of the hill," Charla said. "I'm sure you've noticed her house. I think I ran you off of the place a few years ago with the rest of the kids."

Charla had a corrupt sense of time. It had been at least fifteen years since I'd been up there with anyone else, and at least ten since I'd been called a kid.

"I know *who* she is," I said, scowling. "Why is Mac taking her home?"

"I was walking back to the police station when I saw that crew headed this way with signs." She tilted her head in the direction that Bea's group had gone. "I could tell trouble was brewing so I went and got Mac to help out. We found Neila cowering in the doorway of the bead shop, watching the gang go by."

"Does Mac know her?" It seemed everyone knew Neila except for me.

Charla shook her head. "Not really, he just decided to get her home quickly. She was pretty upset. We didn't know Owen and his buddies were here as well. Mac figured I could deal with a few angry churchgoers on my own."

"What do you mean?"

"The people with the signs. Didn't you get a look at them?"

I shook my head. "Not really. I assumed it was the usual 'Wicca is evil' type of thing that crops up here and there."

Charla nodded. "Yeah, that's about it. Devil worship and sin, that's what they claim. It's that group from Covenant of Grace Church in Grand Rapids. But it wasn't the Wiccans looking like an angry mob." She *tsk*ed, and shook her head.

"Was Neila okay?"

Charla studied me for a moment. "I'm not sure. She seemed confused and she was crying. I haven't seen her in town in years. Maybe she's starting to have some dementia. . . ."

"I don't think so."

Charla shrugged. "You can ask Mac about it next time you see him."

"Thanks, Charla."

She nodded. "I'll just stick around out here for a while to discourage any further shenanigans."

I followed the remaining mourners toward the Reading Room.


**As soon as** Charla turned her back, I veered off to the left around the side of the building. I peeked in the windows to see if I could spot Seth or my dad in the crowd. Seth, because he had a cell phone, and Dad, because I needed his car.

The place was crowded and it was clear that the food was at the far end of the room based on the huge number of people gathered there. Finally, I saw the two of them leaning against the wall with full plates. I called Seth and watched while I waited for him to answer. One ring. He didn't even pause in his shoveling movements. Second ring. The food must be fantastic because he was ignoring his phone. After the fourth ring, it went to voice mail and I glared at Seth through the window even though he couldn't see me.

I dialed again. This time I saw him pat his pocket. He

handed his almost-empty plate to my dad and pulled out his phone.

"Herro?" His mouth was full and he crunched chips in my ear.

"Seth, it's me, Clyde."

He turned and scanned the room, clearly trying to find me in the crowd.

"Where are you?"

"I'm outside. I need to borrow Papa's car without anyone knowing. Can you ask him for me and bring me the keys?"

I saw Seth put the phone against his shoulder and talk to my dad. Dad reached into his pocket and scanned the room at the same time. Seth came back on the line.

"I've got them but he wants to know how long you'll be. He doesn't want to get stuck here all night."

"I won't be more than a half hour." Maybe less, if I couldn't find Mac.

"'Kay. Should I come outside now?"

"Yeah, I'm around the side of the building. Don't let Charla see you."

He clicked off the phone and I saw him make his way through the crowd to the door. A few minutes later I heard him crunching through the leaves and coming toward me. It had gotten fully dark in the time since we first arrived.

"Clyde?" Seth whispered.

"I'm here." I stepped forward so he could see me in the light from the windows.

"Here're the keys." He dropped them into my hand. "Want me to come with you? What are you doing, anyway?"

"I'm just following up on a lead. You go ahead in. I need you to run interference for me with Vi and Nana Rose. Keep telling them you just saw me across the room or something. That will keep them occupied until I get back."

Seth shrugged. "Okay, but the food will be gone pretty soon."

"I'll take my chances."

He turned and melted into the shadows at the side of the building. To avoid being seen by Charla, I walked the long way around the block and down the street to where Dad had parked. I didn't want Mac and Neila spending time together. And I didn't want to be delayed by anyone at the Reading Room.

I pulled out of the parking space and headed to the north end of town and Neila's house. The streetlights only went as far as the bottom of her gravel road and then it was dark forest. This was another reason why the teenagers of Crystal Haven frequented her house on their more daring escapades. It was a sign of true bravery to walk into the woods alone and get as far as the edge of her yard. I was pretty sure most of them just hid behind a tree for ten minutes and then came strolling back out. This time of year, the trees were skeletal and my headlights cast menacing shadows as I bounced the car along the road. I got to the house and saw that Mac's cruiser was still there.

Once I arrived I wasn't sure what I planned to do. I was concerned about Neila, and I really wanted to see Mac. As I sat debating my plan, the door opened. Mac was backlit in the doorway and I saw Neila holding the door and waving him out. I rolled down the window to hear what they were saying.

"Call if you . . ." I heard Mac say.

"Thank . . . ," came a muffled reply.

She swung the door closed and Mac turned on the porch and stopped when he saw me. His face was in shadow and

I couldn't tell what kind of reception to expect until he got right up to the car.

He leaned down with a huge grin on his face and rested his arm on the open window.

"Well, hi. Are you here on a dare, or are you here for me?"

He opened the door and put out a hand to help me out.

"To see you, of course."

"That's a great answer." He pulled me toward him and a few minutes later I started to get embarrassed thinking Neila might be able to see us acting like a couple of overheated teenagers right there in her yard.

I pulled away, and caught the look of confusion on Mac's face.

"Sorry, this place kind of spooks me."

He nodded. "Yeah, I proved my bravery several times over the years just by walking up here. It was a little humiliating when I met her later and she remembered me from those days."

I smiled, but it was so dark he probably couldn't tell.

"I've missed you," I said into his chest and inhaled the scent of pine trees and cool air.

He pulled me closer again and we forgot for a moment that we were standing right outside the Crystal Haven witch's house. This was one thing I hadn't done while a teenager on a dare.

"So, when can I see you?" Mac said into my hair.

"I think you're doing a pretty good job right now."

He laughed and shook his head.

"Let's go do something, just the two of us. I could really use a break from this Rafe Godwin thing. Can you get Seth to hang with your parents for an evening?"

"How about tomorrow night?"

"Great. What do you want to do?" he murmured against my neck.

"Um, dinner?"

"Sure, we should eat." He kissed me and I started to worry I wouldn't be meeting my half-hour deadline.

Then we heard a click and the yard was flooded with light. We jumped apart just as the door swung open.

"Oh, it's you," Neila said from the porch. "I thought it was the kids again. I didn't have the patience for it tonight, after the trouble down at the Reading Room. Lu—a friend installed this floodlight so I can scare them away if they get too loud or come too close."

"Sorry, Ms. Whittle. I was just . . . talking to Clyde Fortune." He grinned at me. "I think someone dared her to come up here to your house."

Neila flapped her hand at him. "Oh, now don't start that. I know what you were doing. At least that's what I hope you were doing, with your faces so red."

I smoothed my hair and zipped my jacket. Now Neila knew our secret as well. At least she was a recluse and never spoke to my family. I didn't know how much longer we could keep up the cloak-and-dagger stuff.

"We'll be on our way, then," Mac said. "I'll call you later," he whispered to me as he brushed a kiss across my cheek.

I waved to Neila and waited until she had closed her door before I got in the Buick and followed Mac back down the driveway. It wasn't until I was halfway back to the reception that I remembered I had gone there to find out what Neila was doing in town. And why Mac had decided to rescue her.

# 29

I returned to the reception without trouble. Mom and Vi didn't even suspect I had been gone, but Seth kept eyeing me as if I had excluded him from a fun adventure. Dad had spent enough years with Vi and my mother to have adopted a low level of curiosity as to the activities of his family members. He took the keys back in silence and nodded pleasantly while sipping his drink.

By the time we got home, had walked the dogs, and provided yet another "routine" treat for them, I was ready for bed. I fell asleep almost immediately and didn't dream.

Friday morning I was well rested and ready to start on a new angle. Bea had seemed so proper when I met her the other night. I was surprised to see her with an angry anti-Wiccan group, especially since her daughter was a member of Rafe's coven. What I had seen earlier when she was spying on Skye (and we were all spying on Lucan) had me wondering what was going on at the Paxton house. Plus, if

Seth was going to be gallivanting with one or both of the sisters, I decided I should have a talk with Bea.

After the usual morning dog-walking and breakfast, I reminded Seth that my dad was going to pick him up at lunchtime, made sure he had homework to do, and set out on my own to find Bea Paxton. Diana had told me she was a preschool teacher at Covenant of Grace Church, which was located between Crystal Haven and Grand Rapids. I Googled it and got directions.

The building itself was gorgeous, and old. It was made of stone with a beautiful bell tower and stained glass. It reminded me of something that would be a tourist stop in Europe. But the growing congregation had needed to expand, and a large, utilitarian, rectangular addition jutted out of the back like a tumor. I wondered how they had gotten it past the historical society. The parking lot was in the rear by the new addition. According to the signs, the offices and a small chapel were in the old building while the classrooms and large sanctuary were in the new. I didn't pay much attention to such things, but I did know that this was one of those megachurches sweeping the Midwest, with multimedia church services and a charismatic preacher. I walked around to the front of the building and up the steps to enter what was originally the front of the church leading into the chapel. Hand-lettered flyers announced the preschool was "now enrolling" and the women's group would sell candied nuts throughout the month of November. By following helpful arrows I found the offices. I wanted to be sure I could go to the preschool area without sending up an alarm.

The woman at the desk was about my mother's age but much more padded and wearing a 1970s-era prairie dress. It had a ruffled collar and her reading glasses rested on her ample chest. A nameplate on her desk read: GLADYS.

"May I help you?" she said.

"I'm Clyde Fortune. I was hoping to speak with Bea Paxton if she's available."

"Are you interested in enrolling your child in the preschool? We have openings."

"Well, I—"

"I know it's hard to answer that until you've seen the place. You know the preschool is only open Monday, Wednesday, and Friday?"

I opened my mouth to answer, but she kept going.

"The church is closed on Tuesdays and Thursdays unless there's an emergency. Are you new in town? I haven't seen you in services, but we're growing so fast, I don't get a chance to meet all the newcomers."

"Not really, I—"

"Just getting back to your roots now that you have a child?" she interrupted again. "It happens all the time. People wander and explore and then they come home when it's time to start a family. We're very family oriented around here."

"You see—"

"You aren't wearing a ring. I assume you're married, if you have a child?" Her tone became frosty with the last comment and I decided the truth wasn't something this woman wanted to hear.

"I . . . was gardening . . . and forgot to put it back on."

"Oh, your husband must be very tolerant. You should be careful—a pretty young woman like yourself. There's no telling what kind of trouble you might attract if the men don't know you're taken." She shook a finger at me, but smiled.

I scanned the room for hidden cameras. Surely she wasn't real?

"Can you check on Mrs. Paxton, please?"

Gladys nodded and slipped her glasses onto her nose. She ran her finger down a row of phone extensions that had been taped to her telephone.

"I'll try her in the classroom. They go outside for exercise around ten thirty. I might just catch her before that."

She picked up the receiver and winked at me, I suppose to indicate our partnership in locating Bea. She covered the receiver and said, "How old is your little one?"

For a moment I didn't understand what she meant and then realized she was talking about my nonexistent preschooler.

The only "little one" I had was Baxter and he almost outweighed me.

"He's three," I said and immediately felt guilty.

"Such a delightful age—" She broke off as someone on the other end picked up the phone.

"Bea, do you have time to speak with a potential preschool parent?" Gladys nodded to herself while listening to Bea's response.

"Okay, I'll let her know." Gladys replaced the receiver in the cradle and smiled at me.

"She said you can meet her out on the playground. They're just getting their coats on to go outside." She pointed in the direction of the new addition.

"Thank you," I said and backed out of the room. Something about Gladys made me want to keep my eye on her.

I found Bea and her small charges in a tiny play area surrounded by a metal fence. Plastic climbing structures took up most of the space and the children swarmed the pieces and fought for turns on the seesaw.

"Oh, it's you; you don't have a preschooler, do you?" Bea said as I approached the fence.

"Sorry, Gladys just assumed I was a parent and then I didn't really get a chance to convince her I just wanted to talk to you."

Bea nodded as if Gladys's habit of conducting her own conversations was well-known.

"It's just as well. The children are cranky today; it wouldn't have set a good example for a new parent. What can I do for you?"

I decided to skip over the preliminaries and get straight to the issue. The swarming mass of small people was making me nervous.

"I saw you at Rafe Godwin's memorial reception last night."

Her eyes narrowed, and she took a step back.

"I didn't see you there. But, yes, I came with some of the members of the congregation." She crossed her arms.

"This may seem like it's none of my business, but why were you there protesting when your daughter was a member of his coven?"

"Shh!" Bea looked back at her class to see if any of them had heard. "We don't talk about things like covens and witches in front of the children. And you're right. It's none of your business," she hissed.

I lowered my voice. "Does your church know about Skye?"

She hesitated and held my gaze for a moment. Then her shoulders relaxed. "Some do, but most don't. My husband and I have been hoping she'll give it up and come back to the church. Especially now that . . . *he*'s dead."

"You think that Skye was only a member of his . . . group . . . because he was the leader?"

"Skye is a very impressionable girl. She has romantic ideas. I thought she might realize her mistake now that he's gone, but she seems as committed as ever to this . . . cult."

I was starting to feel like it takes a cult member to know one when one of the kids came up to us, crying. He appeared to have fallen and scraped up his hand.

"It's okay, Aiden, we'll get some ice for it when we go inside."

Aiden sniffled and ran back to his friends.

"I really have to get back to the children."

She turned and waded into the waist-high crowd, who attached themselves to her while lodging complaints and begging for more time outside.

I turned to go and looked down to see a short blonde girl staring at me with her thumb in her mouth.

"Hello," I said.

"Your eyes are weird," she said around her wet digit.

"Um, thank you?"

"Do you have a kid coming here?"

I shook my head.

"Does your kid have weird eyes, too?"

"No, I don't—"

"Tiffany! Come along and get in line," Bea shouted.

The little girl waved with her free hand and skipped over to the rest of the group, but I was sure her normal eyes followed me all the way to the parking lot.

# 30

❧

I backed out of the parking spot and drove to the road. Left would take me back home; right would take me toward Rafe's house. I felt like there was more to see in his house and the likelihood that I would be interrupted by Mac was low. I decided to take a chance and drive over there for one more look in his office. I hoped to retrieve the family tree I had seen if the police hadn't discovered the secret drawer.

In the three days since I'd been there, the house had gone from abandoned to desolate. Leaves had piled on the porch, the police tape flapped in the wind. I parked along the curb and walked up the front steps. The key was still over the door, where we'd left it last time. I was just about to slide it into the lock when I heard a distinct *thump* from inside the house. I hesitated. Who could be in there?

I turned and looked up and down the street. A navy Suburban and a rusted-out silver Subaru sat by the curb a few houses down, but the street was otherwise deserted. No cop cars to be seen. It was someone else. Obviously, it wasn't Dylan or Diana. Diana had told me she was spending the whole day at the store catching up on paperwork. The only other person I could think of was Skye. Turning back toward the door, I leaned forward, listening for more sounds. All was quiet. Maybe it had just been the wind making the house creak. But I hadn't heard a creak, I'd heard a thump. The last time I'd stood hesitating on a porch, someone had died.

I shoved the key in the lock and opened the door.

"Skye?" I said as I pushed open the door.

I heard a footstep in the office. Then Morgan stood in the doorway. At least I thought it was Morgan. Her dark hair was pulled into a ponytail. She wore minimal makeup, and was garbed in medical scrubs.

"Morgan?"

"Clyde, what are you doing here?"

"Um, picking up something for Diana," I said. "She left a book here and wanted me to come get it for her."

Morgan's eyes narrowed. "That's what I'm doing, too. Rafe must have borrowed a lot of books." She put her hands on her hips.

"How did you get in?" I was still processing her new look and trying to make sense of someone else being in Rafe's house.

"Rafe and I *had* been very close." Her lips curled into a smile I recognized. Even without the makeup, black clothing, and high-heeled boots she exuded menace. "I never returned my key."

"Are you a nurse?" I asked, gesturing to her clothes.

"Physical therapist. I'm on my lunch break."

"I had no idea. I thought you sold daggers and spell kits."

She snorted. "There's not enough demand for those items to keep me clothed and fed. I just do that as a hobby."

"Well, did you find the book you needed?"

"Um, yes." She darted back into the office and reappeared with a small volume clutched in her hands. Short nails, no polish, to go with her new look. And I saw the charm bracelet with only six charms, not seven. "Here it is. Do you want some help finding Diana's book?" She held my gaze and smiled, letting me know she saw through my bluff.

"Thanks, but I don't want to keep you." Now that I knew I was right, and she had lied about being at the ceremony, I was less comfortable being alone with her.

"I hope you find what you're looking for." She took a step closer and held my gaze.

"I'm just looking for a book." I took a step back and scanned the room for anything I could use as a weapon.

"Okay." She crossed her arms. "You should talk to Lucan about this book you need. He knows more about Rafe than he likes to admit."

She brushed past me and went out the front door.

I took a deep breath. Even in nurse's scrubs she made all the hairs on my neck stand on end.

I walked into the office and stood there, trying to get a sense of anything different from last time. Of course, since then both the police and Morgan had been through. I pulled open the secret drawer where I had found the family tree—gone. The will was also missing. I hoped the police had taken it for safekeeping, but worried that someone else had grabbed it. And Morgan was at the top of that list.

**I spent another** hour going through the documents in Rafe's messy office and found nothing of interest. He had an enormous collection of Wiccan books and volumes of witchcraft history, but very little in the way of personal documents. I wished I had taken the family tree when I'd had the chance.

I drove back to my mother's place and found Seth, Dad, Mom, and Vi working with the pendulum again. Well, Mom, Vi, and Seth were working with the pendulum. Dad was sitting at the far end of the dining room table with the newspaper held up as a shield. Baxter gave me his usual sloppy greeting and snorted when I didn't offer any treats. Tuffy hopped on his hind legs, ran in a circle, and then went to lie down in the corner.

Seth grinned. "I taught him to do that. It's better than barking."

"Where have you been all morning?" Vi asked.

"I had a couple of errands," I said.

"You missed lunch," Mom said. "Let me get you something." She put the pendulum back in its bag, for which I was grateful, and headed into the kitchen.

"Did your errands involve finding out anything about the case?" Vi asked.

"I went to talk to Bea Paxton," I said.

"Faith's mom? Why?" Seth asked.

"She was there with the protesters last night."

Seth nodded. "Yeah, Faith says her mom is always protesting something with that church gang."

"When do you have all these conversations with Faith?" I said.

"We text. Sometimes." Seth didn't meet my eyes.

"Here you go," Mom said. She carried a sandwich and a mug of tea, which she placed in front of me.

"Thanks, Mom."

She sat across the table from me.

"So, tell us. Did you find out anything on your 'errands'?" Mom used air quotes for "errands."

I shook my head. "Not really." I told them about meeting

with Bea and the strange vibe I got there. But it felt more like excessive conservatism than anything threatening. I ended by saying, "I may not agree with their beliefs, but they have a right to them."

"They may have a right to them but they should leave everyone else alone." Vi picked up her knitting and viciously stabbed at the stitches.

"That's right, Vi," Mom said. "You don't see the Wiccans picketing their church, do you?" I was surprised by this since my mom had never been a big Wiccan supporter. Maybe after witnessing the fracas at the memorial she had changed her mind.

"Bea doesn't approve of Skye's choice," I said, "but what parent agrees with everything their kid does?" Mom snorted and nodded. Dad rattled his newspaper.

After a moment of uncomfortable silence, I told them about my encounter with Morgan at Rafe's house.

"Do you think she took the will and the family tree?" Seth asked.

I shrugged. "It's possible, but I don't know why she would want them."

"She's a strange one," Vi said, darkly.

"She told you to talk to Lucan?" Dad asked. "Do they even know each other?"

"They were both in Rafe's coven until Rafe kicked her out," I said.

"What does Diana know about that coven?" Vi asked. "Seems like there was an awful lot of drama going on."

"I'll ask her when I see her next. I don't know how much she can tell us. She tried to stay out of that sort of thing. It's not good for business to take sides."

Dad nodded. "She's done a good job with that store. Much better than her father ever did with his used books."

"That's true, Frank." Mom smiled in his direction. "Want to come for dinner tonight, Clyde?"

"I can't, but can Seth hang out here tonight?" I asked.

"Of course." Mom turned to Seth. "Do you want to sleep over, Seth?"

Seth lifted a shoulder and let it drop. "Sure."

"What are you doing?" Vi asked. "Are you going to follow Lucan? I'll go with you. I think we need to keep an eye on him."

"I'm going out . . . with a friend."

"Who? Diana, Alex?" Vi leaned forward.

"No, it's . . ."

Seth interrupted. "It's Tom, isn't it?" He tilted his head and lifted both eyebrows. His less-than-subtle cue that he was going to cover for me.

I smiled and didn't respond.

Seth rolled his eyes. "I don't need a babysitter so you can go out with your *boy*friend."

"He's not her boyfriend," Vi said. Then, almost to herself, she said, "At least, I hope not."

"I could use some help with the computer, Seth. Maybe we could look at your math homework again," Dad said. Dad didn't know what he was covering for, but jumped into the fray.

"Yeah, okay," Seth said.

"Where are you going, Clyde?" Mom asked.

"Just out to dinner. No big deal." I pushed away from the table to end the conversation. I said good-bye and headed toward the front door, but I could feel Vi's inquisitive stare follow me out.

# 31

### ❧❧

I parked in my driveway and opened the back door for Baxter out of habit. Then I remembered I'd left him at my parents' house along with Tuffy and Seth. I raced up the front steps and went into the house. My mind was swirling with suspicions and snippets of conversation. I tried to piece together all the bits of information I had picked up over the past week. So much had happened since Halloween night, only one week ago. I wanted to spend one evening not thinking about any of it. I hoped Mac felt the same way.

Since Mac and I had had a rough start to this new romance, it left me wondering where things stood between us. Our decision to take things slow had started to feel glacial. Had we missed our window of opportunity? Any new relationship, even if it was a second chance, needed momentum. Ours seemed to have skipped the courtship and gone straight to the post-honeymoon (without any honeymoon, I might add). Tonight I hoped to turn things around.

I had to dig through some boxes from my move to find any makeup beyond mascara. Flashes of Morgan's overly made-up eyes had me hesitating as I assessed the situation in the mirror. Barring colored contacts, there was no way to disguise the different-colored eyes. They were very different and I thought it made my face look like a composite of two different people. Sisters, certainly. I didn't resemble Frankenstein, but still, the asymmetry meant that even if I met that mathematical ideal all the magazines talked about, something always appeared "off" about my face. Mac obviously knew about my eyes, so trying to disguise them would only serve to draw attention. I pulled my brown hair out of its usual ponytail and fluffed it. I always hoped Diana's curls would rub off on me, but no luck.

Jeans, a long-sleeved, slightly clingy shirt, and a leather jacket would have to do for a seductive outfit. I never wore skirts. But I chose an old pair of high-heeled boots because I knew Mac liked them. I heard Mac's four-beat knock before I could rethink my outfit or change my shoes. Before I answered the door, I reached for my phone and turned off the volume—no one would be interrupting us tonight.

Mac's blue eyes grew dark when I opened the door. "You look fantastic."

He glanced around the living room and up the stairs.

"Seth's at my parents," I said.

"That's very good news." He pulled me to him and we celebrated our few moments of privacy. Then my stomach growled.

Mac laughed. "Hungry?"

I shrugged and nodded.

"Let's go," he said. Then he leaned toward me and whispered, "I don't want you weak from hunger."

My feet wobbled in my boots as I followed him out the door.

We ended up in Grand Rapids. I didn't want to take any chances of being seen by anyone who would report back to my family.

We spent the next couple of hours happily anonymous at one of the new restaurants downtown that featured multi-course dinners. The benefit was that it took a while and the pace of the evening slowed. I felt my shoulders relax and knew that this is what I had desperately needed. We avoided any mention of Rafe Godwin or Dylan. I didn't want to argue with Mac tonight and even though I did think he could do more to help Dylan, I knew he was doing his job and wouldn't let any personal feelings get in the way of that.

I told him funny stories about the festival and some of the crazy stuff I had seen at the booths. When I got to Morgan and her revenge spell kits, Mac did a dramatic shiver and steered the conversation away from black magick.

By the time the check arrived, we had finished a bottle of wine and were laughing about old times. I leaned on Mac on our way out of the restaurant, feeling unstable on the unfamiliar heels. In his car, we spent a few minutes steaming up the windows until some kids from the art school wandered by, hooting and catcalling. Mac put the car in gear and we headed south toward home.

**We were just** outside of Crystal Haven, listening to oldies on the radio and looking forward to the rest of the evening, when we came around a bend in the road and Mac's headlights caught a light-colored lump on the side of the road. At first I thought it was a dog that had been hit by a car. But it wasn't.

"Shit," Mac said.

He pulled the car over to the side of the road and jumped out to check on the person—because we could see now that it *was* a person—lying on the shoulder.

Mac reached the crumpled form first and I saw him check for a pulse.

"Clyde, call 911."

I had already dialed and was waiting for them to pick up. The person was large, with dark red hair pulled into a ponytail. He was wearing running gear and even as my mind pushed the thought away, I realized it was Lucan.

Mac knelt next to him. "You're going to be fine. We've called for help."

Lucan groaned softly.

"Don't move, just stay where you are," Mac told him. We both knew it was best to keep him still in case he had suffered a neck or back injury.

"Big SUV," Lucan said.

Mac and I exchanged a worried look.

"A car hit you?" Mac asked. But Lucan didn't answer.

Mac felt for a pulse again. "Where's that ambulance?" He glared down the road as if that would bring it more quickly.

Lucan moved his head and coughed.

"Lucan, can you hear me?" Mac said.

"Should we take him to the hospital ourselves?" I said.

"Lucan, can you move at all?" Mac said.

Lucan raised his hand and started to try to sit up. He cried out in pain and lay back down.

I noticed his leg was at an odd angle. "Mac, I think his leg is broken."

"He's breathing okay and I don't know how we'll be able to move him," Mac said. "It's probably best to just wait for the ambulance. You stay here with him. I have some flares in my trunk. I'll put them along the road so we don't have any more accidents."

Feeling completely useless, I sat on the gravel shoulder and watched Lucan.

"It backed up," Lucan said quietly.

"What? What backed up?"

"Car."

"The car that hit you backed into you?"

I thought it must have been going pretty fast in reverse to do this kind of damage.

"Drove over . . . legs."

I gasped. "The car that hit you backed over you?"

He nodded and coughed again.

"Okay, just stay still." I patted his shoulder because it was the only part of him that didn't look beat-up. "We'll get you some help."

"Call Diana, please. I need to see her." Several things clicked into place: the sense he was hiding something when we first met, Vi's photo of him going into the police station when Diana was there, Diana taking his hand and leading him into the Reading Room. Were they dating? I could hardly be mad at her for keeping this from me when I hadn't told her about Mac all summer. But *still*.

Mac came back and sat with us and I told him what Lucan had said. Mac tried to get him to repeat it but Lucan had passed out.

Just when I thought Mac was going to try to drag Lucan to the car on his own and drive him to the hospital, we heard sirens in the distance.

The ambulance pulled past us and parked a short distance away. The fire trucks had also been dispatched and Mac went to send them on their way. Charla arrived and walked down the road to where the flares began so she could direct traffic around the accident. Friday night could be pretty busy along Singapore Highway.

I recognized one of the EMTs from over the summer when I had discovered a shooting victim. I quickly stuffed all of those memories in a small compartment, but not before I had begun to tremble with the flood of adrenaline.

I watched the ambulance workers do their triage. Once they pronounced Lucan stable and had an IV running into his arm, they dosed him up with pain meds and got ready to move him into the ambulance. Mac came back and pulled me away from the activity taking place on the shoulder.

"You don't want to watch when they do this," he said, with an experienced tone.

I looked away but still heard Lucan cry out in pain as they slid him onto the gurney.

Mac put his arm around me. "I should follow them to the hospital; it sounds like a hit-and-run, or worse, and I'll need to file a report."

I nodded, but couldn't make myself speak yet.

"Want me to drop you off at home?" His voice was gentle, but I knew his mind was already working on the case.

"No, I want to go with you. I want to be sure he's okay."

"It could be a long night."

"That's all right. The evening isn't going the way I planned anyway."

Mac's mouth tilted up in a half smile, which was quickly replaced with his cop face.

We followed the ambulance back up the highway toward Grand Rapids, which had the only trauma center in the area.

# 32

❧❧

**The EMTs rushed Lucan through the ambulance** entrance. A burly male nurse stepped in front of us to stop us from following. He silently pointed to the small sitting area and closed the doors.

I turned and surveyed the room. Plastic chairs littered the area, which was anchored by two couches with vinyl seats. The colors had once been bright and festive but had dulled after all the time spent in this purgatory of waiting. Mac and I sat in two of the least wobbly chairs and stared at the television screen playing reruns of *Full House*.

No further word had emanated from the sealed doorway when Diana appeared about half an hour later. I'd called her from the road to tell her about Lucan. I hadn't expected her to drop everything and arrive in the ER. This confirmed my suspicions.

Her orange hair stood out from her head in wild springs

and she looked like she'd been crying again. I didn't know how much more stress she could take.

"Clyde, Mac!" She approached us, breathless. "Have you heard anything?"

Mac shook his head, and I stood up to hug her.

"They haven't come back out yet," I said. "He was conscious at the scene, and asked me to call you."

She blushed and deflected my pointed stare with a question. "You said he was hit while running?"

I nodded. "Based on what he was wearing, I assume that's what he was doing."

"But who would hit a runner and then keep on driving?" She searched both our faces. "What aren't you telling me?"

Mac sighed. I glanced at him and he shrugged and nodded.

"Lucan said the car hit him and then backed over him."

Diana drew in breath quickly and pulled her jacket more tightly around herself.

"We don't have a confirmation on that yet," Mac said. But his tired tone implied that he believed it.

"Who would do that?"

I shook my head. I motioned for Diana to sit.

Mac stood and started pacing. "I'm going to go see what I can find out." He went down the hall to the nurses' desk. I saw him straighten his back and square his shoulders as he approached the counter.

"I can't believe this is happening," Diana said. She leaned forward and put her head in her hands.

I rubbed her shoulder. I was upset about Lucan, too, but obviously he and Diana had become closer than I thought.

Mac returned with a satisfied grimace on his face. "They're going to send someone to talk to us."

A few minutes later, a short, thin young woman wearing

a white lab coat walked toward us down the hall. As she approached I tried to assess her age. Her dark hair escaped from the ponytail she had apparently put in many hours ago, freckles dotted her nose and cheeks, and even though she appeared tired, she had an energy that I envied. Definitely younger than me, she looked barely older than Seth.

"I'm Dr. Baker, the intern taking care of Mr. Reed," she said as she approached. "Are you his family?"

We all glanced at one another and shook our heads. I didn't think he had any family in the area.

"I'm Detective McKenzie. We found him after the accident and I'll be investigating. We're all his . . . friends."

Not really true, but it worked for the doctor.

"He's stable right now, but his right leg is broken in several places. He'll need surgery tonight. We're calling the surgical team in now."

"Can we see him?" Diana's voice cracked.

The doctor nodded. "Very briefly. He's in a lot of pain."

We followed her down the hall and into the brightly lit emergency room. Doctors and nurses rushed past on their way to various curtained cubicles. Dr. Baker led us to a spot at the far end of the room. "Mr. Reed, some friends are here to see you." She whisked the fabric open for us.

Lucan was covered up to his neck in white. Tubes snaked toward the bed and disappeared under the blankets. His face was ashen under his bright red beard. He looked as if he didn't recognize us at first and then his eyes rested on Diana and a hesitant smile formed.

She rushed forward. "Luke, are you in much pain? Is there anything I can do?"

The blanket moved and he fought to pull his hand out from underneath. "Diana, it's good to see you." His voice was so quiet, we all leaned toward him.

She took his hand, and Mac pulled up a chair for her to sit in.

"Lucan, is there anything you can tell me about the car that hit you?" Mac asked. "The sooner I start looking, the better chance I have of finding out who did this."

"It was a big SUV. Dark. I don't know if it was blue or black. I didn't get a good look." Lucan stopped and his breathing became shallow. He was clearly in pain. "I heard it come up behind me, and I realized it was going too fast."

One of the machines started beeping.

"It came right off the road and slammed into me," Lucan said. "Then it stopped and backed up right over my legs." He stopped again.

A nurse came in and glowered at us. She turned off the beeping and turned, taking a deep breath.

"That's enough visiting for now. He needs to rest." The nurse tried to push us out of the room, but Mac pulled out his badge. She *hmph*ed and reminded me of Vi. "Three more minutes," she said and jerked the curtain closed.

"Another car must have come by because the SUV took off. I don't know how long I was there before you found me, but I don't think it was more than a few minutes."

"I don't suppose you have a helpful license plate number?" Mac asked.

Lucan shook his head. "It happened so fast."

"Okay, I'll see what I can do," Mac said. He tilted his head at me to meet him out in the hallway. I followed him out into the busy corridor.

"I need to get back to the station and get started on this." Mac kept his voice low. "Do you want to get a ride home with Diana, or come with me?"

I stole a peek through the slightly open curtain. Diana

clutched Lucan's hand and spoke quietly. The nurse had entered and was putting something into his IV.

"I doubt she's going home anytime soon. I better stay with her."

Mac nodded once, and leaned forward to give me a quick kiss on the cheek.

I pulled the curtain aside far enough to enter and snapped it back into place. The nurse said he would be sleepy soon as she had just given him more pain medicine.

"Clyde. . . ." Lucan opened his eyes and searched the room.

"I'm here."

"Talk to Neila. Tell her . . ."

"Tell her what? Lucan?"

"About me . . . tell her I'm sorry."

Diana's eyes grew wide and she shook his shoulder. "Luke?"

The monitors all beeped and hummed contentedly. Lucan had passed out.

A few minutes later the nurse came to tell us they would take him to the OR soon and we would have to wait in the recovery waiting room or we could leave a phone number to be called when he was out of surgery.

"It could be a while," she said quietly. "They're prepping the room now, and the surgery will be a long one."

Diana refused to leave the hospital and we spent the next several hours dozing and worrying in the family waiting room.

"When were you going to tell me about Mac?" she asked.

"When were you going to tell me about Lucan?" I replied.

"You go first." Diana's stubborn jaw told me not to push it.

"We haven't told anyone because I didn't want my mom and Vi to get wind of it. You remember how they were the last time. Between the tarot and the pendulum, they were planning our wedding before we even went out on our third date, and I was barely twenty-one."

She nodded and grimaced. "Okay, I see your point about them. But, you could have told *me*."

"I know. I should have told you. And I would have. I just . . . I wanted us to have a chance without anyone's expectations getting in the way."

"Well, *I*'ll forgive you. Good luck with Alex."

I nodded and felt my stomach clench. I'd been away from Crystal Haven so long I had forgotten what it was like to have friends who expected sharing. I didn't want to hurt their feelings; I just wanted to figure things out on my own.

"What about you? I didn't even suspect that you were together until Lucan asked me to call you." I fixed her with the same narrowed eyes she had shown me moments before.

"I didn't have anything to tell until recently." She looked away and her cheeks blazed red. "I met him through Rafe and then we worked together on the festival. This past week things changed. He's a really good guy."

I decided not to tell her my whole family had pegged him as a murderer. Anxious to get out of the hospital and talk to Neila, I rethought my stance that Lucan had killed Rafe. If someone had tried to kill Lucan, and it sounded like that had been the case, it had to be connected to Rafe's death. As far as I was concerned, this attack on Lucan was proof that Dylan was not the killer. Mac had provided him with the perfect alibi. At least one good thing would come from Dylan's time in jail.

# 33

❦

**Sore, stiff, and tired, Diana and I had both seen** better mornings. However, we were happy to hear that Lucan's surgery had been a success. The nurse took one look at us and ordered us home to rest.

"He doesn't need to be worrying about you two," she told us with a scowl. "He'll be asleep for at least a few hours."

Diana dropped me off at home and I went straight into the shower. I hadn't even told my family about what had happened to Lucan. Part of me didn't want to wake them, and part didn't want Vi showing up in the waiting room. I'd have to tell them soon, but hoped to get one more thing over with before facing them.

After a very fast shower and a longing look at my bed, I hopped in my Jeep and turned it toward Neila's house. I wasn't sure what her connection was to Lucan, but I was determined to find out.

"How nice to see you again, Clyde," she said as she swung the door wide.

"Ms. Whittle. I have some news."

"Oh. Come in."

We walked back toward her kitchen. This was our usual path and I wasn't sure what the other rooms contained.

After I refused Neila's offers of coffee and tea and cookies, she sat down across from me. "This must be serious," she said.

I nodded. "Lucan Reed was a hit-and-run victim last evening."

Neila didn't react. It was almost as if she hadn't heard me. Then a single tear fell down her cheek. "Is he all right?" she asked with a shaky voice.

I nodded. "He needed surgery for a broken leg. . . ." I hesitated, not wanting to upset her but needing to question her anyway. "The car that hit him . . . backed over him on purpose."

This time she did react with a quick intake of breath. Her fingers turned white on the tabletop. It was as if she gripped the table to keep her balance.

"I had no idea this would be so dangerous," she said quietly and mostly to herself. "What have I done?"

I reached across the table to put a hand on hers. "Ms. Whittle, what do you know about Lucan's accident?"

She met my eyes, but didn't seem to focus. Her mind was far away. And then just as quickly she was back. "Why can't I see this sort of thing happening? Why is it always . . . other things?"

I understood her completely and began to wonder how much she would be able to help me if she had the same concerns I did about her own visions.

"Lucan told me to talk to you. He said to tell you he's sorry."

Several tears were released this time and I glanced around the kitchen, looking for tissues. Neila pulled a handkerchief out of the folds of her apron and scrubbed at her eyes.

"He's right. I can't keep this a secret anymore."

"What is it?"

"We didn't want anyone to know we knew each other," she said. "He was here once when you stopped by. He's been helping me with repairs around the house. But also, Lucan is a private detective."

I sat back in my chair, trying to fit this information into the rest of what I knew about him.

"I hired him a year ago to help me find my son."

"Your . . . son?"

She nodded. "I had a baby boy many years ago. I wasn't married, not that that bothered me at all." She stopped. "Have you ever wondered why I live up here all alone and almost never go into town?"

I thought she was trying to distract me from Lucan's story.

"I guess I never gave it much thought. . . ."

"No one ever does, I suspect. Crystal Haven has all sorts of people who can do amazing things and the idea that there might be a scary witch really isn't so surprising."

I smiled at her. "I don't think you're a scary witch."

"No, but you did. Until you came up here a week ago, if you gave any thought to me at all it would be to wonder if I was still alive, first, and whether I was really a witch, second."

I started to argue, but she held my gaze and I nodded.

"I'm to blame, in part, for the rumors. I never did anything to stop them. In fact, I welcomed them when I decided to retreat from the world. It made it easier that everyone in town was a little afraid of me. No one ever got too curious."

"Why did you decide to retreat?"

"Your grandmother was the only one who stood by me, but it wasn't enough. My kind of talent is one that is guaranteed to keep people at a distance."

I waited.

"I do see some bits of the future, and of course I can read the cards and tea leaves," she said and waved her hand to encompass all of Crystal Haven's offerings. "But my main talent, if you can call it that, is that I can see a woman's children."

"What do you mean?" I leaned toward her.

"I can see how many children she will have, whether there will be boys or girls, or both."

"I don't see how that's such a scary talent." I smiled and wondered where this was going. "I would think people would pay a lot of money to find out that sort of information."

Neila nodded and clasped her hands tightly together on the tabletop. "In some cases, I can also see if the woman will outlive her child."

"Oh." I felt my smile fade, but forced myself not to look horrified.

Neila took in a deep breath and seemed to steady herself. "I can tell if a person is going to lose a child."

I realized that this was why she had sequestered herself. The fewer people she met, the fewer tragedies she would see.

"Who knows about this . . . gift?"

Neila shrugged. "Most of the older members of the city council are aware, I think. They may not have firsthand knowledge, but they've probably heard the rumors."

I grimaced at the word "rumor." It seemed most of what passed for certainty in this town was based on chitchat and hearsay. Unfortunately, there was always a piece of truth buried in the gossip. I thought back to the story about Neila. The kids told the tale of how she was a witch who would take children from their parents and they were never seen again. Much like the "Hansel and Gretel" fable, the witch killed children. In Neila's case, she knew which children would die.

Neila watched me while I struggled with this new information. No wonder she hid herself away. Not only did town legend have her pegged as a child killer, but her visions would show her which kids would die before their parents. I couldn't imagine living with that kind of knowledge. Either as Neila, who had the knowledge, or as the parent, who didn't want it.

"I tried for a long time to keep the information to myself, but that got to be just as bad. If someone's child was in a car accident, they would blame me for not telling them and if I warned them ahead of time, they said I had ruined their last months with the child."

I nodded, thinking about the burden she had carried all these years.

"What would you do?" she asked.

I already knew the answer to that one. I would run, just as I had been doing for the past fifteen years.

We sat quietly for a few minutes and then Neila seemed to gather her strength. She sat up, dried her tears, and took a deep breath.

"Rafe Godwin was my son," she said.

My mouth dropped open and my brain froze. I didn't know what to say.

"What?"

"I gave him up for adoption when he was born." Her voice shook as she spoke. "The minute they placed him in my arms, I knew that I would outlive him. It's amazing to discover what you will do for your child." Her eyes filled again with tears.

"Oh, Neila," I said and laid my hand over hers.

"I thought I'd figured out how to beat the prediction. Maybe if I sent him away, and didn't try to find him, let him disappear into someone else's life, I might be able to protect him." She shook her head.

"What made you look for him now?"

"I guess I just got curious." She lifted a shoulder. "I'm getting old. I wanted to know that he was okay. It never occurred to me that hiring Lucan would lead to anyone's death."

I squeezed her hand to get her to meet my eyes.

"There is nothing to indicate that your investigation of Rafe was related to his death in any way. You can't take the blame for this."

"Maybe not, but I can take the blame for not knowing my son."

I didn't have anything to say to that.

"If it makes you feel any better," I said, "I think he was really proud of who he was. It sounds like he had a very supportive family."

She smiled at me in a pitying way.

"He tried to hide the fact that he was adopted all of his life. Maybe he didn't even know he was adopted until adulthood. I'll never know how he felt about it all except that he didn't want to admit to it."

I nodded. She was right. He didn't want to admit that he was adopted. If Dylan was correct, he'd even killed to keep it a secret. I shuddered to think of how he would have reacted if Neila had tried to contact him after she located him.

"So, all these years that he was living in Grand Rapids—you had no idea?"

She shook her head. "None. I assumed he'd been sent farther away. I don't know why I thought that, but I always imagined him somewhere warm and sunny. I tried not to think about him very much at all."

"How did Lucan find him?"

"He's very good." She shrugged. "I never quizzed him on his methods."

"And he's sure about Rafe?"

She nodded again. "He got close to Rafe through the coven and we sent off a DNA test. It's been confirmed."

"Were you planning to tell Rafe?"

"I wasn't sure what I was going to do." She traced the flowers in her tablecloth with a finger. "I just found out recently that Rafe had been looking into genealogy. He'd been working with that young girl. She apparently knows how to trace things with the computer." She sipped her tea. "If I'd known he was looking for me as well, I would have gone to him immediately."

Neila's lost opportunities and regrets weighed on me. Skye was working on Neila's family tree. Rafe must have known Neila was his mother. I wondered why, after all this time, he'd been trying to locate his birth parents.

"I just hope that Lucan and I didn't trigger all of these events."

"I don't know how you could have. No one even knew what you were doing," I said.

"No, but something got Rafe interested in his birth family."

I wondered whether he would have been pleased in the end to find out that Neila was his mother. She was famous in her own way in Crystal Haven. Would he have found a way to turn that to his advantage? I hated to admit it, but my protectiveness toward Neila had me feeling relieved they'd never met.

# 34

I left Neila's house feeling unsettled and anxious. My list of suspects was rapidly diminishing. My mother always told me to pay attention to my dreams and visions. I'd been dreaming about a woman. It had to be Morgan.

I drove to my parents' to pick up Seth. I knew I'd also have to tell them the story of Lucan's accident. Dad can only learn so much from his police scanner. I prepared myself for the interrogation that would ensue when they heard I had been out with Mac.

The noise from the dogs and the people enveloped me when I opened the front door.

"Where have you been?"

"I knew it!"

"We were worried."

I barely heard these statements over the barking of the dogs. After everyone calmed down, we reconvened in the dining room. Mom had one highly polished extra sense—she always knew when I was starving. She brought some coffee and the leftover bagels and cream cheese the rest of them had eaten for breakfast. I hadn't eaten more than a candy bar since dinner and I gave my food the focus it deserved. For about two bites. Then Vi slapped the table and startled everyone in the room.

"Tell us!"

"Give her a minute, Vi," Mom said. "She needs to eat."

Vi narrowed her eyes at both of us, and crossed her arms.

I swallowed and took a sip of coffee. Then, looking at Vi, I started to take another bite but her steely gaze stopped me. I put the bagel down.

"Lucan was hit by a car last night while he was out running," I said. "He's already had surgery and the doctors say he'll recover nicely."

Vi's shoulders slumped. "You're sure he's okay? Too bad we weren't following him last night—we might have been able to help."

I nodded. "I think so. He's got a broken leg, but he should be all right."

"What happened?" Dad asked. "I heard about a 10-57 on the scanner. The driver didn't stop to help him?"

I shook my head. "He didn't see who the driver was, but they ran into him on purpose . . . and then backed over him."

Mom gasped and reached for her amulet. Seth grimaced and shook his head.

"Is this related to Rafe?"

"I don't know. It might be." I didn't know how much I could tell them without revealing Neila's secret and the fact that I had been visiting her.

"Well, we know Dylan didn't do it," Dad said. "If it *is* connected, that should get Dylan out of jail."

"Who would do something like that? It's horrible," Mom said.

I caught Vi's eye and we both said, "Morgan Lavelle."

Seth shook his head. "I don't know."

We all turned to look at him.

"It seems like you're all just picking on her because she looks different. She might be a very nice person."

"Are you accusing me of . . . of prejudice?" Vi sputtered.

"I don't think so." Seth tilted his head. "Maybe. You said she looks creepy—like Lady Gaga—but she's just trying to make a living and express herself. There's nothing wrong with that." Seth shrugged.

"It's not just how she looks, Seth," I said. "She sells evil spell kits, and I found her mucking around in Rafe's house, and . . . she's creepy."

"Well, you were at Rafe's house, too," he said. "And you're psychic. Some people think that's creepy."

I wondered where all of this protection of Morgan came from. I didn't think he'd ever even met the woman.

"We need more evidence," Vi said.

"Yes, that would be helpful." Mom nodded.

Dad put his head in his hands.

"We aren't going to follow Morgan now, are we?" Seth said. "That hasn't worked out so great in the past."

I decided I needed to talk to Seth alone. He seemed very invested in his life in Crystal Haven and I knew it was time to confront him on his decision to leave New York.

"I have some things to take care of at home," I said.

I thanked Mom for the breakfast and Seth got his things.

"We'll work on a plan," Vi said as we herded the dogs out to the car. "Let's talk this afternoon."

Amazed that I had escaped without talking about Mac, I turned the Jeep toward home. But, about a block away from my parents' house, I pulled over and shut off the engine. The dogs looked at me curiously.

"What are we doing here?" Seth peeked out the window.

"Seth, we need to talk." I knew this was the wrong way to approach a teenager, but I didn't have time for subtle.

"Sure, okay."

"Why did you come back to Crystal Haven?"

His phone buzzed and he pulled it out of his pocket with relief. I put my hand over it and waited until he looked at me.

His shoulders slumped.

"I can't live there anymore," he said.

"Where? In New York?"

He nodded. "Ever since this summer when I . . . heard Baxter. I've felt like I should be here. For one thing, there are a lot of animals in New York City and most of them aren't very happy. It drags me down."

I nodded. I hadn't thought of this, but if he really could sense what the animals were thinking it was probably similar to the way I felt about my own premonitions—assaulted with no way to fight back.

"I thought that there must be other people dealing with this and it's more likely I'll find them here than in New York. Plus, my parents are always gone. There's something going on at work and they're stressed out."

"But, don't you miss them? Don't you miss your sister?" Sophie was seven years younger than Seth, and my own status as a little sibling had me worried about her reaction to his vanishing act.

He nodded. "I do, but I miss them whether I'm here *or* there. I've heard from them more this past week than the whole time I was home. I guess they want to check in with me because I'm out of town. I do miss Sophie. . . ."

"I'm sorry, Seth. I didn't know things were so stressful for your parents. Your mom doesn't tell me very much about her work."

He nodded. "She doesn't talk about it much at all. But it's been worse these past few months." .

I got an uncomfortable tingling feeling in my scalp and I rubbed my head to get rid of it. Grace was in trouble and I didn't know how to help her.

"So, what's your plan?"

He shrugged. "Dunno. I like it here. I'm keeping up with my schoolwork and I don't have to deal with . . . actually going to school."

There was no way Grace and Paul would agree to this. But, Seth clearly wanted to stay here. It would be an uncomfortable conversation—*Hi, sis, your kid wants to come live in the place you've been running from all your life.* I got a queasy feeling just thinking about it.

Seth looked at me with the same sad expression Baxter used when he wanted more dinner.

"Okay, I'm going to have to think about this. It's really going to be up to your parents." .

He nodded, and I caught a fleeting smile as he turned his head away.


*My chest is bursting as I run up the steps. They are twisting around each other and go on and on. I can barely take a breath because the panic fills my lungs.*

*I have one thought: Seth.*

*Light bursts through ahead of me and I realize I am*

*almost at the top. Wind nearly knocks me back down the stairs and rain lashes at my face when I force myself out onto the open tower. My head spins and I have to grip the rough stone wall to keep my balance. I hear the laughing again.*

*A dark, hooded figure steps out of the shadows and approaches me, slowly. I don't want to see what is under the hood, but its hands pull back the fabric. Morgan.*

Someone pounded on the door. I awoke on the couch with afternoon sun streaming in the windows. After we'd arrived home, Seth had taken the dogs for a walk. I'd stretched out on the couch and must have fallen asleep. My scratchy eyes didn't want to open all the way and I felt disoriented after the dream.

I glanced at my watch. Seth had been gone about an hour. The pounding continued and was now punctuated by Diana's urgent voice. "Clyde! Are you there?"

My heart sped up and I felt a jolt as I woke up fully and realized Seth wasn't home yet and Diana was attacking my front entrance.

I jumped up and raced to the door. I wrenched it open such that Diana almost fell on me in her quest to break it down.

"Oh, you *are* here. Good." She straightened up and smoothed her wild hair.

"Where's Seth? Did something happen?"

Diana tilted her head and jerked her thumb over her shoulder. Seth was there in the yard, with Dylan and the dogs. Baxter and Tuffy were welcoming Dylan in their doggy way and Seth laughed at something Dylan said. I felt my body relax. After the dream and the urgent pounding, it took a moment to calm down.

"Why were you pounding on the door like that?"

Diana blushed. "I just . . . got worried when you didn't answer. Seth said you were home and I got a bad feeling. . . ."

I grimaced and swung the door wide so she could enter.

"I take it Mac came to his senses about Dylan?"

Diana nodded. "Charla dropped him off just a little while ago. It seems they have new evidence."

"What new evidence?"

Diana shook her head and shrugged. "She wouldn't say. Just that Dylan wasn't a suspect anymore. Rupert seemed relieved, and maybe a little disappointed that he wouldn't need to go to court."

I sat on the couch and rubbed my forehead.

"Are you okay?" Diana asked.

I nodded and offered her a weak smile. I knew I should be thrilled for Diana that Dylan was out of jail, but the dream lingered with a sense of menace and I was worried about this case. None of it made sense to me and I felt no closer to figuring it out than I had that first day in Mac's office. "I'm so glad Dylan is in the clear, Diana. I just wish they had caught the killer by now."

Diana dropped into the seat next to me. "I know. I was at the hospital earlier visiting Lucan and they have a police officer stationed outside. I had to show my driver's license and get clearance from Mac just to go in the room."

"Mac must think he's still in danger."

"What's going to happen when they let him out of the hospital? Luke will never put up with a babysitter cop hanging around. . . ."

"You seem to know him pretty well," I said.

Diana blushed and dropped her head so her face was hidden behind her hair. "He's . . . not like anyone I've ever met."

I vacillated about whether to tell her he was a private investigator, but decided to wait on that for now. It was his story to tell and she had enough to deal with.

"How long do you think you can keep Mac a secret from your family?" she said.

I had the same worry she did. It wouldn't take long for them to put everything together and figure out that I had been with Mac when Lucan was found on the side of the road.

"Maybe another hour or so?" I sighed.

# 35

❧⚬❧

**Diana and I were making tea in the kitchen when** the front door opened. Expecting to hear Seth's voice, I froze when Vi's "I knew it!" floated into the room. Diana and I exchanged a glance, and I took a deep breath. We heard the dogs jumping and the stomping of multiple feet in the front room.

"Clyde? Where are you?" Seth called.

"I'm here," I said and walked into the living room clutching my tea for support.

"We came over as soon as we heard!" Mom said.

Dad had his arm slung over Dylan's shoulder and a big grin plastered on his face.

"Jillian called your mother to tell her that Dylan was out of jail," Vi said. Jillian, Tom's mother and my mother's best friend, was the main source of gossip in town. Vi turned her frown in my direction. "We had to hear it from the grapevine, like everyone else. Why didn't you call us?"

I held up a hand. "I just found out myself. Diana came by to tell me."

Mom looked me over and *tsk*ed. "You look awful, Clyde. Did you get any sleep?"

I nodded. "About an hour," I said.

"There's no time for sleeping," Vi said. "We need to celebrate. Call Alex and tell him we're on our way."

I took a moment to welcome Dylan home with a quick hug while Vi pushed everyone out the door.

If it hadn't been cold and misty, we could have walked. As it was, we piled into various cars and caravanned downtown. Alex met us at the door of the restaurant. We were lucky that it was in between lunch and dinner, so the place was deserted.

Alex clapped Dylan on the shoulder and waved us toward the back, where he had pulled two tables together.

"Dylan, it's great to see you," Alex said.

"We've been so worried about you, dear," Mom said.

Dylan ducked his head and smiled. "It wasn't so bad. The Crystal Haven jail is pretty nice."

"Weren't you worried?" Seth asked.

"Nah. I knew they'd figure out sooner or later that I didn't do it."

Vi clapped her hands imperiously and gestured at us to sit. "We need to put our heads together and figure this out. Lucan has been attacked—any one of us could be next!"

I was surprised at Lucan's rise from number one murder suspect to "one of us."

"I really don't think we're in danger, Vi," I said.

"How do you know? Lucan probably thought he was safe, too, until someone drove over him—twice!"

"I just mean that we don't know anything, and we aren't involved with Rafe or his death."

"I have a very bad feeling about this," Vi said. "We need to figure it out before someone else gets hurt."

"What do you suggest?" I said.

"We should look at all the clues again, and maybe make a case map like they do on TV. Do you have one of those whiteboards?"

"No, I didn't bring my whiteboard."

"That's okay. We can use this paper." Vi pointed to the paper covering the table. She tossed a new pack of markers and some sticky notes on the table.

"Been shopping, Vi?" I said. She ignored me.

"Okay, everyone pick a color and a topic."

The table erupted in sound, as Seth and my mother fought for the blue marker. Dylan told Diana he knew more about the evidence, and that she was clearly not equipped to write about Lucan. Alex picked up on that and began quizzing Diana and acting huffy that she hadn't told him about Lucan.

"There's nothing to tell," Diana said. "We worked together on the festival and then for Rafe's memorial. . . ." She trailed off and blushed as the table fell silent.

Dylan came to the rescue. "Let's list our suspects and clues," he said.

Just then the door swung open and Tom walked in. I had texted him on the way to the restaurant.

He came over and gave Dylan one of those rough guy-hugs, but his eyes were red and he scrubbed them with his sleeve.

"What's all this?" Tom asked, looking over Diana's shoulder at the markers and notes.

"We're doing a case map like they do on TV," Vi said. "It's good you're here. You can fill in the blanks for us."

Tom squeezed between Vi and Dylan and grabbed a marker. "I'll do what I can, but I've been out of the loop."

After a few minutes of noise, Vi tapped her water glass with her spoon. "We need to be more organized than this. Let's start with clues. We can do those in blue. Seth, you write them down."

Everyone shouted things at the same time, as if it were a game show.

Seth glowered at the table. "Slow down. I'm not a computer."

Our list was longer than I had thought. I wasn't sure we'd make any sense of it. Seth wrote:

*broken EpiPen*
*peanut oil*
*Morgan lying about being at the ceremony*
*Morgan rummaging in Rafe's trash*
*lost charm*
*Rafe fighting with Morgan, Lucan, and Dylan*
*Lucan's SUV accident*
*Baxter's orange*

Seth chuckled at the last one. I started to cross it out with my purple pen.

"I think people use oranges to practice giving an EpiPen injection," Dad said. Seth and I both stared at Dad.

"What's that, dear?" Mom said.

"It was part of a training course I attended a long time ago," Dad said. He seemed surprised to have everyone's attention. "They gave us EpiPens and oranges and we practiced giving an injection just in case we ever had to do it. It also drains the medicine out into the orange." Dad's life as a dentist always took me by surprise. He never talked about it. He was always so focused on his police scanner and staying away from Vi, that I often forgot he had some medical training.

"So, if the killer was at the ceremony, they could have drained the pen right there," Seth said and made a note on the list.

"The killer drained the medicine into the orange, threw it into the bushes where Baxter later found it, and then snapped off the needle?" Diana said.

"It seems like a lot to do with no one seeing them," Alex said.

"I don't know," I said. "It was dark away from the fire. People milled about all over the clearing. It wouldn't take more than a few seconds to drain the medicine and snap off the needle. Then he or she could just slip it back in its case and return it to Rafe's robe pocket."

"Yeah, we didn't put those robes on until after we ate," Vi said. "Rafe's had a fancy gold edge around the hood. I was looking at it and he came and took it from me."

"You messed around with the robes?" I asked.

"I didn't 'mess' with them," she said. "I was just looking. His was right on top and I saw the gold edging."

"Did you see anyone else near them?" Tom asked.

Vi stared into the distance and then shook her head. "I can't remember. There was so much going on, I didn't pay attention." Her shoulders slumped.

I debated with myself about whether to reveal what Neila had told me about Rafe being her son and decided to keep it to myself. I didn't want to distract the crowd and my mother with the story of visiting Neila.

We continued to discuss the clues and suspects. Morgan Lavelle was at the top of the list and just as Vi began a discussion of Morgan's clothing choices, the woman herself walked in the door. She wasn't dressed for work today, but had her black leather and scary makeup back on. Two women who had to be mother and daughter followed in her wake. I remembered seeing Morgan with them at the closing ceremony.

Diana leaned toward me and said, "That's Bronwyn and Ember. I thought they went back to Traverse City."

Morgan cast a dark look in our direction and led her minions to a table across the room. The presence of our number one suspect had cast an uncomfortable silence over the table. Fortunately, the waitress returned with our order and we covered the notes with plates and focused on our food and celebrating Dylan's release.

"How's Lucan?" Mom asked Diana while passing the bread basket down the table.

"He's much better but will need to stay in the hospital for another couple of days," she said.

"I heard he was pretty beat-up from the accident," Tom said. He continued to fork noodles into his mouth.

The table had gone silent in the vicinity of Mom and Vi.

Vi cleared her throat. "Didn't you see Lucan at the accident, Tom?"

Tom looked up and noticed for the first time that all eyes were on him. He scanned the table, searching for the source of trouble.

He shook his head. "No, I haven't seen him since the reception for Rafe."

"Is that so?" Vi said. She turned her narrowed eyes in my direction at the opposite end of the table.

"Weren't you out with Clyde the night she found him?"

Tom blushed and stammered. "N-no. I heard about Lucan from . . . work the next day."

Mom crossed her arms and stared at me.

Seth took a deep breath but I put my hand on his arm to stop him from wading into this situation.

"I was with Mac that night," I said.

"I knew it!" said Vi. She had one finger in the air. "I knew something was up with you two." She leveled the finger in my direction.

"Finally," Alex whispered next to me.

"Oh, Clyde. This is good news," Mom said. "The cards always said you were meant for each other."

Tom turned in his seat to glance toward me down the table. "You and Mac . . . are together?"

I nodded.

"Well, where is he? Why isn't he here helping us?" Vi said. She turned to Mom and said, "We'll have to invite Lucille over for dinner."

I sighed and Seth patted me on the shoulder.


**In the restroom,** grateful for a few minutes away from the mayhem in the dining room, I let the water run and washed my hands slowly. I didn't look up when the door opened and someone else came in the room.

I caught a streak of black out of the corner of my eye and then felt someone standing very close behind me.

"I don't know what your problem is, but you can just back off," she said.

I looked up to meet her eyes in the mirror.

"I don't know what you're talking about, Morgan."

"You went snooping around in the woods and found a charm. The police are trying to link it to me."

I held her gaze and didn't respond. But her presence so close behind me had my heart pounding in fear.

"I didn't kill Rafe," she said. "I . . . wouldn't hurt him."

"Then you have nothing to worry about." I tried to step around her, but she blocked me.

"I think I have you and your gang of amateur detectives to worry about. You're all running in circles trying to find someone to blame for this. I think the police need to look at the people Rafe had threatened, and it wasn't me."

"I don't have any control over what the police are doing."

She gave me a flat stare in the mirror.

"Who was Rafe threatening?" I asked.

"For one thing, your friend's brother was right. Rafe did kill their parents."

"What? How do you know about that?"

Her slow smile showed she was enjoying this. She took a step back and I turned to look at her.

"At least he *thought* he killed them." Morgan shrugged. "He never got over it. He cast a spell and the next day their car crashed." She stepped up to the mirror to trowel on more lipstick.

"Rafe thought a spell killed the Wards?"

She nodded and blotted her lips on a paper towel.

"He liked to test out the spells that were in his mother's grimoire. He was convinced that that one really worked."

"That's ridiculous," I said.

She shrugged. "I didn't say *I* believed it."

"Why did you lie about being at the ceremony?"

Her face went blank. "Who says I lied?"

"You just did. You said the police linked that charm to you."

"No, I said they were trying to. If that's their only proof, I have no worries."

I held my hands out. "Then why are you in here threatening me?"

She blinked. "I'm not threatening you. I'm trying to help

you. Rafe made some enemies along the way. He ran his coven like a dictatorship. I'm not the only person he exiled. Ember and Bronwyn moved all the way to Traverse City to get away from him. They look all sweet and earth-mother-y, but looks can be deceiving."

Diana had said they were above all the drama in Grand Rapids. So, why were they here today with Morgan? And why was she throwing them under the bus?

Morgan continued, "And he was always fighting with that church group. They've been at each other for years."

"The gang that showed up at his memorial?"

Morgan nodded. "He and Bea Paxton go way back, and none of it is friendly."

The door swung open at that moment and Morgan turned on her heel and brushed past the woman, who flattened herself against the wall and stared as Morgan stalked back out to the restaurant.

I nodded at the woman, who scurried into a stall. Morgan had given me a few things to think about. It was true that I had been looking at the case mostly in view of how to prove Dylan's innocence. We'd been focused on finding other people who could have had opportunity, but I didn't know enough about Rafe to know who he might have ticked off.

I went back out to the dining area wondering whether it would be best to let the police do their job. But pulling my family off the scent might prove to be more than I could handle.

# 36

**Sunday morning, after we walked the dogs, I left** Seth with his computer and told him I had some errands.

Mostly, I needed to think. I had too many mysteries, and not enough insight into any of them. Now that Dylan was out of jail, I felt less urgent about figuring out who killed Rafe. Vi's concerns about a roving lunatic aside, I felt like I needed to deal with some mysteries closer to home. Neila's confessions yesterday had been eye-opening but none of it explained why my mother was so against my seeing her that Vi had to go behind her back to get me up there. I understood the recluse excuse, but I didn't understand why she was venturing into town after so many years of self-imposed exile. She must have been trying to get close to Rafe's memorial the night that Mac had driven her home. But why was she causing trouble with Howard and Millie?

I turned my Jeep up the now familiar gravel driveway toward her house. I had grown accustomed to the desolate look of the house, but this time it seemed shut down. I realized the difference was that on my first couple of visits I had smelled wood smoke from her chimney. It was absent this time.

My knock seemed loud in the small clearing and I listened carefully for sounds from within. It was silent. I knocked again and started to get worried. She was over ninety, after all. I had stepped off the porch with a plan to go to the back door when I heard the front door swing open.

"Hello, dear. I'm moving slowly today." She attempted a tired smile that didn't make it to her eyes.

"Hi, Ms. Whittle. I . . . wanted to check on you after our talk yesterday."

She nodded and swung the door open.

Her house seemed colder today, as if the life had been leached out of it. She led me back down the hall to the kitchen, as usual. There was no fire today, as I had surmised while still outside.

"Can I get you anything?" she asked.

I shook my head no, and she settled slowly into her chair.

"Ms. Whittle, I spoke with Millie and Howard last week."

She perked up a bit at this news. "Oh my. Millie doesn't like me very much."

"She thinks you're trying to steal Howard."

The deep laugh that erupted seemed out of place coming from such a tiny person. I smiled along with her.

"She does get ideas," Neila said.

"You're not trying to steal Howard?"

She shook her head. "No, I just wanted to talk to him. We were . . . involved . . . a lifetime ago, but that's been over for longer than you've been alive."

"That's about what Howard said," I agreed. "Can you tell me why, after all this time, you wanted to talk to him?"

She sighed and gestured for me to sit. "He was Rafe's father. I thought he should know that I had found our son. And that he had died."

"I'm sorry. Did you get a chance to tell him before Millie came in?"

She shook her head. "No, and then I had second thoughts. Maybe it would be kinder to let him think . . . whatever it is he thinks. Sometimes the truth isn't as kind as hope."

I took a deep breath. I wasn't sure now whether I wanted to know the answer to my next question, but I plowed on anyway.

"I came to ask you about something else as well. I know you may not want to talk about it, but I really need to know what happened between you and my mother," I said, and leaned my elbows on the table. "You must have known her if you and my grandmother were as close as you say."

Neila glanced at me and looked away. She sighed and seemed to crumple into herself.

"I gave your mother some bad news a long time ago and she's avoided me ever since."

My chest squeezed as I realized the kind of news she must have shared.

"You think my mother will outlive one of her children?"

Neila nodded and wouldn't meet my gaze.

"Do you know which—"

She held up her hand and shook her head.

"I don't know which child it will be. I hope that I'm wrong. I'm sorry, Clytemnestra."

"Well, that explains a lot about my mother," I said. I thought about her overprotectiveness, her insistence that I use my abilities to protect myself, her vocal disapproval of my choice to go to police academy. She must have been concerned I was in constant danger.

"When did you give her this news?"

Neila watched me for a moment. "When you were just a toddler. I don't even think you were talking yet. Your grandmother and mother brought you and Grace to see me. Your grandmother had a knack for reading faces and picking up on subtle things. She knew I'd seen something and badgered me until I told her." Neila hugged herself and pulled her shawls more tightly around her shoulders.

I sensed there was more and waited.

"Your mother gathered up you and your sister and left. I haven't spoken to her since then. Agnes brought you here sometimes, but I never saw Grace or Rose again."

**I left Neila's** house and drove slowly back toward home. It was one of the few times in my life when I wished I had just let things slide. Neila was right—sometimes it's better not to know. I thought about my own premonitions and how they were just gloomy predictions of doom. I knew that because I hadn't honed the talent, or ever fully tested it, I tended to interpret the dreams in the worst light possible. Last summer I had been sure that Mac was in danger and things hadn't turned out that way at all. My efforts to protect him had only complicated matters.

These dreams about Seth really bothered me. I couldn't tell if they were related to what had happened to Rafe, or whatever was going on with Seth in New York, but it seemed pretty clear to me that he was in danger and that I would be useless as a rescuer.

Seth. We'd left things undecided the day before. We had to make a decision, and soon. I pulled into my driveway and shut off the car. I wondered if, when we were done talking, I would feel the same about his truths as I did about Neila's.

I found him camped out in his room, dogs watching his every move as he ate chips and clicked away on his computer.

He looked up when I came in. "Hey," he said, and smiled.

I moved some clothes off the only chair in the room and sat.

His smile faded to a wary line.

"We need to talk about your plans for going back to New York."

He clicked rapidly on the keyboard and then folded up the laptop.

"'Kay."

"You can't just do your homework through e-mail for the rest of the year. You have to be in classes."

I was surprised when he nodded. "Yeah, I know. I looked into transferring to Crystal Haven High."

"What? Do your parents know?"

"Kind of. I told them I didn't want to continue at my own school. A lot of the kids I was with in elementary school go to boarding school now. There are some really good ones, and my mom and dad have mentioned it a bunch of times."

"Boarding school? That's what you want?"

"No, not at all. But I told them it would be no different than if they sent me to boarding school. They couldn't really argue with that."

I sat back and narrowed my eyes at him. "When were you and your mother planning to tell me you had moved in?"

He grinned. "Now seems good. Dylan's out of jail, the Fall Fun Fest is over, so I guess we could talk about it."

I started to wish I hadn't gotten out of bed that morning.

"Your mom is okay with you going to CH High?"

He lifted a shoulder and tilted his head. "She went there."

"That's different. She lived here."

"Yeah, that's why I want to move here. I can't take it in

New York. There's just too much noise, and I'm not talking about traffic. The animals there are . . . well . . . pushy."

I laughed. I couldn't help it.

"How are they pushy?"

"They're constantly complaining about the noise and the other animals and it's just too much. I can't think when I'm there. Ever since last summer when I heard Baxter, I just can't shut it out. I'm not ready to tell my parents about it. I thought maybe you could help me."

I understood his situation only too well, but I hadn't figured out my *own* methods yet. How was I going to help him? Then I remembered the dream. Maybe this is what I was supposed to save him from. New York has a lot of tall buildings. Maybe it was saying I needed to rescue him from New York. Did my sister cackle like a witch? Was I saving him from his own mother?

I must have spaced out for a moment because Seth had gotten up to come snap his fingers in front of me.

"I asked my mom if she would let me stay through till the New Year and see how it goes. I can register at CH High and they can talk to my old school about which classes I should take."

"I'll talk to your mom and we'll see what we can work out."

Seth's smile told me he thought this was a done deal.

# 37

Monday morning Seth and I had just returned home after walking the dogs when a black Tahoe pulled into the driveway. I squinted at the glare shining off the wind-shield and waited.

Skye hopped out and walked toward us.

"Hi," she said and bent to pet Baxter. Her hair fell and covered her face. Baxter wagged his whole body and acted almost as besotted as Seth. Tuffy glowered from under his ponytail until she turned to him and rubbed his ears.

"What's up?" I asked.

Skye pulled a file folder out of her messenger bag.

"I was talking to Diana at work and she told me I should bring these to you." She held the file out to me.

"What is it?" Seth asked.

She bit her lip and wouldn't meet my eyes. "It's Rafe's family tree."

"What?" I snatched the file from her and flipped it open.

It was the same diagram I had seen last week when we searched Rafe's house. "How did you get this?"

She glanced nervously at me and stepped a little closer to Seth.

"I went back after the police left last week. I wanted to see if they had found this." She pointed toward the file.

"You took it?" I tamped down a surge of guilt at having stolen Rafe's grimoire and the knowledge that I would have taken the family tree as well, if it had been there when I went back.

She nodded. "I knew it was important to Rafe and that he didn't want anyone else to see it. He wouldn't even let me look at it, and I was doing research for him."

Seth bounced on his toes and rubbed his arms. "Can we talk about this inside?"

We went in the house and dealt with the dog treats. Baxter would be both spoiled and in another weight class by the time Seth left. *If* he ever left.

"Tell me what this is about," I said when we were settled in the living room.

Skye took the file from me and laid some papers out on the coffee table.

"This is Rafe's family tree according to his grandmother. See the signature in the corner? That's Amity Leal."

Seth and I leaned forward to look.

Skye continued, "According to this diagram, Rafe's grimoire was passed down through the female side of his family, and because he was the only child, he received it from his mother. These notes here show the passage of the grimoire down the female line to Rafe."

Seth and I nodded and I wondered where this was leading. I knew Rafe had the grimoire, as did everyone else. It was how he had claimed his leadership role in the coven.

"This is the part that gets weird. When I showed Diana this family tree, she showed me this other one." Skye reached into her bag and pulled out a copy of the genealogy chart from the back of Dylan's book.

"It looks the same to me," Seth said.

Skye nodded. "It's almost the same. However, the one Diana has clearly shows that Rafe was adopted." She pointed to the dashed line linking Rafe to his adoptive parents.

I nodded. "Did you know he was adopted?"

Skye shook her head. "He never told me. As I said before, he had an interest in Neila Whittle and her family tree. That's what we were working on. He never told me why, just that he had a personal interest."

Seth pointed to the diagram Skye had taken from Rafe's house. "What's this other part?" He pointed to another branch that came off the marriage between Rafe's great-grandparents.

"That's what I wanted you to see," Skye said to me. "This shows that there was another branch of the family, but it went through the son who died in World War II." She pointed to the notation. "And down to this person." Her finger landed on a circle with the name Monica.

I shrugged and looked at Skye. Her finger tracked back to the father of Monica—his name was John Lavelle.

"So?" Seth scooted forward to get a better look.

"Is this Morgan Lavelle?" I asked.

Skye nodded. "I heard them arguing once and Rafe said he liked her old name better. I didn't think much of it at the time because people do change their names sometimes if they join a coven."

"According to this, they're second cousins," I said.

"No offense, Skye, but what does it matter?" Seth said.

"It matters because of this." She pulled out another

document. This one said "Last Will and Testament" at the top. "According to this, the grimoire gets passed down the oldest female line along with 'all my worldly goods,' unless there is no blood relative, in which case it passes down to the other children's children."

"Rafe wasn't a blood relative because he was adopted," I said.

Skye nodded. "Amity Leal tried to cover it up by listing Rafe as a blood relative. I don't know how they managed to trick the great-grandparents, but they must have because Rafe has always had the grimoire."

"But technically, Monica/Morgan should inherit," Seth said.

Skye nodded. "I don't know if this is related to Rafe's death or not, but he had a very good reason to want to keep his adoption a secret. Besides the fact that he claimed control based on his 'bloodline' he also had his inheritance at stake."

"Do you know what he inherited?" I asked.

Skye nodded slowly. "I think it was some land and maybe a house up in Traverse City. He told me a few months ago that he had to go up there to deal with some repairs on a family home. He said he had just inherited it and was fixing it up to sell it." She pulled out the will I had seen that day at Rafe's house. "This will leaves everything to Diana and Dylan, but it's unclear what was actually Rafe's property."

"If Morgan knew about this, it gives her a very good motive for murder," I said.

Skye and Seth waited.

"You have to take this to the police, Skye."

Her shoulders slumped. "I thought you would say that."

"What's the problem? You have evidence that might help them," I said.

"Morgan is my friend. She's always been really support-ive of me and I just can't believe she would hurt Rafe."

Shocked as I was about this statement, I started to see why Seth always defended her.

"If she's innocent, it won't matter."

Seth snorted. "Say that to Dylan."

Skye left with the promise that she would go to the police with all of her charts and notes. I was glad that I had decided to stay out of the investigation. It was getting much too murky for me.

Seth and I spent the rest of the afternoon and evening with the dogs. I attempted to help him with his homework and he ended up teaching me how to do geometry proofs. I never saw the point the first time around, but hid my lack of interest for the sake of being a good role model.

# 38

❦

Tuesday morning I woke early with suspicions and murder plots buzzing in my brain. I texted Mac and asked him to meet me at The Daily Grind. I left a note for Seth and headed off on foot, hoping the brisk air would clear my head. Thunderstorms were forecast for later in the day, but the clouds still looked friendly.

Mac was waiting for me at our usual table and Josh gave me a goofy grin and hooked his thumb toward Mac. Apparently our secret had become common knowledge.

After I sat down, Mac said, "He's acting strange today." He tilted his head in Josh's direction.

I grimaced. "Our secret is out. My family found out we were together the night of Lucan's accident. They jumped to conclusions and I think your mother is going to get a dinner invitation."

Mac nodded. "It's fine. It was getting too hard to cover

up. Plus, I think Andrews has a crush on you. This will let him off the hook."

"He does not."

Mac remained silent but his eyebrows quirked upward.

"How's the case going?" I asked. Any subject would be better.

Mac stiffened and met my eyes. "I can't talk about it. I hope you and your gang have quit trying to 'assist' now that Dylan is out of jail."

I held my hand open on the table. "I don't want to fight about this. I was just asking. I hope you figure it out soon."

Mac glanced at Josh and took my hand. His shoulders relaxed.

"It's been a tough one, as you know. Rafe Godwin had a lot of enemies."

I nodded, debating with myself over whether to tell him about the family tree. Mac was already investigating Morgan; maybe I should just leave it.

"I was thinking we should take a vacation when this case is over," Mac said.

His announcement chased all other thoughts out of my mind. The thought of escaping a Crystal Haven winter and sitting somewhere warm with Mac while sipping drinks decorated with umbrellas seemed too good to be true. I immediately began thinking of what my story would be for the family, when I remembered that they already knew about Mac.

"Where would you want to go?" I asked.

"Somewhere warm where no one knows us."

"That sounds amazing."

We spent the next twenty minutes plotting our escape. We'd narrowed things down to a cruise or an island retreat when Tom burst into the coffee shop. Mac and I, who had literally had our heads together, jumped apart at his interruption.

"Clyde? Detective McKenzie?" He looked from Mac to me and back again. He seemed to have forgotten why he came in. He glanced at our still-clasped hands and his face turned pink.

"Andrews, what do you need?" Mac said.

"I . . . we need you at the station, sir. There's someone who needs to speak to you." Tom came to the table and lowered his voice. "It's Skye Paxton. She says she has some information pertaining to the Rafe Godwin case."

My pulse picked up speed. I hoped she wouldn't tell him that I had known since the day before about Rafe and Morgan and their inheritance dispute.

"Does she have a parent with her?" Mac asked.

Tom shook his head. "She's eighteen, which is good news for us because I wouldn't want to question her with Bea Paxton in the room."

"What's wrong with Bea?" I asked.

"From what I've heard, she takes helicopter parenting to the Black Hawk level."

# 39

❧

**I arrived home to find the dogs waiting at the door.** I called Seth, but received no answer.

"Where's Seth?" I asked Baxter and Tuffy.

Baxter seemed to shrug while Tuffy just glowered.

I found a note in the kitchen: *Had to go out—be back soon.*

I immediately pulled out my phone to see if I had missed a text from him. He never wrote notes. I scrolled through my messages and even checked my e-mail—nothing.

I sent a text: *Where are you?*

Instead of his usual rapid-fire response, it took a full five minutes until I received: *At the mall.*

There was a mall in Grand Rapids, but how did he get there, and why? He hated shopping.

*What mall? How did you get there?*

*I'm with Faith. Skye drove us.*

Something felt wrong. I knew that Skye had gone to the

police station. I doubted she had driven her little sister and Seth to the mall just before coming into Crystal Haven to talk to the police.

*Where are you, really?*

No response. I waited ten minutes and sent several more texts demanding an answer. As each moment passed I got more worried. Seth had never done anything like this, at least not to me. I reminded myself that he had managed to get himself all the way to Michigan without alerting his mother. But this was different, wasn't it? He *wanted* to be here, and he had no reason to hide anything from me.

I didn't want to overreact, but my gut told me that something was seriously wrong.

I called Diana, who was at the hospital visiting Lucan. She pointed out that we used to disappear all the time and our parents had no way of contacting us. That sort of calmed me except that this was unusual for Seth. And I remembered the kind of trouble Diana and Alex and I got into when we disappeared and our parents couldn't find us. Diana said she'd check with me later after she got home from the hospital.

When I called Alex, he agreed it sounded strange.

"He's been texting Faith," he said. "Maybe she talked him into going to the mall. Isn't that what they do these days?"

I admitted that he might be with Faith, but neither of them could drive. I knew that Skye was busy at the police station, so how did he get there?

I decided to drive to the mall myself. It would only take twenty minutes, and I could search for him there. I left the dogs looking more forlorn than usual, and hopped in the Jeep.

An hour later, I'd walked the entire shopping center, investigated any store that I thought would attract a couple of young teens, and sent Seth a text every ten minutes.

Finally, I called Grace.

"Don't freak out," I said when she answered, "but Seth might be missing."

"What do you mean *missing*?" she said. "I thought you were together all the time. How did this happen? You're a police officer!" This from the woman who didn't know if her kid was in New York or Michigan.

I took a deep breath. Arguing with Grace would not help me find Seth. "I went out for an hour this morning and when I came back, he was gone. He's not answering his phone or his texts."

"Let me get to a computer."

I waited while Grace mumbled to herself on the other end of the line.

"I have GPS tracking on his phone in case he loses it," she said. I heard a keyboard clicking in the background. "Let me see where the phone is."

"I'm at the Grand Rapids mall right now. That's where he said he was."

"No, it says here the phone is off, but the last location is not at the mall."

"Where is it?"

"It looks residential. I'll send you the address. Call me as soon as you know anything."

She texted the address to me and I left the mall. I recognized the location, but had no idea why Seth would be there. Then snippets of conversation came back to me. Mom saying parents always want to protect their kids, Neila describing her surprise at what a parent will do, and Morgan's comment that looks can be deceiving. The entire picture shifted for me and I suddenly got very worried.

The early promise of a stormy day had been realized and dark gray clouds seemed to press down on me as I drove to

Covenant of Grace. It was only a few minutes from the mall and when I pulled into the lot, I saw a dark Tahoe parked near the church offices; otherwise the place appeared deserted. I remembered Gladys telling me the church closed on Tuesdays and Thursdays.

Fighting the wind, I tried the door of the old part of the church. Locked. I went to the back and found a small door that led to the back of the sanctuary cracked open. I slipped inside. Dark and silent, none of the usual noises of an electrified building greeted me. The power was out.

In the silence, I heard my own ragged breathing. None of this made sense and I felt more anxious the farther I got inside the church. I called Seth's name but received only an echo from the empty sanctuary. I walked through the whole main floor of the church, peering through the glass into Gladys's office and the other offices on that side of the sanctuary. I saw a small staircase on the other side of the front door and climbed it carefully. Since there were no windows, only a feeble light from the sanctuary's stained glass lit my way. At the top of a short flight I found another door. I held my phone up to the sign in order to read it: BELL TOWER.

I backed away from the door. No way. I wouldn't go up there in *good* weather. I heard the wind howl outside and rain pelted the windows.

I turned and started down the stairs again when I heard a clatter on the stairs on the other side of the door. Sighing, I returned to the entrance to the bell tower.

I pulled the door open slowly, afraid of what I might find on the other side. I thought of my dreams about Seth, and knew I had no choice.

# 40

An ancient stone staircase greeted me and spiraled upward out of sight. The only light in the stairwell seemed to come from above.

I put my foot on the stairs and started climbing. I felt my way along the wall in the dim tower, carefully placing my feet on each step. At about the tenth step my foot kicked something that clattered all the way back down. I cursed to myself and turned around, using my phone's small screen as a flashlight. I found it at the bottom—Seth's dragon statue.

I ran up the stairs again, more frantic than ever.

I started to get dizzy from the constant turning and stopped to catch my breath. The wind howled above me. Either the stairs led directly outside, or a door sat open at the top of the staircase. I continued on, worried about what I would find at the top.

A scrabbling noise from behind stopped me. I made the

mistake of looking back down the stairway. The gray slabs melted into black and then disappeared entirely. My issue with heights kicked in and added to my anxiety about Seth. Fighting to keep my heart rate down, and to breathe calmly, I struggled to remember my police training. *Shut off all emotion and get the job done.* I slowed my pace and prepared to meet the unknown.

A heavy wooden door stood open at the top of the stairs. Rain lashed its way into the opening and onto the top steps. Wind howled in gusts, bringing more icy drops in waves. I reached the doorframe and peered around to the open bell tower.

It was empty. The room was square and the worn dirt floor was wet from the rain. The openings on all four sides of the tower were set high in the wall starting about eight feet off the floor. I looked up into the bells and then noticed the ladder.

Old and rickety, it led to one of the openings. I remembered seeing a balcony with a balustrade running around the tower outside of the bell openings. I had assumed it was a decorative touch by the church architects. The ladder told a different story. Apparently, there was access, albeit rickety, old, and uninviting.

Convinced that Seth needed my help, I tamped down the churning in my gut that accompanied brushes with heights. I tested the ladder and found it to be just as decrepit as it looked. I hoped it would hold my weight. I began to climb, the wind almost drowning out the creaks and groans of protest sent up by the ladder. As I reached the top, I carefully eased my head out into the storm and saw a narrow catwalk running around the tower, enclosed by the balustrade. I struggled up onto the ledge and plastered my body against the tower. I looked to my left briefly and saw nothing, then forced my head around to the right with my eyes closed so I wouldn't look down.

I took slow, shuffling steps along the walkway toward the first corner. I had gotten so turned around, I wasn't even sure which way I was facing. Could I be seen from the road? Would anyone driving by for a fun, storm-lashed jaunt look up and see me? Peering around the first corner, my chest tightened when I didn't see Seth. I wondered if he'd even come up the ladder. Where could he be? My sodden clothing stuck to me and I shivered from the cold and the fear.

"Seth!" I shouted into the wind. My own voice echoed back to me.

I continued shuffling along, gripping the wet stone until I came to the next corner. I edged around the corner and my whole body let out the breath I didn't realize I'd been holding.

"Seth, are you all right?"

I started toward him, and he caught my eye and shook his head ever so slightly. I stopped, wondering if I had misinterpreted him with all the rain in my eyes. I couldn't waste any more time. I was starting to feel that paralyzing tension in my shoulders and my head spun.

I gestured at him to come with me. His eyes got big and he cut them toward the other corner.

"What's going on?" I edged closer, and then I saw what he was trying to warn me about.

A gun, pointed at Seth, and held by Bea Paxton.

"This does complicate things," she said over the wind.

She stepped toward us, holding the gun in both hands and keeping it trained on Seth.

"Mrs. Paxton, what are you doing?"

She glanced at me and then back to Seth. After I found Seth, I felt even dizzier. I had never passed out from my heights issue, but I knew it was possible. I flattened my hands against the rough walls and tried to convince myself that I was safe and close to the ground.

"Faith has been talking to Seth," Bea said. "I can hardly believe my own daughter would turn against me but that seems to be the case. I'll deal with her later. But Seth has to go."

I looked from one to the other. Seth's eyes were wild with terror and Bea's were wild with crazy.

"Mrs. Paxton, let Clyde go," Seth said. "She doesn't know anything and I already told you, I won't say anything."

Bea's lips pressed together and her eyes narrowed.

"No, that won't work," she said. "I'm going to have to change the story. Instead of depressed teen jumps to his death, it'll be brave aunt tries to save nephew . . . and fails."

She took a step forward. I had been inching my way closer to Seth, hoping to get near enough to grab him and . . . something.

"Or do *you* want to be the hero?" Bea took another step toward Seth. "Maybe you followed her up here and tried to talk her down. It's so sad how many suicides there are these days."

Seth leaned away from her. He had his back against one of the posts that ran from the catwalk up to the short ledge that circled the tower, but he was dangerously close to the balustrade. It was only three feet tall and it wouldn't take much to push him over. Just the thought of it had my stomach in knots and my head whirling.

"That's far enough." A voice came from behind Bea.

She whirled toward it and the gun went off. I saw a flap of black fabric disappear behind the corner. The distraction was enough and Seth shoved her hard from behind. She slipped on the wet stones and fell to her hands and knees. The gun clattered away and skittered to the edge of the walkway. I wanted to lunge forward and grab it, but I was frozen in place. I had made the mistake of watching the gun fly to the edge, which led to me looking down. Rooted to the spot, I couldn't even tell Seth to kick the gun off the ledge.

Just then a black-robed figure appeared at the other end of the walkway, its face hidden in the folds of its hood. Bea looked up and saw it and scrabbled away from the gun. Seth seemed rooted to the spot until Bea's backward progress brought her near him again. She started to stand, and in a move that I hadn't realized he knew, he grabbed her right arm and twisted it behind her back. The dark figure stepped forward rapidly, laughing in that shrill way I had heard in my dream, a rope held in its hands.

I finally found my voice, and shouted, "Seth, look out!" But too late. Whoever was in the robes—and at this point I was convinced it was Death herself, or Morgan—was already upon them. I tried to reach for Seth but my hands wouldn't peel away from the wall. *I knew it!* Bea and Morgan were in it together. My breath came in shallow gasps and there were dark spots at the periphery of my vision. The last thing I saw was the figure taking Bea's loose hand and pulling her to a stand.

# 41

### ❧❦

*If* **I blacked out, and that is debatable, it didn't last** long. The next thing I knew, Bea had her hands tied and Morgan pushed her along the balustrade toward me. Seth walked carefully just in front of them. He came toward me with a look of concern and gratitude.

"Clyde, are you okay?" he said.

I nodded and grabbed his hand.

"Are *you* all right?" I asked.

He nodded.

Morgan waited and seemed to be on our side, so I inched my way back toward where I thought I had left the ladder. I kept a tight grip on Seth. Before I knew it, and much faster than it had taken me to get up there, I found myself back down on the stone floor of the bell tower. Seth quickly followed. Then Bea made her way carefully down the ladder, her hands still tied in front of her. Morgan waited until we had a good grip on Bea, and then began climbing. High-heeled black boots stepped on the rungs while the dark fabric billowed in the wind. Once on the ground, she pulled the hood off and there she was, in all her menacing makeup and leather.

All the air that I had finally been able to pull into my lungs after my experience outside rushed out of me and I felt light-headed again.

I instinctively pulled Seth behind me and took a step away from her. She saw this and her red lips curled into her now familiar smirk.

"I'm here to help you, not hurt you," she said.

Bea took a step away from Morgan. Morgan grabbed her by the upper arm and pulled her close.

"Untie me this instant!" Bea glared at Morgan and held out her hands.

Morgan turned her look of disdain onto Bea.

"I don't think so, Mrs. Paxton," she said. "You've been very busy and I just witnessed you trying to kill these people."

Bea shook her head. "You don't know what you're talking about. They dragged me up here and threatened me."

"You pulled a gun on me!" Seth said.

"Gun? I don't see a gun," Bea said. "It's your word against mine. I'm a respected member of this congregation and when I found vandals climbing around inside the bell tower, I did what I had to do to protect the church."

Morgan crossed her arms and tapped her foot. "This is ridiculous. Let's just get you to the police station and you can lie to them. I'm done here." She tightened her grip on Bea and pulled her toward the staircase.

"You can't take me anywhere," Bea said. "That's kidnapping or something. I refuse to go with you. These people are my witnesses."

Seth and I stepped back. I didn't trust either one of them.

I had a thousand questions for Seth whizzing through my brain but this was not the time.

"I'm going to call the police and they can take you in," I said. I glanced at Morgan and she nodded once to agree.

My cell phone had no bars. I showed Seth. He shrugged and gestured at Bea.

"She's got my phone," he said.

"How did she get your phone?" I turned to him.

"She asked to borrow it and then kept it," he said. "She had a gun."

"We can play story time later," Morgan said. "We'll use the phone downstairs in the office. The storm must have knocked out a cell tower."

We trooped slowly down the stairs, Morgan pushing Bea in front, with Seth and me taking up the rear. Now that Seth was safe and we were off the roof, I felt outraged at what Bea had done and it was lucky for Bea that Morgan stood between us. And that we were on a twisty staircase.

When we arrived downstairs, Bea refused to tell us how to unlock the office, so Morgan pulled out a credit card and slid it along the side of the doorframe. I let her make the call. Even though I knew Mac wouldn't actually answer the phone, I was still nervous about his reaction to Seth and me confronting a lunatic *again*.

The storm had slowed, but my mind raced with unanswered questions.

Just as she hung up the phone, we heard pounding on the door outside.

Morgan's eyes grew wide. "That's a quick response," she said.

"Seth! Clyde!" It was Mac and he sounded frantic.

I rushed to the door to let him in.

A wet gust of wind blew Mac, Skye, and Faith into the vestibule. Tom Andrews followed after tripping over the doorstep.

Mac rushed to me and crushed me in a hug. "You're okay," he said.

Seth was enduring his own hugs from Skye and Faith.

Tom ducked his head and took out his handcuffs. He handed them to Morgan, who rolled her eyes and clicked them onto Bea's wrists.

A furor of sound exploded in the small entryway as everyone asked questions at once.

Mac put his fingers to his mouth and blew a shrill whistle.

"Everyone quiet!" he shouted. "We're all going back to the station and sort this out." He nodded at Tom, who took Bea's arm and led her out into the storm.

"Are you okay to drive?" he asked me.

I nodded and put my arm around Seth. He'd been inching in the direction of the girls. Probably thinking he could catch a ride with them and avoid being in a closed vehicle with a livid aunt. I understood how he felt but that didn't sway me.

"I'll take the girls and meet you there," Morgan said.

Seth hung his head and walked in front of me out to the Jeep.

# 42

As soon as we slammed the doors of the Jeep I handed Seth my phone.

"Call your mother and tell her you're safe," I said.

My hands shook as I put the key in the ignition. An adrenaline dump from the heights panic and the following drama had left me feeling shaky and wired.

"There still aren't any bars," Seth said.

I turned to him without starting the engine.

"Seth, what happened? How did you get up there with Bea Paxton?"

He hung his head and didn't look at me.

"It's a long story," he said.

I sat back in my seat and crossed my arms. "I've got time."

"Mac said we should go straight to the station," he said.

I narrowed my eyes even though he wasn't looking at me.

"Okay. Mrs. Paxton came to the house and told me that

Faith and Skye were at the mall. She said she'd drop me off there on her way to the church."

"Had you heard from Skye or Faith?"

He nodded. "I'd gotten a text just a few minutes before she showed up, but now I know that she'd taken Faith's phone. She made me write a note—did you get it?"

"Yeah, that's when I got suspicious," I said.

He clenched his fists on his knees. "Anyway, she claimed her phone battery was dead and asked to see mine. Then she took it! She started lecturing me about Faith and how we were too young to be dating. Which we are absolutely not. Dating, I mean." Seth glanced at me from beneath his bangs. "We drove around for a while looking for Faith. Mrs. Paxton was furious that she couldn't find her. And before I knew it we were here."

"How did she get you into the church?"

"She started saying crazy things about how Faith talks too much and now we're both in trouble and she pulled out a gun. I didn't know what to do so I went into the church with her." Seth had started shivering and I reached out to put an arm around him.

I turned on the engine and cranked up the heat.

"What did she mean, about Faith?"

Seth sighed. "Faith found a bottle of cold-pressed peanut oil in the back of the pantry. She's allergic to peanuts, just like Rafe was. She convinced herself that her mother was going to kill her because she was getting bad grades this term."

"What?"

Seth nodded. "I know, it's nuts. But that house is sketchy. Mrs. Paxton is always quoting the Bible and telling Faith that she better not turn out like Skye. The dad gets mad if he sees her even looking at a boy and won't let her go to any school dances or games."

I had to bring this story back around. "So, Mrs. Paxton thought you knew what the oil meant?"

Seth shrugged. "I guess. I told Faith in a text that it was probably cold-pressed oil that killed Rafe and then Faith went off on how her mother is probably a murderer. It was all on her phone. Mrs. Paxton told me she checks Faith's phone whenever she can and she found all those messages."

I had heard enough to piece the rest together. I put the Jeep in gear and pulled out onto the highway to head to Crystal Haven.

When we were a couple of miles outside of the city limits, my phone started buzzing and vibrating on the dash. Seth said there were forty unread texts, most from Vi, but a few from Grace.

Seth called Grace. The rain had settled into a steady mist and I listened to Seth reassuring his mother over the sound of the beating windshield wipers.

He checked the texts on my phone, which were more and more frantic pleas for information about Seth's and my safety.

We pulled up in front of the police station and my chest squeezed at the sight of the orange smart car parked outside. I went around to the lot and parked. Seth and I both took a moment to steel ourselves.

I had never seen the police station so packed. It seemed the whole town was there.

Vi rushed over to us before we even got in the door and inspected Seth for injury. Mom burst into tears and hugged us both. Dad stood awkwardly to the side, waiting for her to release us. Diana, Dylan, and Alex were there, lobbing questions in our direction.

Mac appeared with a bullhorn. He set off the alarm button and the noise stopped all conversation. Once he had everyone's attention, he directed Seth and me toward the interview rooms and the rest he sent away, grumbling and protesting.

It took a couple of hours to sort out exactly what had happened. Faith had discovered her phone was missing and panicked at the thought that her mother had read all the messages she sent to Seth. The landline wasn't working, no one was home in her immediate neighborhood, and by the time she found someone who would let her use their phone, Skye was at the police station.

The girls and Mac quickly figured out what must have happened and tried to reach Seth and then me. Grace got nervous when she couldn't reach me and called my family, who called Tom, and the address to the church was passed along.

"But how did Morgan end up there?" I asked Mac.

"She claims she saw you at the mall and you looked frantic. She planned to follow you and then she got a text from Skye telling her that Bea was missing and might be dangerous. She followed you to the church and up into the tower."

Mac had confiscated both phones from Bea and the story Seth had told was all true. He'd checked all the texts from Faith.

"Velma and Shaggy had it all figured out," Mac said.

"How did you get into my phone?" Seth asked. "I have a password!"

Mac smiled. "0731?"

Seth's mouth dropped open. "Yeah."

"How did you know that?" I asked. I never would have guessed a random set of numbers.

"It's Harry Potter's birthday," Mac said. "We'll have to

keep this for a couple of days." He slipped the phone into an envelope.

"A couple *days*?" Seth looked panicked for the first time since entering the station. "Aw, man."

# 43

❦

**I knew there would be no chance for peace when I** turned the corner and saw the row of cars outside my house. Seth and I exchanged a grimace, got out of the Jeep, and walked slowly up the steps.

Vi pulled open the door the moment our feet hit the porch.

"What took you so long? We've been waiting for hours."

The smell of something delicious hit me the moment we crossed the threshold and I realized Mom had been working off her stress in her usual way. She and Alex were in the kitchen, jostling for space as she pulled cookies out of the oven and he stirred chicken soup on the stove.

When we were all seated around the table, the questions began. Seth and I did our best to keep up with them, but I felt a bit like a celebrity in the midst of a scandal. Only flashing cameras were missing.

As best as we could, we told the story of Bea and her

plan to rescue Skye from the Wiccans. She and her husband thought that if Rafe was out of the picture, Skye would return to them. Bea was well versed in peanut allergy and what to avoid so she made a plan to purposely expose Rafe to peanuts and disable his medication. The setting of the ceremony was perfect. It was dark, everyone was free to walk around, and no one noticed Bea rummaging among the robes.

Morgan *had* been there that night to continue an argument she'd had with Rafe earlier in the day. She had figured out that Rafe was adopted from talking to Skye and by doing her own investigating. She wanted him to give her the house and land in Traverse City so that she could start her own coven with Bronwyn and Ember. She knew that she could sue him and fight the will. But she wanted to resolve the issue without revealing him to his own coven.

After speaking with Skye, Mac assumed that Rafe was trying to research his biological family tree to see if he would still have claim to a legacy of witchcraft if Morgan did decide to expose him.

Faith and Seth got caught in the middle.

"What about Lucan?" Diana asked. "Why would Bea try to hurt him?"

Vi and I exchanged a glance. "We saw Bea spying on Skye. Lucan met Skye out at Message Circle and the encounter was . . . suspicious. Bea thought that Skye had moved on to another Wiccan in the coven and decided to get rid of him as well."

"But he . . . he's not involved with Skye. Is he?" she looked at Seth.

He shook his head. "No, she met with Lucan to plan the memorial service. She told me she might get back together with Owen. Apparently, drunken spectacles go over big with some people." Seth's expression summed up his low opinion of Owen.

Tom and Dylan had been silent.

"You said Rafe had cast a spell on the Wards?" Tom asked.

I nodded. "That's what Morgan told me. Rafe believed he'd killed them." I glanced at Dylan, who had become very still. "He felt guilty about it, but apparently, it also made him even more certain that he had special powers."

I decided to talk to Dylan later about Rafe's recent discovery about his birth mother. I wasn't quite ready to discuss Neila in front of my mom.

Mom sat very close to Seth and plied him with cookies while he assured her he was fine. "Seth, we were so worried when you went missing." She leaned around him to look at me. "Clyde, I'm surprised you had to use a computer to find him. You used to be so good at finding lost items."

I took a deep breath and let it out slowly. "That's more of a parlor trick, Mom. I didn't have time to mess around with psychic location services."

Mom harrumphed and muttered to herself about wasted talents. I caught Vi watching me with a calculating gleam in her eye.

# 44

A couple of weeks later, on Thanksgiving, I found myself once again surrounded by my crew. We'd added a few to our number as well. Lucan had been invited by Mom, who had taken a much greater interest in Diana's new romance than mine.

"The cards have been telling me about you and Mac for years. Diana and Lucan need my help," she'd said.

Dylan had decided to stick around for a while and had moved into Diana's place. It was unclear whether it was as chaperone, or just that Crystal Haven was more attractive now that the mystery of his parents' death had been put to rest. The lawyers were still arguing over Rafe's property and whether it would go to Diana and Dylan or Morgan.

I had begun visiting Neila a couple of times a week. She had been relieved to find out that Rafe's death was not connected to anything she had done to try to find him. I'd taken her to the woods where he'd died and that seemed to comfort her. We were working together to put the past behind us and make peace with our "gifts."

Lucille McKenzie arrived with Mac. She attached herself to my hip and spent the day offering me recipes and trying to teach me how to knit. After about fifteen minutes of examining a knitting pattern, which consisted of a lot of *k1*'s, *p2*'s and *yo*'s, Vi took pity on me and dragged her off into a corner to speak in some arcane knitting language.

Lucan mouthed a thank-you to me. Vi had been peppering him with questions about surveillance techniques and the best way to tail a suspect.

Seth was due to start school at Crystal Haven High after the break and he sounded like he was looking forward to it. He'd stopped texting Faith after a falling-out over musical tastes. Grace still hadn't told me what was happening in New York, but agreed that Seth could stay through at least the winter holiday to give the new school situation a try.

Alex and Josh brought baked goods. Tom had promised to stop by after a dinner with his own family.

Mac and I escaped into the backyard with the dogs, leaving the noisy party behind for a moment. He pulled me in for a kiss.

Then he took my hand and said, "Let's go."

"Go where?" I said.

He stopped pulling, and turned toward me.

"Do you trust me?"

"Of course."

"Then stop asking questions. Let's go."

He pulled me through the backyard into the neighbor's yard and down the street. It was a glorious crisp day with a hint of snow in the air. We ran down the street laughing like kids.

We arrived at my house out of breath.

"Check the tree," he said.

I smiled. Mac used to leave messages in the tree in my front yard almost every day the first time we'd dated.

"A note?"

He shook his head, and gestured at the tree.

I put my hand inside and felt a plastic bag with an envelope inside. I pulled it out and found two tickets to Mexico.

"Oh, Mac. This is great." I scanned the tickets. "When do we leave?"

"Well, not until February, when we'll really appreciate getting away from the snow."

I put my arms around him and kissed him. "This is a great surprise. Thank you."

I started to walk back toward my parents' house, but he caught my hand.

"Maybe we should put those inside where it's safe."

I smiled. "Maybe we should."

We ran up the steps and into the house. I had barely set the tickets down before I was in his arms.

He kissed my neck, and his hands followed the heat that ran down my spine. His voice was soft when he said, "I think we're alone now."

Exploring the spirit world has never
been this much fun—or this much trouble . . .

## Madelyn Alt

# A Witch in Time

Maggie O'Neill—Stony Mill, Indiana's newest
witch—is dealing with both her burgeoning love
life and her sister's giving birth to twins when she
learns that a local teenager has been found dead.
Later, at the hospital, she hears a whispered conversation that sends chills down her spine. Could the
conversation be related to the teen's death? Or to a
murder that hasn't happened yet? It may take all her
witchy intuition to find out.